THE CAVE GIRL

Suddenly Waldo became conscious that something was creeping up on him from behind out of the dark cave, and he swung his cudgel, aiming a wicked blow at this new enemy as he turned to meet it.

The creature dodged back, and the blow that would have crushed its skull grazed a hair's breadth from its face.

Waldo struck no second blow, and the cold sweat sprang to his forehead when he realized how nearly he had come to murdering a young girl.

There must have been something reassuring in his appearance, for presently she smiled and came out to stand beside him. As she did so a scarlet flush spread over Waldo's face and neck.

'Excuse me,' he said, 'but hadn't you better go in and – er – get your clothes?'

The Cave Girl

Edgar Rice Burroughs

A TANDEM BOOK
published by
Tandem Publishing Ltd

A Tandem Book
Published in 1977
by Tandem Publishing Ltd
a Howard and Wyndham Company
44 Hill Street, London W1X 8LB

First published in America by
Ace Books Inc. by arrangement with Edgar Rice Burroughs Inc.
The Cave Girl copyright © Edgar Rice Burroughs Inc. 1913, 1941
The Cave Man copyright © Edgar Rice Burroughs Inc. 1963

Printed in Great Britain by
Cox & Wyman Ltd, London, Reading and Fakenham

ISBN 0 426 18323 1

Part I

CHAPTER ONE

FLOTSAM

The dim shadow of the thing was but a blur against the dim shadows of the wood behind it.

The young man could distinguish no outline that might mark the presence as either brute or human.

He could see no eyes, yet he knew that somewhere from out of that noiseless mass stealthy eyes were fixed upon him.

This was the fourth time that the thing had crept from out the wood as darkness was settling – the fourth time during those three horrible weeks since he had been cast upon that lonely shore that he had watched, terror-stricken, while night engulfed the shadowy form that lurked at the forest's edge.

It had never attacked him, but to his distorted imagination it seemed to slink closer and closer as night fell – waiting, always waiting for the moment that it might find him unprepared.

Waldo Emerson Smith-Jones was not overly courageous. He had been reared among surroundings of culture plus and ultra-intellectuality in the exclusive Back Bay home of his ancestors.

He had been taught to look with contempt upon all that savored of muscular superiority – such things were gross, brutal, primitive.

It had been a giant intellect only that he had craved – he and a fond mother – and their wishes had been fulfilled. At twenty-one Waldo was an animated encyclopedia – and about as muscular as a real one.

Now he slunk shivering with fright at the very edge of the beach, as far from the grim forest as he could get.

Cold sweat broke from every pore of his long, lank, six-foot-two body. His skinny arms and legs trembled as with palsy. Occasionally he coughed – it had been the cough that had banished him upon this ill-starred sea voyage.

As he crouched in the sand, staring with wide, horror-dilated eyes into the black night, great tears rolled down his thin, white cheeks.

It was with difficulty that he restrained an overpowering desire to shriek. His mind was filled with forlorn regrets that he had not remained at home to meet the wasting death that the doctor had predicted – a peaceful death at least – not the brutal end which faced him now.

The lazy swell of the South Pacific lapped his legs, stretched upon the sand, for he had retreated before that menacing shadow as far as the ocean would permit. As the slow minutes dragged into age-long hours, the nervous strain told so heavily upon the weak boy that toward midnight he lapsed into merciful unconsciousness.

The warm sun awoke him the following morning, but it brought with it but a faint renewal of courage. Things could not creep to his side unseen now, but still they could come, for the sun would not protect him. Even now some savage beast might be lurking just within the forest.

The thought unnerved him to such an extent that he dared not venture to the woods for the fruit that had formed the major portion of his sustenance. Along the beach he picked up a few mouthfuls of sea-food, but that was all.

The day passed, as had the other terrible days which had preceded it, in scanning alternately the ocean and the forest's edge – the one for a ship and the other for the cruel death which he momentarily expected to see stalk out of the dreary shades to claim him.

A more practical and a braver man would have constructed some manner of shelter in which he might have spent his nights in comparative safety and comfort, but Waldo Emerson's education had been conducted along the lines of undiluted intellectuality – pursuits and knowledge which were practical were commonplace, and commonplaces were vulgar. It was preposterous that a Smith-Jones should ever have need of vulgar knowledge.

For the twenty-second time since the great wave had washed him from the steamer's deck and hurled him, choking and spluttering, upon this inhospitable shore, Waldo Emerson saw the sun sinking rapidly toward the western horizon.

As it descended the young man's terror increased, and he kept his eyes glued upon the spot from which the shadow had emerged the previous evening.

He felt that he could not endure another night of the torture he had passed through four times before. That he should go mad he was positive, and he commenced to tremble and whimper even while daylight yet remained. For a time he tried turning his back to the forest, and then he sat huddled up gazing out upon the ocean; but the tears which rolled down his cheeks so blurred his eyes that he saw nothing.

Finally he could endure it no longer, and with a sudden gasp of horror he wheeled toward the wood. There was nothing visible, yet he broke down and sobbed like a child, for loneliness and terror.

When he was able to control his tears for a moment he took the opportunity to scan the deepening shadows once more.

The first glance brought a piercing shriek from his white lips.

The thing was there!

The young man did not fall groveling to the sand this time – instead, he stood staring with protruding eyes at the vague form, while shriek after shriek broke from his grinning lips.

Reason was tottering.

The thing, whatever it was, halted at the first blood-curdling cry, and then when the cries continued it slunk back toward the wood.

With what remained of his ebbing mentality Waldo Emerson realized that it were better to die at once than face the awful fears of the black night. He would rush to meet his fate, and thus end this awful agony of suspense.

With the thought came action, so that, still shrieking, he rushed headlong toward the thing at the wood's rim. As he ran it turned and fled into the forest, and after it went Waldo Emerson, his long, skinny legs carrying his emaciated body in great leaps and bounds through the tearing underbrush.

He emitted shriek after shriek – ear-piercing shrieks that ended in long drawn out wails, more wolfish than human. And the thing that fled through the night before him was shrieking, too, now.

Time and again the young man stumbled and fell. Thorns and brambles tore his clothing and his soft flesh. Blood smeared him from head to feet. Yet on and on he rushed through the semi-darkness of the now moonlit forest.

At first impelled by the mad desire to embrace death and wrest the peace of oblivion from its cruel clutch, Waldo Emerson had come to pursue the screaming shadow before him from an entirely different motive. Now it was for companionship. He screamed now because of a fear that the thing would elude him and that he should be left alone in the depth of this weird wood.

Slowly but surely it was drawing away from him, and as Waldo Emerson realized the fact he redoubled his efforts to overtake it. He had stopped screaming now, for the strain of his physical exertion found his weak lungs barely adequate to the needs of his gasping respiration.

Suddenly the pursuit emerged from the forest to cross a little moonlit clearing at the opposite side of which towered a high and rocky cliff. Toward this the fleeing creature sped, and in an instant more was swallowed, apparently, by the face of the cliff.

Its disappearance was as mysterious and awesome as its identity had been, and left the young man in blank despair.

With the object of pursuit gone, the reaction came, and Waldo Emerson sank trembling and exhausted at the foot of the cliff. A paroxysm of coughing seized him, and thus he lay in an agony of apprehension, fright, and misery until from very weakness he sank into a deep sleep.

It was daylight when he awoke – stiff, lame, sore, hungry, and miserable – but, withal, refreshed and sane. His first consideration was prompted by the craving of a starved stomach; yet it was with the utmost difficulty that he urged his cowardly brain to direct his steps toward the forest, where hung fruit in abundance.

At every little noise he halted in tense silence, poised to flee. His knees trembled so violently that they knocked together; but at length he entered the dim shadows, and presently was gorging himself with ripe fruits.

To reach some of the more luscious viands he had picked from the ground a piece of fallen limb, which tapered from a diameter of four inches at one end to a trifle over an inch at the other. It was the first practical thing that Waldo Emerson had done since he had been cast upon the shore of his new home – in fact, it was, in all likelihood, the nearest approximation to a practical thing which he had ever done in all his life.

Waldo had never been allowed to read fiction, nor had he ever cared to so waste his time or impoverish his brain, and nowhere in the fund of deep erudition which he had accumulated could he recall any condition analogous to those which now confronted him.

Waldo, of course, knew that there were such things as step-ladders, and had he had one he would have used it as a means to reach the fruit above his hand's reach; but that he could knock the delicacies down with a broken branch seemed indeed a mighty discovery – a valuable addition to the sum total of human knowledge. Aristotle himself had never reasoned more logically.

Waldo had taken the first step in his life toward independent mental action – heretofore his ideas, his thoughts, his acts, even, had been borrowed from the musty writing of the ancients, or directed by the immaculate mind of his superior mother. And he clung to his discovery as a child clings to a new toy.

When he emerged from the forest he brought his stick with him.

He determined to continue the pursuit of the creature that had eluded him the night before. It would, indeed, be curious to look upon a thing that feared him.

In all his life he had never imagined it possible that any creature could flee from him in fear. A little glow suffused the young man as the idea timorously sought to take root.

Could it be that there was a trace of swagger in that long, bony figure as Waldo directed his steps toward the cliff? Perish the thought! Pride in vulgar physical prowess! A long line of Smith-Joneses would have risen in their graves and rent their shrouds at the veriest hint of such an idea.

For a long time Waldo walked back and forth along the foot of the cliff, searching for the avenue of escape used by the fugitive of yesternight. A dozen times he passed a well-defined trail that led, winding, up the cliff's face; but Waldo knew nothing of trails – he was looking for a flight of steps or a doorway.

Finding neither, he stumbled by accident into the trail; and, although the evident signs that marked it as such revealed nothing to him, yet he followed it upward for the simple reason that it was the only place upon the cliff side where he could find a foothold.

Some distance up he came to a narrow cleft in the cliff into which the trail led. Rocks dislodged from above had fallen into it, and, becoming wedged a few feet from the bottom, left only a small cavelike hole, into which Waldo peered.

There was nothing visible, but the interior was dark and forbidding. Waldo felt cold and clammy. He began to tremble. Then he turned and looked back toward the forest.

The thought of another night spent within sight of that dismal place almost overcame him. No! A thousand times no! Any fate were better than that, and so after several futile efforts he forced his unwilling body through the small aperture.

He found himself on a path between two rocky walls – a path that rose before him at a steep angle. At intervals the blue sky was visible above through openings that had not been filled with debris.

To another it would have been apparent that the cleft had been kept open by human beings – that it was a thoroughfare which was used, if not frequently, at least sufficiently often to warrant considerable labor having been expended upon it to keep it free from the debris which must be constantly falling from above.

Where the path led, or what he expected to find at the other end, Waldo had not the remotest idea. He was not an imaginative youth. But he kept on up the ascent in the hope that at the end he would find the creature which had escaped him the night before.

As it had fled for a brief instant across the clearing beneath the moon's soft rays, Waldo had thought that it bore a remarkable resemblance to a human figure; but of that he could not be positive.

At last his path broke suddenly into the sunlight. The walls on either side were but little higher than his head, and a moment later he emerged from the cleft onto a broad and beautiful plateau.

Before him stretched a wide, grassy plain, and beyond towered a range of mighty hills. Between them and him lay a belt of forest.

A new emotion welled in the breast of Waldo Emerson Smith-Jones. It was akin to that which Balboa may have felt when he gazed for the first time upon the mighty Pacific from the Sierra de Quarequa. For the moment, as he contemplated this new and beautiful scene of rolling meadowland, distant forest, and serrated hilltops, he almost forgot to be afraid. And on the impulse of the instant he set out across the tableland to explore the unknown which lay beyond the forest.

Well it was for Waldo Emerson's peace of mind that no faint conception of what lay there entered his unimaginative mind. To him a land without civilization – without cities and towns peopled by humans with manners and customs similar to those which obtain in Boston – was beyond belief.

As he walked he strained his eyes in every direction for some indication of human habitation – a fence, a chimney – anything that would be man-built; but his efforts were unrewarded.

At the verge of the forest he halted, fearing to enter; but at last, when he saw that the wood was more open than that near the ocean, and that there was but little underbrush, he mustered sufficient courage to step timidly within.

On careful tiptoe he threaded his way through the park-like grove, stopping every few minutes to listen, and ready at the first note of danger to fly screaming toward the open plain.

Notwithstanding his fears, he reached the opposite boundary of the forest without seeing or hearing anything to arouse suspicion, and, emerging from the cool shade, found himself a little distance from a perpendicular white cliff, the face of which was honeycombed with the mouths of many caves.

There was no living creature in sight, nor did the very apparent artificiality of the caves suggest to the impractical Waldo that they might be the habitations of perhaps savage human beings.

With the spell of discovery still upon him, he crossed the open toward the cliffs; but he had by no means forgotten his chronic state of abject fear. Ears and eyes were alert for hidden dangers; every few steps were punctuated by a timid halt and a searching survey of his surroundings.

It was during one of these halts, when he had crossed half the distance between the forest and the cliff, that he discerned a slight movement in the wood behind him.

For an instant he stood staring and frozen, unable to de-

CHAPTER TWO

THE WILD PEOPLE

The creature was naked except for a bit of hide that hung from a leathern waist thong.

If Waldo viewed the newcomer with wonder, it was no less than the wonder which the sight of him inspired in the breast of the hairy one, for what he saw was as truly remarkable to his eyes as was his appearance to those of the cultured Bostonian. And Waldo did indeed present a most startling exterior. His six-feet-two was accentuated by his extreme skinniness; his gray eyes looked weak and watery within the inflamed circles which rimmed them, and which had been produced by loss of sleep and much weeping.

His yellow hair was tangled and matted, and streaked with dirt and blood. Blood stained his soiled and tattered ducks. His shirt was but a mass of frayed ribbons held to him at all only by the neck-band.

As he stood helplessly staring with bulging eyes at the awful figure glowering at him from the forest his jaw dropped, his knees trembled, and he seemed about to collapse from sheer terror.

Then the hideous man crouched and came creeping warily toward him.

With an agonized scream Waldo turned and fled toward the cliff. A quick glance over his shoulder brought another series of shrieks from the frightened fugitive, for it revealed not alone the fact that the awful man was pursuing him, but that behind him raced at least a dozen more equally frightful.

Waldo ran toward the cliffs only because that direction lay straight away from his pursuers. He had no idea what he should do when he reached the rocky barrier – he was far too frightened to think.

His pursuers were gaining upon him, their savage yells mingling with his piercing cries and spurring him on to undreamed-of pinnacles of speed.

As he ran, his knees came nearly to his shoulders at each frantic bound; his left hand was extended far ahead, clutching wildly at the air as though he were endeavoring to pull himself ahead, while his right hand, still grasping the cudgel, described a rapid circle, like the arm of a windmill gone mad. In action Waldo was an inspiring spectacle.

At the foot of the cliff he came to a momentary halt, while he glanced hurriedly about for a means of escape; but now he saw that the enemy had spread out toward the right and left, leaving no means of escape except up the precipitous side of the cliff. Up this narrow trails led steeply from ledge to ledge.

In places crude ladders scaled perpendicular heights from one tier of caves to the next above; but to Waldo the thing which confronted him seemed absolutely unscalable, and then another backward glance showed him the rapidly nearing enemy; and he launched himself at the face of that seemingly inpregnable barrier, clutching desperately with fingers and toes.

His progress was impeded by the cudgel to which he still clung, but he did not drop it; though why it would have been difficult to tell, unless it was that his acts were now purely mechanical, there being no room in his mind for aught else than terror.

Close behind him came the foremost cave man; yet though he had acquired the agility of a monkey through a lifetime of practice, he was amazed at the uncanny speed with which Waldo Emerson clawed his shrieking way aloft.

Half-way up the ascent, however, a great hairy hand came almost to his ankle.

It was during the perilous negotiation of one of the loose and wobbly ladders – little more than small trees leaning precariously against the perpendicular rocky surface – that the nearest foeman came so close to the fugitive; but at the top chance intervened to save Waldo, for a time at least. It was at the moment that he scrambled frantically to a tiny ledge from the frightfully slipping sapling.

In his haste he did by accident what a resourceful man would have done by intent – by pushing himself onto the ledge he kicked the ladder outward – for a second it hung toppling in the balance, and then with a lunge crashed down the cliff's face with its human burden, in its fall scraping others of the pursuing horde with it.

A chorus of rage came up from below him, but Waldo had not even turned his head to learn of his temporary good fortune. Up, ever up he sped, until at length he stood upon the topmost ledge, facing an overhanging wall of blank rock that towered another twenty-five feet above him to the summit of the bluff. Time and again he leaped futilely against the smooth surface, tearing at it with his nails in a mad endeavor to climb still higher.

At his right was the low opening to a black cave, but he did not see it – his mind could cope with but the single idea: to clamber from the horrible creatures which pursued him. But finally it was borne in on his half-mad brain that this was the end – he could fly no farther – here, in a moment more, death would overtake him.

He turned to meet it, and below saw a number of the cave men placing another ladder in lieu of that which had fallen. In a moment they were resuming the ascent after him.

On the narrow ledge above them the young man stood, chattering and grinning like a madman. His pitiful cries were now punctuated with the hollow coughing which his violent exercise had induced.

Tears rolled down his begrimed face, leaving crooked, muddy streaks in their wake. His knees smote together so violently that he could barely stand, and it was into the face of this apparition of cowardice that the first of the cave men looked as he scrambled above the ledge on which Waldo stood.

And then, of a sudden, there rose within the breast of Waldo Emerson Smith-Jones a spark that generations of overrefinement and emasculating culture had all but extinguished – the instinct of self-preservation by force. Heretofore it had been purely by flight.

With the frenzy of the fear of death upon him, he raised his cudgel, and, swinging it high above his head, brought it down full upon the unprotected skull of his enemy.

Another took the fallen man's place – he, too, went down with a broken head. Waldo was fighting now like a cornered rat, and through it all he chattered and gibbered; but he no longer wept.

At first he was horrified at the bloody havoc he wrought with his crude weapon. His nature revolted at the sight of blood, and when he saw it mixed with matted hair along the side of his cudgel, and realized that it was human hair and human blood, and that he, Waldo Emerson Smith-Jones, had struck the blows that had plastered it there so thickly in all its hideousness, a wave of nausea swept over him, so that he almost toppled from his dizzy perch.

For a few minutes there was a lull in hostilities while the cave men congregated below, shaking their fists at Waldo and crying out threats and challenges. The young man stood looking down upon them, scarcely able to realize that alone he had met savage men in physical encounter and defeated them.

He was shocked and horrified; not, odd to say, because of the thing he had done, but rather because of a strange and unaccountable glow of pride in his brutal supremacy over brutes. What would his mother have thought could she have seen her precious boy now?

Suddenly Waldo became conscious from the corner of his eye that something was creeping upon him from behind out of the dark cave before which he had fought. Simultaneously with the realization of it he swung his cudgel in a wicked blow at this new enemy as he turned to meet it.

The creature dodged back, and the blow that would have crushed its skull grazed a hairbreadth from its face.

Waldo struck no second blow, and the cold sweat sprang to his forehead when he realized how nearly he had come to murdering a young girl. She crouched now in the mouth of the cave, eyeing him fearfully. Waldo removed his tattered cap, bowing low.

'I crave your pardon,' he said. 'I had no idea that there was a lady here. I am very glad that I did not injure you.'

There must have been something either in his tone or manner that reassured her, for she smiled and came out upon the ledge beside him.

As she did so a scarlet flush mantled Waldo's face and neck and ears – he could feel them burning. With a nervous cough he turned and became intently occupied with the distant scenery.

Presently he cast a surreptitious glance behind him. Shocking! She was still there. Again he coughed nervously.

'Excuse me,' he said. 'But – er – ah – you – I am a total stranger, you know; hadn't you better go back in, and – er – get your clothes?'

She made no reply, and so he forced himself to turn toward her once more. She was smiling at him.

Waldo had never been so horribly embarrassed in all his life before – it was a distinct shock to him to realize that the girl was not embarrassed at all.

He spoke to her a second time, and at last she answered; but in a tongue which he did not understand. It bore not the slightest resemblance to any language, modern or dead, with which he was familiar, and Waldo was more or less master of them all – especially the dead ones.

He tried not to look at her after that, for he realized that he must appear very ridiculous.

But now his attention was required by more pressing affairs – the cave men were returning to the attack. They carried stones this time, and, while some of them threw the missiles at Waldo, the others attempted to rush his position.

It was then that the girl hurried back into the cave, only to reappear a moment later carrying some stone utensils in her arms.

There was a huge mortar in which she had collected a pestle and several smaller pieces of stone. She pushed them along the ledge to Waldo.

At first he did not grasp the meaning of her act; but presently she pretended to pick up an imaginary missile and hurl it down upon the creatures below – then she pointed to the things she had brought and to Waldo.

He understood. So she was upon his side. He did not understand why, but he was glad.

Following her suggestion, he gathered up a couple of the smaller objects and hurled them down upon the men beneath.

But on and on they came – Waldo was not a very good shot. The girl was busy now gathering such of the cave men's missiles as fell upon the ledge. These she placed in a pile beside Waldo.

Occasionally the young man would strike an enemy by accident, and then she would give a little scream of pleasure – clapping her hands and jumping up and down.

It was not long before Waldo was surprised to find that this applause fell sweetly upon his ears. It was then that he began to take better aim.

In the midst of it all there flashed suddenly upon him a picture of his devoted mother and the select coterie of intellectual young people with which she had always surrounded him.

Waldo felt a new pang of horror as he tried to realize with what emotions they would look upon him now as he stood upon the face of a towering cliff beside an almost naked girl hurling rocks down upon the heads of hairy men who hopped about, screaming with rage, below him.

It was awful! A great billow of mortification rolled over him.

He turned to cast a look of disapprobation at the shameless young woman behind him – she should not think that he countenanced such coarse and vulgar proceedings. Their eyes met – in hers he saw the sparkle of excitement and the joy of life and such a look of comradeship as he never before had seen in the eyes of another mortal.

Then she pointed excitedly over the edge of the ledge.

Waldo looked.

A great brute of a cave man had crawled, unseen, almost to their refuge.

He was but five feet below them, and at the moment that he looked up Waldo dropped a fifty-pound stone mortar full upon his upturned face.

The young woman emitted a little shriek of joy, and Waldo Emerson Smith-Jones, his face bisected by a broad grin, turned toward her.

CHAPTER THREE

THE LITTLE EDEN

The mortar ended hostilities – temporarily, at least; but the cave men loitered about the base of the cliff during the balance of the afternoon, occasionally shouting taunts at the two above them.

These the girl answered, evidently in kind. Sometimes she would point to Waldo and make ferocious signs, doubtless indicative of the horrible slaughter which awaited them at his hands if they did not go away and leave their betters alone. When the young man realized the significance of her pantomime he felt his heart swell with an emotion which he feared was pride in brutal, primitive, vulgar physical prowess.

As the long day wore on Waldo became both very hungry very thirsty. In the valley below he could see a tiny brooklet purling, clear and beautiful, toward the south. The sight of it drove him nearly mad, as did also that of the fruit which he glimpsed hanging ripe for eating at the edge of the forest.

By means of signs he asked the girl if she, too, were hungry, for he had come to a point now where he could look at her almost without visible signs of mortification. She nodded her head and, pointing toward the descending sun, made it plain to him that after dark they would descend and eat.

The cave men had not left when darkness came, and it seemed to Waldo a very foolhardy thing to venture down while they might be about; but the girl made it so evident that she considered him an invincible warrior that he was torn with the conflicting emotions of cowardice and an unaccountable desire to appear well in her eyes, that he might by his acts justify her belief in him.

It seemed very wonderful to Waldo that any one should look upon him in the light of a tower of strength and a haven of refuge; he was not quite certain in his own mind but that the reputation might lead him into most uncomfortable and embarrassing situations. Incidentally, he wondered if the girl was a good runner; he hoped so.

It must have been quite near midnight when his companion intimated that the time had arrived when they should fare forth and dine. Waldo wanted her to go first, but she shrank close to him, timidly, and held back.

There was nothing else for it, then, than to take the plunge, though had the sun been shining it would have revealed a very pale and wide-eyed champion, who slipped gingerly over the side of the ledge to grope with his feet for a foothold beneath.

Half-way down the moon rose above the forest – a great, full, tropic moon, that lighted the face of the cliff almost as brilliantly as might the sun itself. It shone into the mouth of a cave upon the ledge that Waldo had just reached in his descent, revealing to the horrified eyes of the young man a great, hairy form stretched in slumber not a yard from him.

As he looked, the wicked little eyes opened and looked straight into his.

With difficulty Waldo suppressed a shriek of dismay as he turned to plunge madly down the precipitous trail. The girl had not yet descended from the ledge above.

She must have sensed what had happened, for as Waldo turned to fly she gave a little cry of terror. At the same instant the cave man leaped to his feet. But the girl's voice had touched something in the breast of Waldo Emerson which generations of disuse had almost atrophied, and for the first time in his life he did a brave and courageous thing.

He could easily have escaped the cave man and reached the valley – alone; but at the first note of the young girl's cry he wheeled and scrambled back to the ledge to face the burly, primitive man, who could have crushed him with a single blow.

Waldo Emerson no longer trembled. His nerves and muscles were very steady as he swung his cudgel in an arc that brought it crashing down upon the upraised guarding arm of the cave man.

There was a snapping of bone beneath the blow, a scream of pain – the man staggered back, the girl sprang to Waldo's side from the ledge above, and hand in hand they turned and fled down the face of the cliff.

From a dozen cave-mouths above issued a score of cave men, but the fleeing pair were half-way across the clearing before the slow-witted brutes were fully aware of what had happened. By the time they had taken up the pursuit Waldo and the girl had entered the forest.

For a few yards the latter led Waldo straight into the shadows of the wood, then she turned abruptly toward the north, at right angles to the course they had been pursuing.

She still clung to the young man's hand, nor did she slacken her speed the least after they had entered the darkness beneath the trees. She ran as surely and confidently through the impenetrable night of the forest as though the way had been lighted by flaming arcs; but Waldo was continually stumbling and falling.

The sound of pursuit presently became fainter; it was apparent that the cave men had continued on straight into the wood; but the girl raced on with the panting Waldo for what seemed to the winded young man an eternity. Presently, however, they came to the banks of the little stream that had been visible from the caves. Here the girl fell into a walk, and a moment later dragged the Bostonian down a shelving bank into water that came above his knees.

Up the bed of the stream she led him, sometimes floundering through holes so deep that they were entirely submerged.

Waldo had never learned the vulgar art of swimming, so it was that he would have drowned but for the strong, brown hand of his companion, which dragged him, spluttering and coughing, through one awful hole after another, until half-strangled and entirely panic-stricken, she hauled him safely upon a low, grassy bank at the foot of a rocky wall which formed one side of a gorge, through which the river boiled.

It must not be assumed that when Waldo Emerson returned to face the hairy brute who threatened to separate him from his new-found companion that by a miracle he had been transformed from a hare into a lion – far from it.

Now that he had a moment in which to lie quite still and speculate upon the adventures of the past hour, the reaction came, and Waldo Emerson thanked the kindly night that obscured from the eyes of the girl the pitiable spectacle of his palsied limbs and trembling lip.

Once again he was in a blue funk, with shattered nerves that begged to cry aloud in the extremity of their terror.

It was not warm in the camp canyon, through which the wind swept over the cold water, so that to Waldo's mental anguish was added the physical discomfort of cold and wet. He was indeed a miserable figure as he lay huddled upon the sward, praying for the rising of the sun, yet dreading the daylight that might reveal him to his enemies.

But at last dawn came, and after a fitful sleep Waldo awoke to find himself in a snug and beautiful little paradise hemmed in by the high cliffs that flanked the river, upon a sloping grassy shore that was all but invisible except from a short stretch of cliff-top upon the farther side of the stream.

A few feet from him lay the girl.

She was still asleep. Her head was pillowed upon one firm, brown arm. Her soft black hair fell in disorder across one cheek and over the other arm, to spread gracefully upon the green grass about her.

As Waldo looked he saw that she was very comely. Never before had he seen a girl just like her. His young women friends had been rather prim and plain, with long, white faces and thin lips that scarcely ever dared to smile and scorned to unbend in plebeian laughter.

This girl's lips seemed to have been made for laughing – and for something else, though at the time it is only fair to Waldo to say that he did not realize the full possibilities that they presented.

As his eyes wandered along the lines of her young body his Puritanical training brought a hot flush of embarrassment to his face, and he deliberately turned his back upon her.

It was indeed awful to Waldo Emerson to contemplate, to say the least, the unconventional position into which fate had forced him. The longer he pondered it the redder he became. It was frightful – what would his mother say when she heard of it?

What would this girl's mother say? But, more to the point, and – horrible thought – what would her father or her brothers do to Waldo if they found them thus together – and she with only a scanty garment of skin about her waist – a garment which reached scarcely below her knees at any point, and at others terminated far above?

Waldo was chagrined. He could not understand what the girl could be thinking of, for in other respects she seemed quite nice, and he was sure that the great eyes of her reflected only goodness and innocence.

While he sat thus, thinking, the girl awoke and with a merry laugh addressed him.

'Good morning,' said Waldo quite severely.

He wished that he could speak her language, so that he could convey to her a suggestion of the disapprobation which he felt for her attire.

He was on the point of attempting it by signs, when she rose, lithe and graceful as a tigress, and walked to the river's brim. With a deft movement of her fingers she loosed the thong that held her single garment, and as it fell to the ground Waldo, with a horrified gasp, turned upon his face, burying his tightly closed eyes in his hands.

Then the girl dived into the cool waters for her matutinal bath.

She called to him several times to join her, but Waldo

could not look at the spectacle presented; his soul was scandalized.

It was some time after she emerged from the river before he dared risk a hesitating glance. With a sigh of relief he saw that she had donned her single garment, and thereafter he could look at her unashamed when she was thus clothed. He felt that by comparison it constituted a most modest gown.

Together they strolled along the river's edge, gathering such fruits and roots as the girl knew to be edible. Waldo Emerson gathered those she indicated – with all his learning he found it necessary to depend upon the untutored mind of this little primitive maiden for guidance.

Then she taught him how to catch fish with a bent twig and a lightninglike movement of her brown hands – or, rather, tried to teach him, for he was far too slow and awkward to succeed.

Afterward they sat upon the soft grass beneath the shade of a wild fig-tree to eat the fish she had caught. Waldo wondered how in the world the girl could make fire without matches, for he was quite sure that she had none; and even should she be able to make fire it would be quite useless, since she had neither cooking utensils nor stove.

He was not left long in wonderment.

She arranged the fish in a little pile between them, and with a sweet smile motioned to the man to partake; then she selected one for herself, and while Waldo Emerson looked on in horror, sunk her firm, white teeth into the raw fish.

Waldo turned away in sickening disgust.

The girl seemed surprised and worried that he did not eat. Time and again she tried to coax him by signs to join her; but he could not even look at her. He had tried, after the first wave of revolt had subsided, but when he discovered that she ate the entire fish, without bothering to clean it or remove the scales, he became too ill to think of food.

Several times during the following week they ventured from their hiding-place, and at these times it was evident from the girl's actions that she was endeavoring to elude their enemies and reach a place of safety other than that in which they were concealed. But at each venture her quick ears or sensitive nostrils warned her of the proximity of danger, so that they had been compelled to hurry back into their little Eden.

During this period she taught Waldo many words of her native tongue, so that by means of signs to bridge the gaps between, they were able to communicate with a fair degree of satisfaction. Waldo's mastery of the language was rapid.

On the tenth day the girl was able to make him understand that she wished to escape with him to her own people; that these men among whom he had found her were enemies of her tribe, and that she had been hiding from them when Waldo stumbled upon her cave.

'I fled,' she said. 'My mother was killed. My father took another mate, always cruel to me. But when I had wandered into the land of these enemies I was afraid, and would have returned to my father's cave. But I had gone too far.

'I would have to run very fast to escape them. Once I ran down a narrow path to the ocean. It was dark.

'As I wandered through the woods I came suddenly out upon a beach, and there I saw a strange figure on the sand. It was you. I wanted to learn what manner of man you were. But I was very much afraid, so that I dared only watch you from a distance.

'Five times I came down to look at you. You never saw me until the last time, then you set out after me, roaring in a horrible voice.

'I was very much afraid, for I knew that you must be very brave to live all alone by the edge of the forest without any shelter, or even a stone to hurl at Nagoola, should he come out of the woods to devour you.'

Waldo Emerson shuddered.

'Who is Nagoola?' he asked.

'You do not know Nagoola!' the girl exclaimed in surprise.

'Not by that name,' replied Waldo.

'He is as large,' she began in description, 'as two men, and black, with glossy coat. He has two yellow eyes, which see as well by night as by day. His great paws are armed with mighty claws. He—'

A rustling from the bushes which fringed the opposite cliff-top caused her to turn, instantly alert.

'Ah,' she whispered, 'there is Nagoola now.'

Waldo looked in the direction of her gaze.

It was well that the girl did not see his pallid face and popping eyes as he looked into the evil mask of the great black panther that crouched watching them from the river's further bank.

Into Waldo's breast came great panic. It was only because his fear-prostrated muscles refused to respond to his will that he did not scurry, screaming, from the sight of that ferocious countenance.

Then, through the fog of his cowardly terror, he heard again the girl's sweet voice: 'I knew that you must be very brave to live all alone by the edge of that wicked forest.'

For the first time in his life a wave of shame swept over Waldo Emerson.

The girl called in a taunting voice to the panther, and then turned, smiling, toward Waldo.

'How brave I am now,' she laughed. 'I am no longer afraid of Nagoola. You are with me.'

'No,' said Waldo Emerson, in a very weak voice, 'you need not fear while I am with you.'

'Oh!' she cried. 'Slay him. How proud I should be to return to my people with one who vanquished Nagoola, and wore his hide about his loins as proof of his prowess.'

'Y-yes,' acquiesced Waldo faintly.

'But,' continued the girl, 'you have slain many of Nagoola's brothers and sisters. It is no longer sport to kill one of his kind.'

'Yes – yes,' cried Waldo. 'Yes, that is it – panthers bore me now.'

'Oh!' The girl clasped her hands in ecstasy. 'How many have you slain?'

'Er – why, let me see,' the young man blundered. 'As a matter of fact, I never kept any record of the panthers I killed.'

Waldo was becoming frantic. He had never lied before in his life. He hated a lie and loathed a liar. He wondered why he had lied now.

Surely it were nothing to boast of to have butchered one of God's creatures – and as for claiming to have killed so many that he could not recall the number, it was little short of horrible. Yet he became conscious of a poignant regret that he had not killed a thousand panthers, and preserved all the pelts as evidence of his valor.

The panther still regarded them from the safety of the farther shore. The girl drew quite close to Waldo in the instinctive plea for protection that belongs to her sex. She laid a timid hand upon his skinny arm and raised her great, trusting eyes to his face in reverent adoration.

'How do you kill them?' she whispered. 'Tell me.'

Then it was that Waldo determined to make a clean breast of it, and admit that he never before had seen a live panther. But as he opened his mouth to make the humiliating confession he realized, quite suddenly, why it was that he had lied – he wished to appear well in the eyes of this savage, half-clothed girl.

He, Waldo Emerson Smith-Jones, craved the applause of a barbarian, and to win it had simulated that physical prowess which generations of Smith-Joneses had viewed from afar – disgusted, disapproving.

The girl repeated her question.

'Oh,' said Waldo, 'it is really quite simple. After I catch them I beat them severely with a stick.'

The girl sighed.

'How wonderful!' she said.

Waldo became the victim of a number of unpleasant emotions – mortification for this suddenly developed moral turpitude; apprehension for the future, when the girl might discover him in his true colors; fear, consuming, terrible

30

fear, that she might insist upon his going forth at once to slay Nagoola.

But she did nothing of the kind, and presently the panther tired of watching them and turned back into the tangle of bushes behind him.

It was with a sigh of relief that Waldo saw him depart.

CHAPTER FOUR

DEATH'S DOORWAY

Late in the afternoon the girl suggested that they start that night upon the journey toward her village.

'The bad men will not be abroad after dark,' she said. 'With you at my side, I shall not fear Nagoola.'

'How far is it to your village?' asked Waldo.

'It will take us three nights,' she replied. 'By day we must hide, for even you could not vanquish a great number of bad men should they attack you at once.'

'No,' said Waldo; 'I presume not.'

'It was very wonderful to watch you, though,' she went on, 'when you battled upon the cliff-side, beating them down as they came upon you. How brave you were! How terrible! You trembled from rage.'

'Yes,' admitted Waldo, 'I was quite angry. I always tremble like that when my ire is excited. Sometimes I get so bad that my knees knock together. If you ever see them do that you will realize how exceedingly angry I am.'

'Yes,' murmured the girl.

Presently Waldo saw that she was laughing quietly to herself.

A great fear rose in his breast. Could it be that she was less gullible than she had appeared? Did she, after all, penetrate the bombast with which he had sought to cloak his cowardice?

He finally mustered sufficient courage to ask: 'Why do you laugh?'

'I think of the surprise that awaits old Flatfoot and Korth and the others when I lead you to them.'

'Why will they be surprised?' asked Waldo.

'At the way you will crack their heads.'

Waldo shuddered.

'Why should I crack their heads?' he asked.

'Why should you crack their heads!' It was apparently incredible to the girl that he should not understand.

'How little you know,' she said. 'You cannot swim, you do not know the language which men may understand, you would be lost in the woods were I to leave you, and now you say that you do not know that when you come to a strange tribe they will try to kill you, and only take you as one of them when you have proven your worth by killing at least one of their strongest men.'

'At least one!' said Waldo, half to himself.

He was dazed by this information. He had expected to be welcomed with open arms into the best society that the girl's community afforded. He had thought of it in just this way, for he had not even yet learned that there might be a whole people living under entirely different conditions than those which existed in Boston, Massachusetts.

Her reference to his ignorance also came as a distinct shock to him. He had always considered himself a man of considerable learning. It had been his secret boast and his mother's open pride.

And now to be pitied for his ignorance by one who probably thought the earth flat, if she ever thought about such matters at all – by one who could neither read nor write. And the worst of it all was that her indictment was correct – only she had not gone far enough.

There was little of practical value that he did know. With the realization of his limitations Waldo Emerson took, unknown to himself, a great stride toward a broader wisdom than his narrow soul had ever conceived.

That night, after the sun had set and the stars and moon come out, the two set forth from their retreat toward the northwest, where the girl said that the village of her people lay.

They walked hand in hand through the dark wood, the

33

girl directing their steps, the young man grasping his long cudgel in his right hand and searching into the shadows for the terrible creatures conjured by his cowardly brain, but mostly for the two awesome spots of fire which he had gathered from the girl's talk would mark the presence of Nagoola.

Strange noises assailed his ears, and once the girl crouched close to him as her quick ears caught the sound of the movement of a great body through the underbrush at their left.

Waldo Emerson was almost paralyzed by terror; but at length the creature, whatever it may have been, turned off into the forest without molesting them. For several hours thereafter they suffered no alarm, but the constant tension of apprehension on the man's already over-wrought nerves had reduced him to a state of such abject nervous terror that he was no longer master of himself.

So it was that when the girl suddenly halted him with an affrighted little gasp and, pointing straight ahead, whispered, 'Nagoola,' he went momentarily mad with fear.

For a bare instant he paused in his tracks, and then breaking away from her, he raised his club above his head, and with an awful shriek dashed – straight toward the panther.

In the minds of some there may be a doubt as to which of the two – the sleek, silent, black cat or the grinning, screaming Waldo – was the most awe-inspiring.

Be that as it may, it was quite evident that no doubt assailed the mind of the cat, for with a single answering scream, he turned and faded into the blackness of the black night.

But Waldo did not see him go. Still shrieking, he raced on through the forest until he tripped over a creeper and fell exhausted to the earth. There he lay panting, twitching, and trembling until the girl found him, an hour after sunrise.

At the sound of her voice he would have struggled to his feet and dashed on into the woods, for he felt that he could never face her again after the spectacle of cowardice with which he had treated her a few hours before.

But even as he gained his feet her first words reassured him, and dissipated every vestige of his intention to elude her.

'Did you catch him?' she cried.

'No,' panted Waldo Emerson quite truthfully. 'He got away.'

They rested a little while, and then Waldo insisted that they resume their journey by day instead of by night. He had positively determined that he never should or could endure another such a night of mental torture. He would much rather take the chance of meeting with the bad men than suffer the constant feeling that unseen enemies were peering out of the darkness at him every moment.

In the day they would at least have the advantage of seeing their foes before they were struck. He did not give these reasons to the girl, however. Under the circumstances he felt that another explanation would be better adapted to her ears.

'You see,' he said, 'if it hadn't been so dark Nagoola might not have escaped me. It is too bad – too bad.'

'Yes,' agreed the girl, 'it is too bad. We shall travel by day. It will be safe now. We have left the country of the bad men, and there are few men living between us and my people.'

That night they spent in a cave they found in the steep bank of a small river.

It was damp and muddy and cold, but they were both very tired, and so they fell asleep and slept as soundly as though the best of mattresses lay beneath them. The girl probably slept better, since she had never been accustomed to anything much superior to this in all her life.

The journey required five days, instead of three, and during all the time Waldo was learning more and more woodcraft from the girl. At first his attitude had been such that he could profit but little from her greater practical knowledge, for he had been inclined to look down upon her as an untutored savage.

Now, however, he was a willing student, and when Waldo

Emerson elected to study there was nothing that he could not master and retain in a remarkable manner. He had a well-trained mind – the principal trouble with it being that it had been crammed full of useless knowledge. His mother had always made the error of confusing knowledge with wisdom.

Waldo was not the only one to learn new things upon this journey. The girl learned something, too – something which had been threatening for days to rise above the threshold of her conscious mind, and now she realized that it had lain in her heart almost ever since the first moment that she had been with this strange young man.

Waldo Emerson had been endowed by nature with a chivalrous heart, and his training had been such that he mechanically accorded to all women the gallant little courtesies and consideration which are of the fine things that go with breeding. Nor was he one whit less punctilious in his relations with this wild cave girl than he would have been with the daughter of the finest family of his own aristocracy.

He had been kind and thoughtful and sympathetic always, and to the girl, who had never been accustomed to such treatment from men, nor had ever seen a man accord it to any woman, it seemed little short of miraculous that such gentle tenderness could belong to a nature so warlike and ferocious as that with which she had endowed Waldo Emerson. But she was quite satisfied that it should be so.

She would not have cared for him had he been gentle with her, yet cowardly. Had she dreamed of the real truth – had she had the slightest suspicion that Waldo Emerson was at heart the most arrant poltroon upon whom the sun had ever shone, she would have loathed and hated him, for in the primitive code of ethics which governed the savage community which was her world there was no place for the craven or the weakling – and Waldo Emerson was both.

As the realization of her growing sentiment toward the man awakened, it imparted to her ways with him a sudden coyness and maidenly aloofness which had been entirely

36

wanting before. Until then their companionship, in so far as the girl was concerned, had been rather that of one youth toward another; but now that she found herself thrilling at his slightest careless touch, she became aware of a paradoxical impulse to avoid him.

For the first time in her life, too, she realized her nakedness, and was ashamed. Possibly this was due to the fact that Waldo appeared so solicitous in endeavoring to coerce his rags into the impossible feat of entirely covering his body.

As they neared their journey's end Waldo became more and more perturbed.

During the last night horrible visions of Flatfoot and Korth haunted his dreams. He saw the great, hairy beasts rushing upon him in all the ferocity of their primeval savagery – tearing him limb from limb in their bestial rage.

With a shriek he awoke.

To the girl's startled inquiry he replied that he had been but dreaming.

'Did you dream of Flatfoot and Korth?' she laughed. 'Of the things that you will do to them tomorrow?'

'Yes,' replied Waldo; 'I dreamed of Flatfoot and Korth.' But the girl did not see how he trembled and hid his head in the hollow of his arm.

The last day's march was the most agonizing experience of Waldo Emerson's life. He was positive that he was going to his death, but to him the horror of the thing lay more in the manner of his coming death than in the thought of death itself. As a matter of fact, he had again reached a point when he would have welcomed death.

The future held for him nothing but a life of discomfort and misery and constant mental anguish, superinduced by the condition of awful fear under which he must drag out his existence in this strange and terrible land.

Waldo had not the slightest conception as to whether he was upon some mainland or an unknown island. That the tidal wave had come upon them somewhere in the South Pacific was all that he knew; but long since he had given up hope that succor would reach him in time to prevent him perishing miserably far from his home and his poor mother.

He could not dwell long upon this dismal theme, because it always brought tears of self-pity to his eyes, and for some unaccountable reason Waldo shrunk from the thought of exhibiting this unmanly weakness before the girl.

All day long he racked his brain for some valid excuse whereby he might persuade his companion to lead him elsewhere than to her village. A thousand times better would be some secluded little garden such as that which had harbored them for the ten days following their escape from the cave men.

If they could but come upon such a place near the coast, where Waldo could keep a constant watch for passing vessels, he would have been as happy as he ever expected it would be possible for him in such a savage land.

He wanted the girl with him for companionship; he was more afraid when he was alone. Of course, he realized that she was no fit companion for a man of his mental attainments; but then she was a human being, and her society much better than none at all. While hope had still lingered that he might live to escape and return to his beloved Boston, he had often wondered whether he would dare tell his mother of his unconventional acquaintance with this young woman.

Of course, it would be out of the question for him to go at all into details. He would not, for example, dare to attempt a description of her toilet to his prim parent.

The fact that they had been alone together, day and night, for weeks was another item which troubled Waldo considerably. He knew that the shock of such information might prostrate his mother, and for a long time he debated the wisdom of omitting any mention of the girl whatever.

At length he decided that a little, white lie would be permissible, inasmuch as his mother's health and the girl's reputation were both at stake. So he had decided to mention that the girl's aunt had been with them in the capacity of chaperone; that fixed it nicely, and on this point Waldo's mind was more at ease.

Late in the afternoon they wound down a narrow trail that led from the plateau into a narrow, beautiful valley. A tree-bordered river meandered through the center of the level plain that formed the valley's floor, while beyond rose precipitous cliffs, which trailed off in each direction as far as the eye could reach.

'There live my people,' said the girl, pointing toward the distant barrier.

Waldo groaned inwardly.

'Let us rest here,' he said, 'until tomorrow, that we may come to your home rested and refreshed.'

'Oh, no,' cried the girl; 'we can reach the caves before dark. I can scarcely wait until I shall have seen how you shall slay Flatfoot, and maybe Korth also. Though I think that after one of them has felt your might the others will be glad to take you into the tribe at the price of your friendship.'

'Is there not some way,' ventured the distracted Waldo, 'that I may come into your village without fighting? I should dislike to kill one of your friends,' said Waldo solemnly.

The girl laughed.

'Neither Flatfoot nor Korth are friends of mine,' she replied; 'I hate them both. They are terrible men. It would be better for all the tribe were they killed. They are so strong and cruel that we all hate them, since they use their strength to abuse those who are weaker.

'They make us all work very hard for them. They take other men's mates, and if the other men object they kill them. There is scarcely a moon passes that does not see either Korth or Flatfoot kill someone.

'Nor is it always men they kill. Often when they are angry they kill women and little children just for the pleasure of killing; but when you come among us there will be no more of that, for you will kill them both if they be not good.'

Waldo was too horrified by this description of his soon-to-be antagonists to make any reply – his tongue clave to the roof of his mouth – all his vocal organs seemed paralyzed.

But the girl did not notice. She went on joyously, ripping Waldo's nervous system out of him and tearing it into shreds.

'You see,' she continued, 'Flatfoot and Korth are greater than the other men of my tribe. They can do as they will. They are frightful to look upon, and I have often thought that the hearts of others dried up when they saw either of them coming for them.

'And they are so strong! I have seen Korth crush the skull of a full-grown man with a single blow from his open palm; while one of Flatfoot's amusements is the breaking of men's arms and legs with his bare hands.'

They had entered the valley now, and in silence they continued on toward the fringe of trees which grew beside the little river.

Nadara led the way toward a ford, which they quickly crossed. All the way across the valley Waldo had been searching for some avenue of escape.

He dared not enter that awful village and face those terrible men, and he was almost equally averse to admitting to the girl that he was afraid.

He would gladly have died to have escaped either alternative, but he preferred to choose the manner of his death.

The thought of entering the village and meeting a horrible end at the hands of the brutes who awaited him there and of being compelled to demonstrate before the girl's eyes that he was neither a mighty fighter nor a hero was more than he could endure.

Occupied with these harrowing speculations, Waldo and Nadara came to the farther side of the forest, whence they could see the towering cliffs rising steeply from the valley's bed, three hundred yards away.

Along their face and at their feet Waldo descried a host of half-naked men, women, and children moving about in the consummation of their various duties. Involuntarily he halted.

The girl came to his side. Together they looked out upon the scene, the like of which Waldo Emerson never before had seen.

It was as though he had been suddenly snatched back through countless ages to a long-dead past and dropped into the midst of the prehistoric life of his paleolithic progenitors.

Upon the narrow ledges before their caves, women, with long, flowing hair, ground food in rude stone mortars.

Naked children played about them, perilously close to the precipitous cliff edge.

Hairy men squatted, gorillalike, before pieces of flat stone, upon which green hides were stretched, while they scraped, scraped, scraped with the sharp edge of smaller bits of stone.

There was no laughter and no song.

Occasionally Waldo saw one of the fierce creatures address another, and sometimes one would raise his thick lips in a nasty snarl that exposed his fighting fangs; but they were too far away for their words to reach the young man.

CHAPTER FIVE

AWAKENING

'Come,' said the girl, 'let us make haste. I cannot wait to be home again! How good it looks!'

Waldo gazed at her in horror. It did not seem credible that this beautiful young creature could be of such clay as that he looked upon. It was revolting to believe that she had sprung from the loins of one of those half-brutes, or that a woman as fierce, repulsive, such as those he saw before him, could have borne her. It made him sick with disgust.

He turned from her.

'Go to your people, Nadara,' he said, for an idea had come to him.

He had evolved a scheme for escaping a meeting with Flatfoot and Korth, and the sudden disgust which he felt for the girl made it easier for him to carry out his design.

'Are you not coming with me?' she cried.

'Not at once,' replied Waldo, quite truthfully. 'I wish you to go first. Were we to go together they might harm you when they rushed out to attack me.'

The girl had no fear of this, but she felt that it was very thoughtful of the man to consider her welfare so tenderly. To humor him, she acceded to his request.

'As you wish, Thandar,' she answered, smiling.

Thandar was a name of her own choosing, after Waldo had informed her in answer to a request for his name, that she might call him Mr Waldo Emerson Smith-Jones. 'I shall call you Thandar,' she had replied; 'it is shorter, more easily remembered, and describes you. It means the Brave One.' And so Thandar he had become.

The girl had scarcely emerged from the forest on her way

toward the cliffs when Thandar the Brave One, turned and ran at top speed in the opposite direction. When he came to the river he gave immediate evidence of the strides he had taken in woodcraft during the brief weeks that he had been under the girl's tutorage, for he plunged immediately into the water, setting out up-stream upon the gravelly bottom where he would leave no spoor to be tracked down by the eagle eyes of these primitive men.

He supposed that the girl would search for him; but he felt no compunction at having deserted her so scurvily. Of course, he had no suspicion of her real sentiments toward him – it would have shocked him to have imagined that a low-born person, such as she, had become infatuated with him.

It would have been embarrassing and unfortunate, but, of course, quite impossible – since Waldo Emerson Smith-Jones could never form an alliance beneath him. As for the girl herself, he might as readily have considered the possibility of marrying a cow, so far from any such thoughts of her had he been.

On and on he stumbled through the cold water. Sometimes it was above his head, but Waldo had learned to swim – the girl had made him, partly by pleas, but largely by fear that she would ridicule him.

As night came on he commenced to become afraid, but his fear now was not such a horribly prostrating thing as it had been a few weeks before. Without being aware of the fact, Waldo had grown a trifle less timid, though he was still far from lion-like.

That night he slept in the crotch of a tree. He selected a small one, which, though less comfortable, was safer from the approach of Nagoola than a larger tree would have been. This also had he learned from Nadara.

Had he paused to consider, he would have discovered that all he knew that was worth while he had had from the savage little girl whom he, from the high pinnacle of his erudition, regarded with such pity. But Waldo had not as yet learned enough to realize how very little he knew.

In the morning he continued his flight, gathering his breakfast from tree and shrub as he fled. Here again was he wholly indebted to Nadara, for without her training he would have been restricted to a couple of fruits, whereas now he had a great variety of fruits, roots, berries, and nuts to choose from in safety.

The stream that he had been following had now become a narrow, rushing, mountain torrent. It leaped suddenly over little precipices in wild and picturesque waterfalls; it rioted in foaming cascades; and ever it led Waldo farther into high and rugged country.

The climbing was difficult and oftentimes dangerous. Waldo was surprised at the steeps he negotiated -- perilous ascents from which he would have shrunk in palsied fear a few weeks earlier. Waldo was coming on.

Another fact which struck him with amazement at the same time that it filled him with rejoicing, was that he no longer coughed. It was quite beyond belief, too, since never in his life had he been so exposed to cold and wet and discomfort.

At home, he realized, he would long since have curled up and died had he been subjected to one-tenth the exposure that he had undergone since the great wave had lifted him bodily from the deck of the steamer to land him unceremoniously in the midst of this new life of hardships and terrors.

Toward noon Waldo began to travel with less haste. He had seen or heard no evidence of pursuit. At times he stopped to look back along the trail he had passed, but though he could see the little valley below him for a considerable distance he discovered nothing to arouse alarm.

Presently he realized that he was very lonely. A dozen times in as many minutes he thought of observations he would have been glad to make had there been some one with him to hear. There were queries, too, relative to this new country that he should have liked very much to propound, and it flashed upon him that in all the world there was only

44

one whom he knew who could give him correct answers to these queries.

He wondered what the girl had thought when he did not follow her into the village, and set upon Flatfoot and Korth. At the thought he found himself flushing in a most unaccountable manner.

What would the girl think! Would she guess the truth? Well, what difference if she did? What was her opinion to a cultured gentleman such as Waldo Emerson Smith-Jones? But yet he found his mind constantly reverting to this unhappy speculation; it was most annoying.

As he thought of her he discovered with what distinctness he recalled every feature of her piquant little face, her olive skin tinged beautifully by the ruddy glow of health; her fine, straight nose and delicate nostrils, her perfect eyes, soft, yet filled with the fire of courage and intelligence. Waldo wondered why it was that he recalled these things now, and dwelt upon them; he had been with her for weeks without realizing that he had particularly noticed them.

But most vividly he conjured again the memory of her soft, liquid speech, her ready retorts, her bright, interesting observations on the little happenings of their daily life; her thoughtful kindliness to him, a stranger within her gates, and – again he flushed hotly – her sincere, though remarkable, belief in his prowess.

It took Waldo a long time to admit to himself that he missed the girl; it must have been weeks before he finally did so unreservedly. Simultaneously he determined to return to her village and find her. He had even gone so far as to start the return journey when the memory of her description of Flatfoot and Korth brought him to a sudden halt – a most humiliating halt.

The blood surged to his face – he could feel it burning there. And then Waldo did two things which he had never done before: he looked at his soul and saw himself as he was, and – he swore.

'Waldo Emerson Smith-Jones,' he said aloud, 'you're a

darned coward! Worse than that, you're an unthinkable cad. That girl was kind to you. She treated you with the tender solicitude of a mother. And how have you returned her kindness? By looking down upon her with arrogant condescension. By pitying her.

'Pitying her! You – you miserable weakling – ingrate, pitying that fine, intelligent, generous girl. You, with your pitiful little store of secondhand knowledge, pitying that girl's ignorance. Why, she's forgotten more real things than you ever heard of, you – you—' Words utterly failed him.

Waldo's awakening was thorough – painfully thorough. It left no tiny hidden recess of his contemptible little soul unrevealed from his searching self-analysis. Looking back over the twenty-one years of his uneventful life, he failed to resurrect but a single act of which he might now be proud, and that, strange to say, in the light of his past training, had to do neither with culture, intellect, birth, breeding, nor knowledge.

It was a purely gross, physical act. It was hideously, violently, repulsively animal – it was no other than the instant of heroism in which he had turned back upon the cliff's face to battle with the horrible, hairy man who had threatened to prevent Nadara's escape.

Even now Waldo could not realize that it had been he who ventured so foolhardy an act; but none the less his breast swelled with pride as he recalled it. It put into the heart of the man a new hope and into his head a new purpose – a purpose that would have caused his Back Bay mother to seek an early grave could she have known of it.

Nor did Waldo Emerson lose any time in initiating the new regime which was eventually to fit him for the consummation of his splendid purpose. He thought of it as splendid now, though a few weeks before the vulgar atrocity of it would have nauseated him.

Far up in the hills, near the source of the little river, Waldo had found a rocky cave. This he had chosen as his new home. He cleaned it out with scrupulous care, littering the floor with leaves and grasses.

Before the entrance he piled a dozen large boulders, so arranged that three of them could be removed or replaced either from within or without, thus forming a means of egress and ingress which could be effectually closed against intruders.

From the top of a high promontory, a half mile beyond his cave, Waldo could obtain a view of the ocean, some eight or ten miles distant. It was always in his mind that some day a ship would come, and Waldo longed to return to the haunts of civilization, but he did not expect the ship before his plans had properly matured and been put into execution. He argued that he could not sail away from this shore forever without first seeing Nadara, and restoring the confidence in him which he felt his recent desertion had unquestionably shaken to its foundation.

As a part of his new regime, Waldo required exercise, and to this end he set about making a trip to the ocean at least once each week. The way was rough and hazardous, and the first few times Waldo found it almost beyond his strength to make even one leg of the journey between sunrise and dark.

This necessitated sleeping out over night; but this, too, accorded with the details of the task he had set himself, and so he did it quite cheerfully and with a sense of martyrdom that he found effectually stilled his most poignant fits of cowardice.

As time went on he was able to cover the whole distance to the ocean and return in a single day. He never coughed now, nor did he glance fearfully from side to side as he strode through the woods and open places of his wild domain.

His eyes were bright and clear, his head and shoulders were thrown well back, and the mountain climbing had expanded his chest to a degree that appalled him – the while it gave him much secret satisfaction. It was a very different Waldo from the miserable creature which had been vomited up by the ocean upon the sand of that distant beach.

The days that Waldo did not make a trip to the ocean he spent in rambling about the hills in the vicinity of his cave. He knew every rock and tree within five miles of his lair.

He knew where Nagoola hid by day, and the path that he took down to the valley by night. Nor did he longer tremble at sight of the great, black cat.

True, Waldo avoided him, but it was through cool and deliberate caution, which is quite another thing from the senseless panic of fear. Waldo was biding his time.

He would not always avoid Nagoola. Nagoola was a part of Waldo's great plan, but Waldo was not ready for him yet.

The young man still bore his cudgel, and in addition he had practised throwing rocks until he could almost have hit a near-by bird upon the wing. Besides these weapons Waldo was working upon a spear. It had occurred to him that a spear would be a mighty handy weapon against either man or beast, and so he had set to work to fashion one.

He found a very straight young sapling, a little over an inch in diameter and ten feet long. By means of a piece of edged flint he succeeded in tapering it to a sharp point. A rawhide thong, plaited from many pieces of small bits of hide taken from the little animals that had fallen before his missiles, served to sling the crude weapon across his shoulders when he walked.

With his spear he practised hour upon hour each day, until he could transfix a fruit the size of an apple three times out of five, at a distance of fifty feet, and at a hundred hit a target the size of a man almost without a miss.

Six months had passed since he had fled from an encounter with Flatfoot and Korth.

Then Waldo had been a skinny, cowardly weakling; now his great frame had filled out with healthy flesh, while beneath his skin hard muscles rolled as he bent to one of the many Herculean tasks he had set for himself.

For six months he had worked with a single purpose in view, but still he felt that the day was not yet come when he might safely venture to put his newfound manhood to the test.

Down, far down, in the depth of his soul he feared that he was yet a coward at heart – and he dared not take the risk. It was too much to expect, he told himself, that a man should be entirely metamorphosed in a brief half year. He would wait a little longer.

It was about this time that Waldo first saw a human being after his last sight of Nadara.

It was while he was on his way to the ocean, on one of the trips that had by this time become thrice weekly affairs, that he suddenly came face to face with a skulking, hairy brute.

Waldo halted to see what would happen.

The man eyed him with those small, cunning, red-rimmed eyes that reminded Waldo of the eyes of a pig.

Finally Waldo spoke in the language of Nadara.

'Who are you?' he said.

'Sag the Killer,' replied the man. 'Who are you?'

'Thandar,' answered Waldo.

'I do not know you,' said Sag; 'but I can kill you.'

He lowered his bull head and came for Waldo like a battering ram.

The young man dropped the point of his ready spear, bracing his feet. The point entered Sag's breast below the collar-bone, stopping only after it had passed entirely through the savage heart. Waldo had not moved; the momentum of the man's body had been sufficient to impale him.

As the body rolled over, stiffening after a few convulsive kicks, Waldo withdrew his spear from it. Blood smeared its point for a distance of a foot, but Waldo showed no sign of loathing or disgust.

Instead he smiled. It had been so much easier than he had anticipated.

Leaving Sag where he had fallen he continued toward the ocean. An hour later he heard unusual noises behind him.

He stopped to listen. He was being pursued. From the

sounds he estimated that there must be several in the party, and a moment later, as he was crossing a clearing, he got his first view of them as they emerged from the forest he had just quitted.

There were at least twenty powerfully muscled brutes. In skin bags thrown across their shoulders each carried a supply of stones, and these they began to hurl at Waldo as they raced toward him. For a moment the man held his ground, but he quickly realized the futility of pitting himself against such odds.

Turning, he ran toward the forest upon the other side of the clearing while a shower of rocks whizzed about him.

Once within the shelter of the trees there was less likelihood of his being hit by one of the missiles, but occasionally a well-aimed rock would strike him a glancing blow. Waldo hoped that they would tire of the chase before the beach was reached, for he knew that there could be but one outcome of a battle in which one man faced twenty.

As the pursued and the pursuers raced on through the forest one of the latter, fleeter than his companions, commenced to close up the gap which had existed between Waldo and the twenty. On and on he came, until a backward glance showed Waldo that in another moment this swift foeman would be upon him. He was younger than his fellows and more active, and, having thrown all his stones, was free from any burden of weight other than the single garment about his hips.

Waldo still clung to his tattered ducks, which from lack of support and more or less rapid disintegration were continually slipping down from his hips, so that they tended to hinder his movements and reduce his speed.

Had he been as naked as his pursuer he would doubtless have distanced him; but he was not, and it was evident that because of this fact he must take a chance in a hand-to-hand encounter that might delay him sufficiently to permit the balance of the horde to reach him – that would be the end of everything.

But Waldo Emerson neither screamed in terror nor trembled. When he wheeled to meet the now close savage there was a smile upon his lips, for Waldo Emerson had 'killed his man', and there was no longer the haunting fear within his soul that at heart he was a coward.

As he turned with couched spear the cave man came to a sudden stop.

This was not what Waldo had anticipated. The other savages were running rapidly toward him, but the fellow who had first overhauled him remained at a safe twenty feet from the point of his weapon.

Waldo was being cleverly held until the remainder of the enemy could arrive and overwhelm him. He knew that if he turned to run the fellow who danced and yelled just beyond his reach would plunge forward and be upon his back in an instant.

He tried rushing the man, but the other retreated nimbly, drawing Waldo still closer to those who were coming on.

There was no time to be lost. A moment more and the entire twenty would be upon him; but there were possibilities in a spear that the cave man in his ignorance dreamed not of. There was a lightninglike movement of Waldo's arm, and the aborigine saw the spear darting swiftly through space toward his breast. He tried to dodge, but was too late. Down he went, clutching madly at the slender thing which protruded from his heart.

Although one of the dead man's companions was now quite close, Waldo could not relinquish his weapon without an effort – it had cost him considerable time to make, and twice today it had saved his life. Forgetful that he had ever been a coward he leaped toward the fallen man, reaching his side at the same instant as his foremost pursuer.

The two came together like mad bulls – the savage reaching for Waldo's throat, Waldo wielding his light cudgel. For a moment they struggled backward and forward, turning and twisting, the cave man in an effort to close upon Waldo's wind, Waldo to hold the other at arm's length for the brief instant that would be necessary for one sudden, effective blow from the cudgel.

The other savages were almost upon them when the young man found his antagonist's throat. Throwing all his weight and strength into the effort, Waldo forced the cave man back until there was room between them for the play of the stick. A single blow was sufficient.

As the limp body of his foeman slipped from his grasp, Waldo snatched his precious spear from the heart of its victim, and with the hands of the infuriated pack almost upon him, turned once more into his flight toward the ocean.

The howling band was close upon his heels now, nor could he greatly increase the distance that separated him from them. He wondered what the outcome of the matter was to be; he did not wish to die. His thoughts kept reverting to his boyhood home, to his indulgent mother, to the friends that had been his. He felt that at the last moment he was about to lose his nerve – that, after all, his hard earned manliness was counterfeit.

Then there came to him a vision of an oval, olive face framed by a mass of soft, black hair; and before it the fear of death dissolved into a grim smile. He did not pause to analyze the reason for it – nor could he have done so then had he tried. He only knew that with those eyes upon him he could not be aught else than courageous.

A moment later he burst through the last fringe of underbrush to emerge upon the clearing that faced the sea.

There by a tiny rivulet he saw a sight that filled him with thanksgiving, and farther out upon the ocean that which he had been waiting and hoping for for all these long, hard months – a ship.

CHAPTER SIX

A CHOICE

Seamen upon the beach were filling watercasks.

There were a dozen of them, and as Waldo plunged from the forest they looked with startled apprehension at the strange apparition. A great, brown giant they saw, clad in a few ragged strings of white duck, for Waldo had kept his apparel as immaculately clean as hard rubbing in cold water would permit.

In one hand the strange creature carried a long, bloody spear, in the other a light cudgel. Long, yellow hair streamed back over his broad shoulders.

Several of the men — those who were armed — leveled guns and revolvers at him; but when, as he drew closer, they saw a broad grin upon his face, and heard in perfectly good English, 'Don't shoot; I'm a white man,' they lowered their weapons and awaited him.

He had scarcely reached them when they saw a swarm of naked men dash from the forest in his wake. Waldo saw their eyes directed past him and knew that his pursuers had come into view.

'You'll have to shoot at them, I imagine,' he said. 'They're not exactly domesticated. Try firing over their heads at first; maybe you can scare them away without hurting any of them.'

He disliked the idea of seeing the poor savages slaughtered. It didn't seem just like fair play to mow them down with bullets.

The sailors followed his suggestion. At the first reports the cave men halted in surprise and consternation.

'Let's rush 'em,' suggested one of the men, and this was all that was needed to send them scurrying back into the woods.

Waldo found that the ship was English, and that all the men spoke his mother tongue in more or less understandable fashion. The second mate, who was in charge of the landing party, proved to have originated in Boston. It was much like being at home again.

Waldo was so excited and wanted to ask so many questions all at once that he became almost unintelligible. It seemed scarcely possible that a ship had really come.

He realized now that he had never actually entertained any very definite belief that a ship ever would come to this out-of-the-way corner of the world. He had hoped and dreamed, but down in the bottom of his heart he must have felt that years might elapse before he would be rescued.

Even now it was difficult to believe that these were really civilized beings like himself.

They were on their way to a civilized world; they would soon be surrounded by their families and friends, and he, Waldo Emerson Smith-Jones, was going with them!

In a few months he would see his mother and his father and all his friends – he would be among his books once more.

Even as the last thought flashed through his mind it was succeeded by mild wonderment that this outlook failed to raise his temperature as he might have expected that it would. His books had been his real life in the past – could it be that they had lost something of their glamour? Had his brief experience with the realities of life dulled the edge of his appetite for second-hand hopes, aspirations, deeds, and emotions?

It had.

Waldo yet craved his books, but they alone would no longer suffice. He wanted something bigger, something more real and tangible – he wanted to read and study, but even more he wanted to do. And back there in his own world there would be plenty awaiting the doing.

His heart thrilled at the possibilities that lay before the new Waldo Emerson – possibilities of which he never would have dreamed but for the strange chance which had snatched him bodily from one life to throw him into this new one, which had forced upon him the development of attributes of self-reliance, courage, initiative, and resourcefulness that would have lain dormant within him always but for the necessity which had given birth to them.

Yes, Waldo realized that he owed a great deal to this experience – a great deal to – And then a sudden realization of the truth rushed in upon him – he owed everything to Nadara.

'I was never shipwrecked on a desert island,' said the second mate, breaking in upon Waldo's reveries, 'but I can imagine just about how good you feel at the thought that you are at last rescued and that in an hour or so you will see the shoreline of your prison growing smaller and smaller upon the southern horizon.'

'Yes,' acquiesced Waldo in a far away voice: 'It's awfully good of you, but I am not going with you.'

Two hours later Waldo Emerson stood alone upon the beach, watching the diminishing hull of a great ship as it dropped over the rim of the world far to the north.

A vague hint of tears dimmed his vision; then he threw back his shoulders, swallowed the thing that had risen into his throat, and with high held head turned back into the forest.

In one hand he carried a razor and a plug of tobacco – the sole mementos of his recent brief contact with the world of civilization. The kindly sailors had urged him to reconsider his decision, but when he remained obdurate they had insisted that they be permitted to leave some of the comforts of life with him.

The only thing that he could think of that he wanted very badly was a razor – firearms he would not accept, for he had worked out a rather fine chivalry of his own here in this savage world – a chivalry which would not permit him to take any advantage over the primeval inhabitants he had found here other than what his own hands and head might give him.

At the last moment one of the seamen, prompted by a generous heart and a keen realization of what life must be without even bare necessities, had thrust upon Waldo the plug of tobacco. As he looked at it now the young man smiled.

'That would indeed be the last step, according to mother's ideas,' he soliloquized. 'No lower could I sink.'

The ship that bore away Waldo's chance of escape carried also a long letter to Waldo's mother. In portions it was rather vague and rambling. It mentioned, among other things, that he had an obligation to fulfil before he could leave his present habitat; but that the moment he was free he should 'take the first steamer for Boston'.

The skipper of the ship which had just sailed away had told Waldo that in so far as he knew there might never be another ship touch his island, which was so far out of the beaten course that only the shore-line of it had ever been explored, and scarce a score of vessels had reported it since Captain Cook discovered it in 1773.

Yet it was in the face of this that Waldo had refused to leave. As he walked slowly through the wood on his way back toward his cave he tried to convince himself that he had acted purely from motives of gratitude and fairness – that as a gentleman he could do no less than see Nadara and thank her for the friendly services she had rendered him; but for some reason this seemed a very futile and childish excuse for relinquishing what might easily be his only opportunity to return to civilization.

His final decision was that he had acted the part of a fool; yet as he walked he hummed a joyous tune, and his heart was full of happiness and pleasant expectations of what he could not have told.

To one thing he had made up his mind, and that was that the next sun would see him on his way to the village of Nadara. His experience with the savages that day had convinced him that he might with reasonable safety face Flat-foot and Korth.

The more he dwelt upon this idea the more light-hearted he became – he could not understand it. He should be plunged into the blackest despair, for had he not within a day or two to enter the village of the ferocious Flatfoot and the mighty Korth? Even so, his heart sang.

Waldo saw nothing of his enemies of the earlier part of the day as he moved cautiously through the forest or crossed the little plains and meadows which lay along the route between the ocean and his lair; but his thoughts often reverted to them and to his adventures of the morning, and the result was that he became aware of a deficiency in his equipment – a deficiency which his recent battle made glaringly apparent.

In fact, there were two points that might be easily rem-edied. One was the lack of a shield. Had he had protection of this nature he would have been in comparatively little danger from the shower of missiles that the savages had flung at him.

The other was a sword. With a sword and shield he could have let his enemies come to very close quarters with perfect impunity to himself and then have run them through with infinite ease.

This new idea would necessitate a delay in his plans; he must finish both shield and sword before he departed for the village of Flatfoot. What with his meditation and his plan-ning, Waldo had made poor time on the return journey from the coast, so that it was after sunset when he entered the last deep ravine beyond the farther summit of which lay his rocky home. In the depths of the ravine it was already quite dark, though a dim twilight still hung upon the surrounding hill-tops.

He had about completed the arduous ascent of the last steep trail, at the crest of which was his journey's end, when above him, silhouetted against the darkening sky, loomed a great black, crouching mass, from the center of which blazed two balls of fire.

It was Nagoola, and he occupied the center of the only trail that led over the edge of the ridge from the ravine below.

'I had almost forgotten you, Nagoola,' murmured Waldo Emerson. 'I could never have gone upon my journey without first interviewing you, but I could have wished a different time and place than this. Let us postpone the matter for a day or so,' he concluded aloud; but the only response from Nagoola was an ominous growl. Waldo felt rather uncomfortable.

He could not have come upon the great, black panther at a more inopportune time or place. It was too dark for Waldo's human eyes, and the cat was above him and Waldo upon a steep hillside that under the best of conditions offered but a precarious foothold. He tried to shoo the formidable beast away by shouts and menacing gesticulations, but Nagoola would not shoo.

Instead he crept slowly forward, edging his sinuous body inch by inch along the rocky trail until it hung poised above the waiting man a dozen feet below him.

Six months before Waldo would long since have been shrieking in meteorlike flight down the bed of the ravine behind him. That a wonderful transformation had been wrought within him was evident from the fact that no cry of fright escaped him, and that, far from fleeing, he edged inch by inch upward toward the menacing creature hanging there above him. He carried his spear with the point leveled a trifle below those baleful eyes.

He had advanced but a foot or two, however, when, with an awful shriek, the terrible beast launched itself full upon him.

As the heavy body struck him Waldo went over backward down the cliff, and with him went Nagoola.

Clawing, tearing, and scratching the two rolled and bounded down the rocky hillside until, near the bottom, they came to a sudden stop against a large tree.

The growling and screeching ceased, the clawing paws

and hands were still. Presently the tropic moon rose over the hill-top to look down upon a little tangled mound of man and beast that lay very quiet against the bole of a great tree near the bottom of a dark ravine.

CHAPTER SEVEN

THANDAR, THE SEEKER

For a long time there was no sign of life in that strange pile of flesh and bone and brawn and glossy black fur and long, yellow hair and blood. But toward dawn it moved a little, down near the bottom of the heap, and a little later there was a groan, and then all was still again for many minutes.

Presently it moved again, this time more energetically, and after several efforts a yellow head streaked and matted with blood emerged from beneath. It required the better part of an hour for the stunned and lacerated Waldo to extricate himself from the entangling embrace of Nagoola.

When, finally, he staggered to his feet he saw that the great cat lay dead before him, the broken shaft of the spear protruding from the sleek, black breast.

It was quite evident that the beast had lived but the barest fraction of an instant after it had launched itself upon the man; but during that brief interval of time it had wrought sore havoc with its mighty talons, though fortunately for Waldo the great jaws had not found him.

From breast to knees ghastly wounds were furrowed in the man's brown skin where the powerful hind feet of the beast had raked him.

That he owed his life to the chance that had brought about the encounter upon a steep hillside rather than on the level seemed quite apparent, for during their tumble down the declivity Nagoola had been unable to score with any degree of accuracy.

As Waldo looked down upon himself he was at first horrified by the frightful appearance of his wounds; but when a closer examination showed them to be superficial he realized that the only danger lay in infection. Every bone and muscle in his body ached from the man-handling and the fall, and the wounds themselves were painful, almost excruciatingly so when a movement of his body stretched or tore them; but notwithstanding his suffering he found himself smiling as he contemplated the remnants of his long-suffering ducks.

There remained of their once stylish glory not a shred – the panther's sharp claws had finished what time and brambles had so well commenced. And of their linen partner – the white outing shirt – only the neckband remained, with a single fragment as large as one's hand depending behind.

'Nature is a wonderful leveler,' thought Waldo. 'It is evident that she hates artificiality as she does a vacuum. I shall really need you now,' he concluded, looking at the beautiful, black coat of Nagoola.

Despite his suffering, Waldo crawled to his lair, where he selected a couple of sharp-edged stones from his collection and returned to the side of Nagoola.

Leaving his tools there he went on down to the bottom of the ravine, where in a little crystal stream he bathed his wounds. Then he returned once more to his kill.

After half a day of the most arduous labor Waldo succeeded in removing the panther's hide, which he dragged laboriously to his lair, where he fell exhausted, unable even to crawl within.

The next day Waldo worked upon the inner surface of the hide, removing every particle of flesh by scraping it with a sharp stone, so that there might be no danger of decomposition.

He was still very weak and sore, but he could not bear the thought of losing the pelt that had cost him so much to obtain.

When the last vestige of flesh had been scraped away he crawled into his lair, where he remained for a week, only emerging for food and water. At the end of that time his wounds were almost healed, and he had entirely recovered from his lameness and the shock of the adventure, so that it was with real pleasure and exultation that he gloated over his beautiful trophy.

Always as he thought of the time that he should have it made ready for girting about his loins he saw himself, not through his own eyes, but as he imagined that another would see him, and that other was Nadara.

For many days Waldo scraped and pounded the great skin as he had seen the cave men scrape and pound in the brief instant he had watched them with Nadara from the edge of the forest before the village of Flatfoot. At last he was rewarded with a pelt sufficiently pliable for the purpose of the rude apparel he contemplated.

A strip an inch wide he trimmed off to form a supporting belt. With this he tied the black skin about his waist, passed one arm through a hole he had made for that purpose near the upper edge; bringing the fore paws forward about his chest, he crossed and fastened them to secure the garment from falling from the upper part of his body.

It was a very proud Waldo that strutted forth in the finery of his new apparel; but the pride was in the prowess that had won the thing for him – vulgar, gross, brutal, physical prowess – the very attribute upon which he had looked with supercilious contempt six months before.

Next Waldo turned his attention toward the fashioning of a sword, a new spear, and a shield. The first two were comparatively easy of accomplishment – he had them both completed in half a day, and from a two-inch strip of panther hide he made also a sword belt to pass over his right shoulder and support his sword at his left side; but the shield almost defied his small skill and newborn ingenuity.

With small twigs and grasses he succeeded, after nearly a week of painstaking endeavor, in weaving a rude, oval buckler three feet long by two wide, which he covered with the skins of several small animals that had fallen before his death-dealing stones. A strip of hide fastened upon the back of the shield held it to his left arm.

With it Waldo felt more secure against the swiftly thrown missiles of the savages he knew he should encounter on his forthcoming expedition.

At last came the morning for departure. Rising with the sun, Waldo took his morning 'tub' in the cold spring that rose a few yards from his cave, then he got out the razor that the sailor had given him, and after scraping off his scanty, yellow beard, hacked his tawny hair until it no longer fell about his shoulders and in his eyes.

Then he gathered up his weapons, rolled the boulders before the entrance to his cave, and turning his back upon his rough home set off down the little stream toward the distant valley where it wound through the forest along the face of the cliffs to Flatfoot and Korth.

As he stepped lightly along the hazardous trail, leaping from ledge to ledge in the descent of the many sheer drops over which the stream fell, he might have been a re-incarnation of some primeval hunter from whose savage loins had sprung the warriors and the strong men of a world.

The tall, well-muscled, brown body; the clear, bright eyes; the high-held head; the sword, the spear, the shield were all a far cry from the weak and futile thing that had lain groveling in the sand upon the beach, sweating and shrieking in terror six short months before. And yet it was the same.

What one good but mistaken woman had smothered another had brought out, and the result of the influence of both was a much finer specimen of manhood than either might have evolved alone.

In the afternoon of the third day Waldo came to the forest opposite the cliffs where lay the home of Nadara. Cautiously he stole from tree to tree until he could look out unseen upon the honey-combed face of the lofty escarpment.

All was lifeless and deserted. The cave mouths looked out upon the valley, sad and lonely. There was no sign of life in any direction as far as Waldo could see.

Coming from the forest he crossed the clearing and approached the cliffs. His eye, now become alert in woodcraft, detected the young grass growing in what had once been well-beaten trails. He needed no further evidence to assure him that the caves were deserted, and had been for some time.

One by one he entered and explored several of the cliff dwellings. All gave the same mute corroboration of what was everywhere apparent – the village had been evacuated without haste in an orderly manner. Everything of value had been removed – only a few broken utensils remaining as indication that it had ever constituted human habitation.

Waldo was utterly confounded. He had not the remotest idea in which direction to search. During the balance of the afternoon he wandered along the various ledges, entering first one cave and then another.

He wondered which had been Nadara's. He tried to imagine her life among these crude, primitive surroundings; among the beastlike men and women who were her people. She did not seem to harmonize with either. He was convinced that she was more out of place here than Flatfoot would have been in a Back Bay drawing-room.

The more his mind dwelt upon her the sadder he became. He tried to convince himself that it was purely disappointment in being thwarted in his desire to thank her for her kindness to him, and demonstrate that her confidence in his prowess had not been misplaced; but always he discovered that his thoughts returned to Nadara rather than to the ostensible object of his adventure.

In short he began to realize, rather vaguely it is true, that he had come because he wanted to see the girl again; but why he wanted to see her he did not know.

That night he slept in one of the deserted caves, and the next morning set forth upon his quest for Nadara. For three days he searched the little valley, but without results. There was no sign of any other village within it.

Then he passed over into another valley to the north. For

weeks he wandered hither and thither without being rewarded by even a sight of a human being.

Early one afternoon as he was topping a barrier in search of other valleys he came suddenly face to face with a great, hairy man. Both stopped – the hairy one glaring with his nasty little eyes.

'I can kill you,' growled the savage.

Waldo had no desire to fight – it was information he was searching. But he almost smiled at the ready greeting of the man. It was the same that Sag the Killer had accorded him that day he had gone down to the sea for the last time.

It came as readily and as glibly from these primitive men as 'good morning' falls from the lips of the civilized races, yet among the latter he realized that it had its counterpart in these stony stares which Anglo Saxon strangers vouchsafe one another.

'I have no quarrel with you,' replied Waldo. 'Let us be friends.'

'You are afraid,' taunted the hairy one.

Waldo pointed to his sable garment.

'Ask Nagoola,' he said.

The man looked at the trophy. There could be no mightier argument for a man's valor than that. He came a step closer that he might scrutinize it more carefully.

'Full-grown and in perfect health,' he grunted to himself. 'This is no worn and mangy hide peeled from the rotting carcass of one dead of sickness.

'How did you slay Nagoola?' he asked suddenly.

Waldo indicated his spear, then he drew his garment aside and pointed to the vivid, new-healed scars that striped his body.

'We met at dusk at a cliff-top. He was above, I below. When we reached the bottom of the ravine Nagoola was dead. But it was nothing for Thandar. I am Thandar.'

Waldo rightly suspected that a little bravado would make a good impression on the intellect primeval, nor was he mistaken.

'What do you here in my country?' asked the man, but his tone was less truculent than before.

'I am searching for Flatfoot and Korth – and Nadara,' said Waldo.

The other's eyes narrowed.

'What would you of them?' he asked.

'Nadara was good to me – I would repay her.'

'But Flatfoot and Korth – what of them?' insisted the man.

'My business is with them. When I see them I shall transact it,' Waldo parried, for he had seen the cunning look in the man's eyes and he did not like it. 'Can you lead me to them?'

'I can tell you where they are, but I am not bound thither,' replied the man. 'Three days toward the setting sun will bring you to the village of Flatfoot. There you will find Korth also – and Nadara,' and without further parley the savage turned and trotted toward the east.

CHAPTER EIGHT

NADARA AGAIN

Waldo watched him out of sight, half minded to follow, for he was far from satisfied that the fellow had been entirely honest with him. Why he should have been otherwise Waldo could not imagine, but nevertheless there had been an indefinable suggestion of duplicity in the man's behavior that had puzzled him.

However, Waldo took up his search toward the west, passing down from the hills into a deep valley, the bottom of which was overgrown by a thick tangle of tropical jungle.

He had forced his way through this for nearly half a mile when he came to the bank of a wide, slow-moving river. Its water was thick with sediment – not clean, sparkling, and inviting, as were the little mountain streams of the hills and valleys farther south.

Waldo traveled along the edge of the river in a north-westerly direction, searching for a ford. The steep, muddy banks offered no foothold, so he dared not venture a crossing until he could be sure of a safe landing upon the opposite shore.

A couple of hundred yards from the point at which he had come upon the stream he found a broad trail leading down into the water, and on the other side saw a similar track cutting up through the bank.

This, evidently, was the ford he sought, but as he started toward the river he noticed the imprints of the feet of many animals – human and brute.

Waldo stooped to examine them minutely. There were the broad pads of Nagoola, the smaller imprints of countless rodents, but back and forth among them all were old and new signs of man.

There were the great, flat-foot prints of huge adult males, the smaller but equally flat-footed impresses of the women and children; but one there was that caught his eye particularly.

It was the fine and dainty outline of a perfect foot, with the arch well defined. It was new, as were many of the others, and, like the other newer ones, it led down to the river and then back again, as though she who made it had come for water and then returned from whence she had come. Waldo knew that the tracks leading away from the river were newer, because where the two trails overlapped those coming up from the ford were always over those which led downward.

The multiplicity of signs indicated a considerable community, and their newness the proximity of the makers.

Waldo hesitated but a moment before he reached a decision, and then he turned up the trail away from the river, and at a rapid trot followed the spoor along its winding course through the jungle to where it emerged at the base of the foothills, to wind upward toward their crest.

He found that the trail he was following crossed the hills but a few yards from the spot at which he had met the cave man a short time before. Evidently the man had been returning from the river when he had espied Waldo.

The young man could see where the fellow's tracks had left the main trail, and he followed them to the point where the man had stood during his conversation with Waldo; from there they led toward the east for a short distance, and then turned suddenly north to reenter the main trail.

Waldo could see that as soon as the man had reached a point from which he would be safe from the stranger's observation he had broken into a rapid trot, and as he already had two hours' start Waldo felt that he would have to hurry were he to overtake him.

Just why he wished to do so he did not consider, but intuitively possibly, he felt that the surly brute could give him much more and accurate information than he had. Nor could Waldo eliminate the memory of those dainty feminine footprints.

It was foolish, of course, and he fully realized the fact; but his silly mind would insist upon attributing them to the cave girl – Nadara.

For two hours he trotted doggedly along the trail, which for the most part was well defined. There were places, of course, which taxed his trailing ability, but by circling widely from these points he always was able to pick up the tracks again.

He had come down from the hills and entered an open forest, where the trail was entirely lost in the mossy carpet that lay beneath the trees, when he was startled by a scream – a woman's scream – and the hoarse gutturals of two men, deep and angry.

Hastening toward the sound, Waldo came upon the authors of the commotion in a little glade half hidden by surrounding bushes.

There were three actors in the hideous tragedy – a hairy brute dragging a protesting girl by her long, black hair and an old man, who followed, protesting futilely against the outrage that threatened the young woman.

None of them saw Waldo as he ran toward them until he was almost upon them, and then the beast who grasped the girl looked up, and Waldo recognized him as the same who had sent him toward the west earlier in the day.

At the same instant he saw the girl was Nadara.

In the brief interval that the recognition required there sloughed from the heart and mind and soul of Waldo Emerson Smith-Jones every particle of the civilization and culture and refinement that had required countless ages in the building, stripping him naked, age on age, down to the primordial beast that had begot his first human progenitor.

He saw red through blood as he leaped for the throat of the man-beast whose ruthless hands were upon Nadara.

His lip curled in the fighting snarl that exposed his long-unused canine fangs.

He forgot sword and shield and spear.

He was no longer a man, but a terrible beast; and the hairy brute that witnessed the metamorphosis blanched and shrank back in fear.

But he could not escape the fury of that mad charge or the raging creature that sought his throat.

For a moment they struggled in a surging, swaying embrace, and then toppled to the ground — the hairy one beneath.

Rolling, tearing, and biting, they battled — each seeking a death hold upon the other.

Time and again the gleaming teeth of the once-fastidious Bostonian sank into the breast and shoulder of his antagonist, but it was the jugular his primal instinct sought.

The girl and the old man had drawn away where they could watch the battle in safety. Nadara's eyes were wide in fascination.

Her slim, brown hands were tight pressed against her rapidly rising and falling breasts as she leaned a little forward with parted lips, drinking in every detail of the conflict between the two beasts.

Ah, but was the yellow-haired giant really fighting for possession of her, or merely in protection, because she was a woman?

She could readily conceive from her knowledge of him that he might be acting now solely from some peculiar sense of duty which she realized that he might entertain, although she could not herself understand it.

Yes, that was it, and when he had conquered his rival he would run away again, as he had months before. At the thought Nadara felt herself flush with mortification. No, he should never have another opportunity to repeat that terrible affront.

As she allowed her mind to dwell on the humiliating moment that had witnessed the discovery that Thandar had fled from her at the very threshold of her home Nadara found herself hating him again as fiercely as she had all these long months – a hatred that had almost dissolved at sight of him as he rushed out of the underbrush a moment before to wrest her from the clutches of her hideous tormentor.

Waldo and his antagonist were still tearing futilely at one another in mad efforts to maim or kill. The giant muscles of the cave man gave him but little if any advantage over his agile, though slightly less-powerful, adversary.

The hairy one used his teeth to better advantage, with the result that Waldo was badly torn and bleeding from a dozen wounds.

Both were weakening now, and it seemed to the girl who watched that the younger man would be the first to succumb to the terrific strain under which both had been. She took a step forward and, stooping, picked up a stone.

Her small strength would be ample to turn the scales as she might choose – a sharp blow upon the head of either would give his adversary the trifling advantage that would spell death for the one she struck.

The two men had struggled to their feet again as she approached with raised weapon.

At the very moment that it left her hand they swung completely round, so that Waldo faced her, and in the instant before the missile struck his forehead he saw Nadara in the very act of throwing – upon her face an expression of hatred and loathing.

Then he lost consciousness and went down, dragging with him the cave man, upon whose throat his fingers had just found their hold.

CHAPTER NINE

THE SEEKER

When the old man saw what had happened he ran forward and grasped Nadara by the wrist.

'Quick!' he cried – 'quick, my daughter! You have killed him who would have saved you, and now nothing but flight may keep Korth from having his way with you.'

As in a trance the girl turned and departed with him.

They had scarcely disappeared within the underbrush when Waldo returned to consciousness, so slight had been the effect of the blow upon his head.

To his surprise he found the cave man lying very still beside him, but an instant later he read the reason for it in the little projecting ridge of rock upon which lay his foe's forehead – in falling the savage man had struck thus and lost consciousness.

Almost immediately the hairy one opened his eyes, but before he could gather his scattered senses sinewy fingers found his throat, and he lapsed once more into oblivion – from which there was no awakening.

As Waldo staggered to his feet he saw that the girl had vanished, and there swept back into his mind the memory of the hate that had been in her face as she struck him down.

It seemed incredible that she should have turned against him so, and at the very moment, too, when he had risked his life in her service; but that she had there could be no doubt, for he had seen her cast the stone – with his own eyes he had seen her, and, too, he had seen the hatred and loathing in her face as she looked straight into his. But what he had not seen was the look of horror that followed as the missile struck him instead of Korth, sending him crumpling to earth.

Slowly Waldo turned away from the scene of battle, and without even a second look at his vanquished enemy limped painfully into the brush. His heart was very heavy and he was weak from exhaustion and loss of blood, but he staggered on, back toward his mountain lair, as he thought, until unable to go further he sank down upon a little grassy knoll and slept.

When Nadara recovered from the shock of the thing she had done sufficiently to reason for herself she realized that after all Thandar might not be dead, and though the old man protested long and loudly against it, she insisted upon retracing her steps toward the spot where they had left the yellow giant in the clutches of Korth.

Very cautiously the girl threaded her way through the maze of shrubbery and creepers that filled the intervening space between the forest trees, until she came silently to the edge of the clearing in which the two had fought.

As she peered anxiously through the last curtain of foliage she saw a single body lying quiet and still upon the sward, and an instant later recognized it as Korth's. For several minutes she watched it before she became convinced that the man who had so terrorized her whole childish life could never again offer her harm.

She looked about for Thandar, but he was nowhere to be seen. Nadara could scarcely believe that her eyes were not deceiving her.

It was incredible that the yellow one could have gone down to unconsciousness before her unintentional blow and yet have mastered the mighty Korth; but how else could Korth have met his death and Thandar be gone?

She approached quite close to the dead man, turning the body over with her foot until the throat was visible. There she saw the finger-marks that had done the work, and with a little thrill of pride she turned back into the forest, calling Thandar's name aloud.

But Thandar did not hear. Half a mile away he lay weak and unconscious from loss of blood.

Morning found Nadara sleeping in a sturdy tree upon the trail along which Waldo had followed Korth. She had discovered the footprints of the two men the evening before while she had been searching unsuccessfully for the trail which Waldo had followed after the battle. She hoped now that the spoor might lead her to Thandar's cave, to which she felt it quite possible he might have returned by another way.

When the girl awoke she again took up her journey, following the tracks as unerringly as a hound up through the hilly country, across the divide and down into the jungle to the very watering place at which her tribe had drank a few days earlier. Here she made a brief stay.

Then on again down the river, back through the jungle and onto the divide once more. She was much mystified by the windings of the trail, but for days she followed the fading spoor until, becoming fainter and fainter as it grew older, she lost it entirely at last.

She was quite sure by now, however, that it led from her tribe's former territory, and so she kept on, hoping against hope, that soon she would come across the fresh track of Thandar where he had passed her on his return journey to his home.

Nadara had eluded the old man when she started upon her search for Thandar, so it was that the old fellow returned to the dwellings of his people alone the following day.

Flatfoot was the first to greet him.

'Where is the girl?' he growled. 'And where is Korth? Has he taken her? Answer me the truth or I will break every bone in your carcass.'

'I do not know where the girl is,' answered the old man truthfully enough, 'but Korth lies dead in the little glade beyond the three great trees. A mighty man killed him as he was dragging Nadara off into the thicket—'

'And the man has taken the girl for himself?' yelled Flatfoot. 'You old thief you. This is some of your work. Always have you tried to cheat me of this girl since first you knew

74

that I desired her. Whither went they? Quick! Before I kill you.'

'I do not know,' replied the old man. 'For hours I searched, until darkness came, but neither of them could I find, and my old eyes are no longer keen for trailing, so I was forced to abandon my hunt and return here when morning came.'

'By the three trees the trail starts, you say?' cried Flatfoot. 'That is enough – I shall find them. And when I return with the girl it will be time enough to kill you; now it would delay me too much,' and with that the cave man hurried away into the forest.

It took him half a day to find Nadara's trail, but at last his search was rewarded, and as she had made no effort to hide it he moved rapidly along in the wake of the unsuspecting girl; but he was not as swift as she, and the chase bid fair to be a long one.

When Waldo woke he found the sun beating down upon his face, and though he was lame and sore he felt quite strong enough to continue his journey; but whither he should go he did not know.

Now that Nadara had turned against him the island held nothing for him, and he was on the point of starting back toward his far distant lair from where he might visit the ocean often to watch for a passing ship, when the sudden decision came to him to see the girl again, regardless of her evident hostility, and learn from her own lips the exact reason of her hatred for him.

He had no idea that the loss of her friendship would prove such a blow to him, so that his pride suffered as well as his heart as he contemplated his harrowed emotions.

Of course he was reasonably sure that Nadara's attitude was due to his ungallant desertion, for which act he had long suffered the most acute pangs of remorse and contrition. Yet he felt that her apparent vindictiveness was not warranted by even the grave offense against chivalry and gratitude of which he had been guilty.

It presently occurred to him that by the traitorous attack which he believed that she had made upon him while he was acting in her defense she had forfeited every claim which her former kindness might have given her upon him, but with this realization came another – a humiliating thought – he still wished to see her!

He, Waldo Emerson Smith-Jones, had become so devoid of pride that he would voluntarily search out one who had wronged and outraged his friendship, with the avowed determination of seeking a reconciliation. It was unthinkable, and yet, as he admitted the impossibility of it, he set forth in search of her.

Waldo wondered not a little at the strange emotion – inherent gregarious instinct, he thought it – which drew him toward Nadara.

It did not occur to him that during all the past solitary months he had scarcely missed the old companionship of his Back Bay friends; that for once that they had been the subject of his reveries the cave girl had held the center of that mental stage a thousand times.

He failed to realize that it was not the companionship of the many that he craved; that it was not the community instinct, or that his strange longing could be satisfied by but a single individual. No, Waldo Emerson did not know what was the matter with him, nor was it likely that he ever would find out before it was too late.

The young man attempted to retrace his steps to the battle-ground of the previous day, but he had been so dazed after the encounter that he had no clear recollection of the direction he had taken after he quitted the glade.

So it was that he stumbled in precisely the opposite direction, presently emerging from the underbrush almost at the foot of a low cliff tunneled with many caves. All about were the morose, unhappy community whose savage lives were spent in almost continual wandering from one filthy, comfortless warren to another equally foul and wretched.

At sight of them Waldo did not flee in dismay, as most

certainly would have been the case a few months earlier. Instead, he walked confidently toward them.

As he approached they ceased whatever work they were engaged upon and eyed him suspiciously. Then several burly males approached him warily.

At a hundred yards they halted.

'What do you want?' they cried. 'If you come to our village we can kill you.'

Before Waldo could reply an old man crawled from a cave near the base of the cliff, and as his eyes fell upon the stranger he hurried as rapidly as his ancient limbs would carry him to the little knot of ruffians who composed the reception committee.

He spoke to them for a moment in a low tone, and as he was talking Waldo recognized him as the old man who had accompanied Nadara on the previous day at the battle in the glade. When he had finished speaking one of the cave men assented to whatever proposal the decrepit one had made, and Waldo saw that each of the others nodded his head in approval.

Then the old man advanced slowly toward Waldo. When he had come quite close he spoke.

'I am an old man,' he said. 'Thandar would not kill an old man?'

'Of course not; but how know you that my name is Thandar?' replied Waldo.

'Nadara, she who is my daughter, has spoken of you often. Yesterday we saw you as you battled with that son of Nagoola – Nadara told me then that it was you. What would Thandar among the people of Flatfoot?'

'I come as a friend,' replied Waldo, 'among the friends of Nadara. For Flatfoot I care nothing. He is no friend of Nadara, whose friends are Thandar's friends, and whose enemies are Thandar's enemies. Where is Nadara – but first where is Flatfoot? I have come to kill him.'

The words and the savage challenge slipped as easily from the cultured tongue of Waldo Emerson Smith-Jones as though he had been born and reared in the most rocky and barren cave of this savage island, nor did they sound strange or unusual to him. It seemed that he had said the most natural and proper thing under the circumstances that there was to say.

'Flatfoot is not here,' said the old man, 'nor is Nadara. She—' but here Waldo interrupted him.

'Korth, then,' he demanded. 'Where is Korth? I can kill him first and Flatfoot when he returns.'

The old man looked at the speaker in unfeigned surprise.

'Korth!' he exclaimed. 'Korth is dead. Can it be that you do not know that he, whom you killed yesterday, was Korth?'

Waldo's eyes opened as wide in surprise as had the old man's.

Korth! He had killed the redoubtable Korth with his bare hands – Korth, who could crush the skull of a full-grown man with a single blow from his open palm.

Clearly he recollected the very words in which Nadara had described this horrible brute that time she had harrowed his poor, coward nerves, as they approached the village of Flatfoot. And now he, Waldo Emerson Smith-Jones, had met and killed the creature from whom he had so fearfully fled a few months ago!

And, wonder of wonders, he had not even thought to use the weapons upon which he had spent so many hours of handicraft and months of practice in preparation for just this occasion. Of a sudden he recalled the old man's statement that Nadara was not there.

'Where is she – Nadara?' he cried, turning so suddenly upon the ancient one that the old fellow drew back in alarm.

'I have done nothing to harm her,' he cried. 'I followed and would have brought her back, but I am old and could not find her. Once, when I was young, there was no better trailer or mighty warrior among my people than I, but—'

'Yes, yes,' exclaimed Waldo impatiently; 'but Nadara! Where is she?'

'I do not know,' replied the old man. 'She has gone, and I could not find her. Well do I remember how, years ago, when the trail of an enemy was faint or the signs of game hard to find, men would come to ask me to help them, but now—'

'Of course,' interrupted Waldo; 'but Nadara. Do you not even know in what direction she has gone?'

'No; but since Flatfoot has set forth upon her trail it should be easy to track the two of them.'

'Flatfoot set out after Nadara!' cried Waldo. 'Why?'

'For many moons he has craved her for his mate, as has Korth,' explained Nadara's father; 'but I think that each feared the other, and because of that fact Nadara was saved from both; but at last Korth came upon us alone and away from the village, and then he grasped Nadara and would have taken her away, for Flatfoot was not about to prevent.

'You came then, and the rest you know. If I had been younger neither Flatfoot nor Korth would have dared menace Nadara, for when I was a young man I was very terrible and the record of my kills was a—'

'How long since did Flatfoot set out after Nadara?' Waldo broke in.

'But a few hours since,' replied the old man. 'It would be an easy thing for me to overtake him by night had I the speed of my youth, for I well remember—'

'From where did Flatfoot start upon the trail?' cried the young man. 'Lead me to the place.'

'This way then, Thandar,' said the other, starting off toward the forest. 'I will show you if you will save Nadara from Flatfoot. I love her. She has been very kind and good to me. She is unlike the rest of our people.

'I should die happy if I knew that you have saved her from Flatfoot, but I am an old man and may not live until Nadara returns. Ah, that reminds me; there is that in my cave which belongs to Nadara, and were I to die there would be none to protect it for her.

'Will you wait for the moment that it will take me to run

and fetch it, that you may carry it to her, for I am sure that you will find her; though I am not as sure that you will overcome Flatfoot if you meet him. He is a very terrible man.'

Waldo hated to waste a minute of the precious time that was allowing Flatfoot to win nearer and nearer Nadara; but if it were in a service for the girl who had been so kind to him and for the happiness of her old father he could not refuse, so he waited impatiently while the old fellow tottered off toward the caves.

Those who had come halfway to meet Waldo had hovered at a safe distance while he had been speaking to Nadara's father, and when the two turned toward the forest all had returned to their work in evident relief; for the old man had told them that the stranger was the mighty warrior who had killed the terrible Korth with his bare hands, nor had the story lost anything in the telling.

After what seemed hours to the waiting Waldo the old man returned with a little package carefully wrapped in the skin of a small rodent, the seams laboriously sewed in a manner of lacing with pieces of gut.

'This is Nadara's,' he said as they continued their way toward the forest. 'It contains many strange things of which I know not the meaning or purpose. They all were taken from the body of her mother when the woman died. You will give them to her?'

'Yes,' said Waldo. 'I will give them to Nadara, or die in the trying of it.'

CHAPTER TEN

THE TRAIL'S END

Soon they came upon the trail of Flatfoot in the glade by the three great trees; they had not searched for it sooner, for the old man knew that it would start from that point upon its quest for the girl.

The tracks circled the glade a dozen times in widening laps until at last, at the point where Flatfoot must have picked up the spoor of Nadara, they broke suddenly away into the underbrush. Once the way was plain Waldo bid the old man be of good heart, for he would surely bring his daughter back to him unharmed if the thing lay in the power of man.

Then he hurried off upon the new-made trail that lay as plain and readable before him as had the printed page of his former life; but never had he bent with such keen interest to the reading of his favorite author as he did to this absorbing drama written in the turned leaves, the scattered twigs, and the soft mud of a primeval forest by the feet of a savage man and a savage maid.

Toward mid-afternoon Waldo became aware that he was much weaker from the effects of his battle with Korth than he had supposed. He had lost much blood from his wounds, and the exertion of following the trail at a swift pace had reopened some of the worse ones, so that now, as he ran, he was leaving a little trail of blood behind him.

The discovery made him almost frantic, for it seemed to presage failure. His condition would handicap him in the race after the two whose track he pursued so that it would be a miracle were he to reach Flatfoot before the brute overtook Nadara.

And if he did overtake him in time – what then? Would he be physically able to cope with the brawny monster? He feared that he would not, but that he kept doggedly to the grueling chase augured well for the new manhood that had been so recently born within him.

On and on he stumbled, until at dusk he slipped and fell exhausted to the earth. Twice he struggled to his feet in an attempt to go on, but he was forced to give in, lying where he was until morning.

Slightly refreshed, he ate of the roots and fruit which abounded in the forest, taking up the chase again, but this time more slowly.

He was now convinced that the way led back along the same trail which he had followed into the country, and when he reached the point at which he had first met Korth on the previous day he cut across the little space which intervened between the cave man's tracks and the point at which he had stood before he went down over the divide into the jungle toward the river and the ford.

A moment later he was rewarded by the sight of Nadara's dainty footprints as well as those of Flatfoot leading away along his old trail. The act had saved him several miles of needless tracking.

All that day he followed as rapidly as his weakened condition would permit, but his best efforts seemed dismally snail-like.

Along the way he bowled over a couple of large rodents, which he ate raw, for he had long since learned the desirability of a meat diet for one undergoing severe physical exertion, and had conquered his natural aversion for the uncooked flesh. He even had come to relish it, though often as he dined thus upon meat a broad grin illumined his countenance at the thought of the horror with which his mother and his Boston friends would view such a hideous performance.

As he continued trailing the two he was at first surprised to discover the fidelity with which Nadara had clung to his old trail, and because of this fact he often was able to save miles at a time by taking cross-cuts where, on his way in, he had made wide detours.

But at last, on the third day, when he attempted this at a place which would have saved him fully ten miles, he was dismayed by the discovery that he could not again pick up either Nadara's trail or that of the cave man. Even his own old trail was entirely obliterated.

It was this fact which caused him the greatest concern, for it meant that if Nadara really had been following it she must now be wandering rather aimlessly, possibily in an attempt to again locate it. In which event her speed would be materially reduced, and the probability of her capture by Flatfoot much enhanced.

It was possible, too, that the beast already had overtaken her – this, in fact, might be the true cause of the cessation of the pursuit along the way which it had proceeded up to this point.

The thought sent Waldo back along his former route, which he was able to follow by recollection, though the spoor was seldom visible.

He came upon no sign of those he sought that day, but the next morning he found the point at which Nadara had lost his old trail upon a rocky ridge. The girl evidently assumed that it would lead into the valley below where she might pick it up again in the soft earth, and so her footprints led down a shelving bluff, while plain above them showed the huge imprints of Flatfoot.

Up to this point at least he had not caught up with her. Waldo breathed a sigh of relief at the discovery. The trail was at least two days old, for Nadara and Flatfoot had traveled much more rapidly than the wounded man who haunted their footsteps like a grim shadow.

About noon Waldo came to a little stream at which both those who preceded him had evidently stopped to drink – he could see where they had knelt in the soft grass at the water's edge.

As Waldo stopped to quench his own thirst his eyes rested

for an instant upon the farther bank, which at that point was little more than ten feet from him. He saw that the opposite shore was less grassy, and that it sloped down to the water, forming a muddy beach partially submerged.

But what riveted his attention were several deep imprints in the mud.

He could not be certain, of course, at that distance, but he was sure enough that he had recognized them to cause him to leap to his feet, forgetful of his thirst, and plunge through the stream for a closer inspection.

As he bent to examine the spoor at close range he could scarce repress a cry of exultation – they had been made by the hands and knees of Nadara as she had stopped to drink at the very spot not twenty-four hours before.

She must have circled back toward the brook for some reason; but by far the greatest cause for rejoicing was the fact that Nadara's trail alone was there. Flatfoot had not yet come upon her, and Waldo now was between them.

The knowledge that he might yet be in time, and that he was gaining sufficiently in strength to make it reasonably certain that he could overhaul the girl eventually, filled Waldo with renewed vigor. He hastened along Nadara's trail now with something of the energy that had been his directly before his battle with Korth.

His wounds had ceased bleeding, and for several days he had eaten well, and by night slept soundly for he had reasoned that only by conserving his energy and fortifying himself in every way possible could he succor the girl.

That night he slept in a little thicket which had evidently harbored Nadara the night before.

The following day the way lay across a rolling country, cut by numerous deep ravines and lofty divides. That the pace was telling on the girl Waldo could read in the tell-tale spoor that revealed her lagging footsteps. Upon each eminence the man halted to strain his eyes ahead for a sight of her.

About noon he discerned far ahead a shimmering line

which he knew must be the sea. Surely his long pursuit must end there.

As he was about to plunge on again along Nadara's trail something drew his eyes toward the rear, and there upon another hilltop a mile or two behind he saw the stocky figure of a half-naked man – it was Flatfoot.

The cave man must have seen Waldo at the same instant, for, with a menacing wave of his huge fist, he increased his gait to a run, an instant later disappearing into the ravine which lay at the bottom of the hill upon he had come into view.

Waldo was undecided whether to wait for the encounter where he was or hasten on in an effort to overtake Nadara, that she might not escape him entirely. He knew that he stood a good chance of being killed in the conflict, and he also knew that were he victorious it might easily be at such a terrible price that he would be physically incapable of continuing his search for the girl for many days.

As he meditated his eyes wandered back and forth across the landscape before him searching for Nadara.

To his right lay, at a little distance, a level plain which stretched to the foot of low-lying cliffs at the valley's southern rim, some three or four miles distant. In this direction his view was almost unobstructed, but it was not in the direction of the girl's flight, so that it was but by accident that Waldo's eyes swept casually across the peaceful scene which would, at another time, have chained his attention with its quiet and alluring beauty.

It was as he swept a backward glance in the direction of Flatfoot that his eye was arrested by the thing far out across the valley, a little behind his own position.

To the Waldo of a few months previous it would not have been visible, but the new woodcraft of the man scented the abnormal in the vague suggestion of movement out among the long-waving grasses of the plain.

And now, with every sense alert and riveted upon the spot, he was quick to perceive that it was an animal moving slowly

85

toward the cliffs at the upper end of the valley. Presently a little rise of ground, less thickly grassed, brought the creature into full view for an instant; but in that instant Waldo saw that the thing he watched was a woman.

As he turned to hurry after her he saw Flatfoot top another hill a half mile nearer than he had before been, and as the cave man came into view he turned his eyes in the direction that Waldo had been looking. A second later and he had abandoned the pursuit of Waldo and was running rapidly toward the woman.

Nadara had apparently circled back once more, this time from the sea, and coming up the valley had passed Waldo and come opposite Flatfoot before either of them had discovered her. The young man gave a little cry of alarm as he realized that the cave man was nearer to the girl than he – by a good half mile, he judged, and so he put every ounce of his speed into the wild dash he made down the hill into a gully which led out upon the valley.

On and on he raced unable to see either Flatfoot or Nadara; hoping, ever hoping, that he would be the first to win to her side; for Nadara had told him of the atrocities that such a creature as Flatfoot might perpetrate upon a woman rather than permit her to escape him or fall into the hands of another.

Nadara, being up wind, caught neither scent nor noise of the two who were racing madly toward her. The first knowledge she had that she was not alone in the valley was the sight of Flatfoot as he broke suddenly through a clump of tall grass not fifty paces from her.

She gave a little scream and started to run; but she was very tired from the days of unremitting flight which had so sorely taxed her endurance, and thus it was no wonder that she slipped and fell before she had taken a dozen steps.

Scarcely had she gained her feet when Flatfoot was upon her, one hand grasping her by the arm.

'Come with me in peace or I will kill you!' he cried.

'Kill me, then,' retorted the despairing girl, 'for I shall never come with you; first will I kill myself.'

Flatfoot did not wish to kill her, nor did he wish her to escape, as she would be very likely to do should he be interrupted by the fellow who must even now be quite close to them.

Possibly if he could keep the girl quiet they might hide in the grass until their pursuer had gone by, and so Flatfoot, acting upon the idea, clapped a rough hand over Nadara's mouth and dragged her back along the trail he had just made.

The girl struggled – striking and clawing at the hairy brute that pulled her along at his side – but she was as helpless in his clutches as if she had been a day-old babe.

She did not know that help was so close at hand, or she would have found the means to free her mouth and cry out once at least. As it was, she wondered that Flatfoot should attempt to silence her in this way if there were none to hear her screams.

For days she had known that the cave man was on her trail, for once in doubling back upon herself she had passed but a short distance from a ridge she had traversed the preceding day, and had seen the man's squat figure and recognized his awkward, shuffling trot.

It was this knowledge that had turned her away from the old village toward which she had been traveling since she lost Thandar's trail, and sent her in search of a new country in which she might lose herself from Flatfoot.

As the man dragged her roughly on through the grass Nadara racked her brain for some means of escape, or a way to end her misery before the beast could have his way with her. But there came no ray of hope to her poor, unhappy heart.

If Thandar were but there! He would save her, even if it were but to desert her the next instant.

But did she wish to be saved again by him? Now that she pondered the idea she was quite sure that she would rather die than see him again, for had he not twice run away from her?

In her misery she put this interpretation upon the remarkable disappearance of Thandar after his battle with Korth — he had waited until she was out of sight and then he had risen and fled for fear she might return and discover him. She wondered why he should dislike her so much.

She was quite sure that she had been very good to him, and had tried not to annoy him while they were together. Maybe he looked down upon her, for surely he was of a superior race; of that she was quite positive.

And so Nadara was very miserable and unhappy and hopeless as the brutal Flatfoot dragged her far into the tall jungle-grass. Presently she noticed that the cave man repeatedly cast glances toward the rear.

What could he expect from that direction, or from any direction whatever, so far as that was concerned? Were they not days and days from their own people, in a land where there seemed no men at all?

Flatfoot heard no sign of pursuit. He was growing more confident. The stranger had lost their trail. The cave man moved less rapidly, and as he went he looked now for a burrow into which he might crawl with the maiden. Then there would be no further danger whatever.

Tomorrow Flatfoot would come out and find the fellow and kill him, but now he had pleasanter work in view, nor did he wish to be disturbed.

And at that very moment he caught a stealthy movement in the grasses a few yards to his right. Waldo had come upon the spot at which Flatfoot had overtaken Nadara but a few moments after the brute had dragged her away, and on the instant had sought a higher piece of ground from which he could overlook the tall grass.

Nor had he been long in finding a spot that, coupled with his six feet two, brought his eyes above the level of the surrounding jungle.

There he watched for a little until he discerned a movement of the grasstops at a little distance from him. After that it was but a matter of trailing.

When Flatfoot saw what he took to be his enemy he threw Nadara across his shoulder and started on a run in the opposite direction – at right angles to the way he had been going.

The ruse proved good, for when Waldo came to the point at which he had figured his path would cross the cave man's he found no sign of the latter, and in searching about to locate the trail lost many minutes of valuable time. But at last he came upon that which he sought, and with redoubled speed set out at a rapid run through the tall grasses.

He had proceeded but a short distance when the trail broke suddenly into the open, close by the base of the cliffs that he had seen from the hill that had given him his fleeting glimpse of Nadara.

Ahead of him he saw the two he sought – Nadara across the burly shoulders of Flatfoot – and the cave man was making for the caves that dotted the face of the cliff. Were he to reach these he might defend one of them against a single antagonist indefinitely.

CHAPTER ELEVEN

CAPTURE

Almost at the moment that Waldo emerged from the jungle Nadara saw him, and with a lunge threw herself from Flatfoot's shoulder.

The man turned with a fierce growl of rage, and his eyes fell upon the giant rushing toward them.

The girl was now struggling madly to escape or delay her captor. There could be but one outcome, as Flatfoot knew. He must fight now, but the girl should never escape him.

Raising the huge fist that had killed many a full-grown man with a single blow he aimed a wicked one at the side of Nadara's head.

The first one she dodged, and as the arm went up to strike again, Thandar threw his spear-arm far back and with a mighty forward surge drove his light weapon across the hundred feet that separated him from Flatfoot.

It was an awful risk – there was not a foot to spare between the hairy breast that was his target and the beautiful head of the fair captive. Should either move between the time the spear left his hand and the instant that it found its mark it might pierce the one it had been sped to save.

Flatfoot's fist was crashing down toward that lovely face at the instant that the spear found him; but he had moved – just enough to place his arm before his breast – so that it was the falling arm that received the weapon instead of the heart that it had been intended for.

But it served its purpose. With a howl of pain and rage, Flatfoot, forgetful of the girl in the madness of his anger, dropped her and sprang toward Waldo.

The latter had drawn his sword – naught but a sharpened

stick of hard wood – and stood waiting to receive his foe. It was his first attempt to put either sword or shield into practical use, and he was anxious to discover their value.

As Flatfoot came toward his antagonist he pulled the spear from the muscles of his arm, and, stooping, gathered up one of the many rocks that lay scattered about at the base of the cliff.

The cave man was roaring like a mad bull; hate and murder shot from his close-set eyes; his upper lip curled back, showing his fighting fangs, and a light froth flecked his bristling beard.

Waldo was sure there had never existed a more fearsome creature, and he marveled that he was not afraid. The very thought of what the effect of this terrible monster's mad charge would have been upon him a short while ago brought a smile to his lips.

At sight of that taunting smile Flatfoot hurled the rock full at the maddening face. With a quick movement of his left arm Waldo caught the missile on his buckler, from whence it dropped harmlessly to the ground.

Flatfoot did not throw again, and an instant later he was upon the Bostonian – the pride and hope of the cultured and aristocratic Back Bay Smith-Joneses.

When he reached for the agile, blond giant he found a thin sheet of hide-covered twigs in his way, and when he tried to tear down this barrier the point of a sharpened stick was thrust into his abdomen.

This was no way to fight!

Flatfoot was scandalized. He jumped back a few feet and glared at Waldo. Then he lowered his head and came at him once more with the very evident intention of rushing him off his feet by the very weight and impetuosity of his charge.

This time the sharp stick slipped quickly over Flatfoot's neck just where it joined his thick skull.

Burying a foot of its point beneath the muscles of the shoulder, it brought a scream of pain and rage from the hairy beast.

Before Waldo could withdraw his weapon from the tough sinews, Flatfoot had straightened up with a sudden jerk that snapped the sword short, leaving but a short stub in his antagonist's hand.

Nadara had been watching the battle breathlessly, ready to flee should it turn against her champion, yet at the same time searching for an opportunity to aid him.

Like Flatfoot, the girl had never before seen spear or sword or shield in use, and while she marveled at the advantage which they gave Thandar, she became dubious as to the result of the encounter when she saw the sword broken, for the spear had been snapped into kindling-wood by Flatfoot when he tore it from his arm.

But Waldo still had his cudgel, fastened by a thong to his sword-belt, and as the cave man rushed upon him again he swung a mighty blow to the low, brutal forehead.

Momentarily stunned, the fellow reeled backward for a step, and again Waldo wielded his new weapon.

Flatfoot trembled, his knees smote together, he staggered drunkenly, and then, when Waldo looked to see him go down, the brute power that was in him, responding to nature's first law, sent him hurtling at the Bostonian's throat in the snarling, blind rage of the death-smitten beast.

Catapulted by all the enormous strength of his mighty muscles, the squat, bearlike animal bore Waldo to earth, and at the same instant each found the other's throat with sinewy, viselike fingers.

They lay very still now, choking with firm, relentless clutch. Every ounce of muscle was needed, every grain of endurance.

Waldo was suffering agonies after a moment of that awful death-grip. He could feel his gasping, pain-racked lungs struggling for air.

He tried to wriggle free from those horrible fingers, but not once did he loosen his own hold upon the throat of Flatfoot; instead he tried to close a little tighter each second that he felt his own life ebbing. He became weaker and weaker. The pain was unendurable now.

A haze obscured his vision – everything became black – his brain was whizzing about at frightful velocity within the awful darkness of his skull.

The girl was bending close above them now, for both were struggling less violently. She had been minded to come to Thandar's rescue when suddenly she recalled his desertion of her, and all the wild hatred of the primitive mind surged through her.

Let him die, she thought. He had spurned her, cast her off; he looked down upon her.

Well, let him take care of himself, then, and she turned deliberately away to leave the two men to decide the out-come of their own battle, and started back upon the trail in the direction of her tribe's village.

But she had taken scarce a score of steps when something flamed up in her heart that withered the last remnant of her malice toward Thandar. As she turned back again toward the combatants she attempted to justify this new weakness by the thought that it was only fair that she should give the yellow one aid in return for the aid that he had rendered her; that done, she could go on her way with a clear con-science.

She wished never to see him again, but she could not have his blood upon her hands. At that thought she gave a little cry and ran to where the men lay.

Both were almost quiet now; their struggles had nearly ceased. Just as she reached them Flatfoot relaxed, his hands slipped from Waldo's throat and he lay entirely motionless.

Then the fair giant struggled convulsively once or twice; he gasped, his eyes rolled up and set, and with a sudden twitching of his muscles he stiffened rigidly and was very still.

Nadara gave one horrified look at the ghastly face of her companion, and fled into the jungle.

She stumbled on for a quarter of a mile as fast as her tired

93

limbs would carry her through the entangling grasses, and then she came to that which she sought – a little stream, winding slowly through the valley down toward the ocean.

Dropping to her knees beside it she filled her mouth with the refreshing water. In an instant she was up again and off in the direction from which she had just come.

Throwing herself at Waldo's side, she wet his face with the water from her mouth. She chafed his hands, shook him, blew upon his face when the water was exhausted, and then, tears streaming from her eyes, she threw herself upon him, covering his face with kisses, and moaning inarticulate words of love and endearment that were half stifled by anguished sobs of grief.

Suddenly her lamentations ceased as quickly as they had begun. She raised her head from where it had been buried beside the man's and looked intently into his face.

Then she placed her ear upon his breast; with a delighted cry she resumed chafing his hands, for she had heard the beating of his heart.

Presently Waldo gasped, and for a moment suffered the agonies of returning respiration. When he opened his eyes in consciousness he saw Nadara bending over him – a severely disinterested expression upon her beautiful face. He turned his head to one side; there lay Flatfoot quite dead.

It was several moments before he could speak. Then he rose, very unsteadily, to his feet.

'Nadara,' he said, 'Korth lies dead beside the three great trees in the glade that is near the village that was Flatfoot's. Here is the dead body of Flatfoot, and about my loins hangs the pelt of Nagoola, taken in fair fight.

'I have done all that you desired of me; I have tried to repay you for your kindness to me when I was a stranger in your land. I do not know why you should have tried to kill me while I battled with Korth.

'No more do I know why you have allowed me to live today when it would have been so easy to have dispatched me as I lay unconscious here beside Flatfoot.

'I read dislike upon your face, and I am sorry, for I would have parted with you in friendship, so that when the time comes that I return to my own land I should be able to carry away with me only the pleasant memory of it. When we have rested and are refreshed I shall take you back to your father.'

All that had been surging to the girl's lips of love and gratitude from a heart that was filled with both was congealed by the cold tone which marked this dispassionate recital of the discharge of a moral obligation.

Possibly Waldo's tone was colored by the vivid memory of the look of hate that he had seen in the girl's eyes at the instant that he went down before her missile as he battled with Korth, for it was not even tinged with friendliness.

And so the girl's manner was equally distant when she replied; in fact, it was even colder, for it was fraught with bitterness.

'Thandar owed nothing to Nadara,' she said, 'and though it matters not at all, it is only fair to say that the stone that struck you as you battled in the glade was intended for Korth.'

Waldo's face brightened. A load that he had not realized lay there was lifted from his heart.

'You did not want to hurt me, then?' he cried.

'Why should I want to hurt you?' returned the girl.

'I thought' – and here Waldo spoiled the fair start they had made at a reconciliation – 'I thought,' he said, 'that you were angry because I ran away from you after we had come to your village that time, months ago.'

Nadara's head went high and she laughed aloud.

'I angry? I was surprised that you did not come to the village, but after an hour I had forgotten the matter – it was with difficulty that I recognized you when I next saw you, so utterly had the occurrence departed from my thoughts.'

Waldo wondered why he should feel such humiliation at this frank avowal. Of what moment to him was this girl's estimation of him? Why did he feel a flush suffuse his face at the knowledge that he was of so little moment to her that she had entirely forgotten him within a few months?

Waldo was mortified and angry. He changed the subject brusquely, hereafter he should eschew personalities.

'Let us find a cave at a distance from the dead man,' he said, 'and there we may rest until you are ready to attempt the return journey.'

'I am ready now,' replied Nadara; 'nor do I need or desire your company. I can return alone, as I came.'

'No,' remonstrated Waldo doggedly; 'I shall go with you whether you wish it or not. I shall see you safely with your father. I promised him.'

Nadara had been delighted with the first clause of his reply, but when it became evident that his only desire to return with her was to fulfil a promise made her father she became furious, though she was careful not to let him see it.

'Very well,' she replied; 'you may come if you wish, though it is neither necessary nor as I would have it. I prefer being alone.'

'I shall not force my company upon you,' said Waldo haughtily. 'I can follow a few paces behind you.'

There was an injured air in his last words which did not escape the girl. She wondered if he really deserved the harsh attitude she had maintained.

They found a cave a half-mile down the valley, where they took up their quarters against the time that Waldo should be rested, for the girl insisted that she was fully able to commence the return journey at once.

The man knew better, and so he let her have it that the delay was on his account rather than hers, for he doubted her ability to cope with the hardships of the long journey without an interval for recuperation.

The next morning found them both rested and in better spirits, so that there was no return to their acrimonious encounter of the previous day.

As they walked out toward the forest that lay down the valley in the direction of the ocean Waldo dropped a few paces behind the girl in polite deference to her expressed wish of the day before.

As he walked he watched the graceful movements of her lithe figure and the lines of her clear-cut profile as she turned her head this way and that in search of food.

How beautiful she was! It was incredible that this wild cave girl should have greater beauty and a more regal carriage than the queens and beauties of civilization, and yet Waldo was forced to admit that he had never even dreamed, much less seen, such absolute physical perfection.

He wished that he could say as much for her disposition; that was atrocious. It was unbelievable that such a wondrous exterior could harbor so much ingratitude and coldness.

Presently they came among the trees where the ripe fruit hung, and as Waldo climbed nimbly among the branches and tossed the most luscious down to her, the girl, in her turn, watched him.

She noted more closely the marvelous change that a few months had wrought. She had thought him wonderful before, but now he was a very god. She did not think just this, for she knew nothing of gods – other than the demons that were supposed to enter the bodies of the sick; but she thought of him as some superior creature, and then she ceased to feel aggrieved that he should care so little for her.

He was not a man – he was something more than a man, and she had been very wicked to have treated him so shamefully. She would make amends.

So she tried to be more kind thereafter, though there still remained a trace of aloofness.

Together they sat upon the turf and ate the fruit, and as they ate they talked a little, for it is difficult for two young people to harbor animosity for a great time, especially when there is none other for them to talk to.

'When you have returned with me to my father, Thandar,' the girl asked, 'where shall you go then?'

'I shall return to the sea where I may watch for a ship to take me back to my own land,' he replied.

'I have seen but one ship in all my life,' said Nadara, 'and that was years ago. It was when we lived close by the big water that it stopped a long way from shore and sent many smaller boats to land.

'There were many men in the boats, and when they landed, my father and mother took me far into the forest away from the sea, and there we stayed for many days until the strangers had sailed. They wandered up and down the coast and came back into the forests and the jungles for a few miles.

'My mother said that they were searching for me, and that if they found me they would take me away. I was very much frightened.'

At the mention of her mother Waldo recalled the little parcel that Nadara's father had given into his custody for the girl. He unfastened it from the thing that circled his waist, where it had hung beneath his pantherskin garment.

'Here is something your father asked me to bring you,' he said, handing the package to Nadara.

The girl took it and examined it as though it was entirely unfamiliar.

'What is it?' she asked.

'Your father did not say, other than that it contained articles that your mother wore when she died,' he said tenderly, for a great pity had welled up in his heart for this poor, motherless girl.

'That my mother wore!' Nadara repeated, her brows contracted in a puzzled frown. 'When my mother died she wore nothing but a single garment of many small skins – very old and worn – and that was buried with her. I do not understand.'

She made no effort to open the package, but sat gazing far off toward the ocean which was just visible through the trees, entirely absorbed in the reverie which Waldo's words had engendered.

'Could the thing that the old woman told me have been

true?' the girl mused half aloud. 'Could it have been because it was true that my mother fell upon her with tooth and nail until she had nearly killed her? I wonder if—'

But here she stopped, her eyes riveted in sudden fear and hopelessness upon a thing that she had just espied in the distance.

A great lump rose in her throat, tears came to her eyes, and with them the full measure of realization of what that thing beyond the forest meant to her.

She turned her eyes toward the man. He was sitting with bowed head, playing idly with a large beetle that he had penned within a tiny palisade of small twigs.

At length he made an opening in the barrier.

'Go your way, poor thing,' he murmured. 'Heaven knows I realize too well the horrors of captivity to keep any other creature from its fellows and its home.'

A choking sigh that was almost a sob racked the girl. At the sound Waldo looked up to see her pathetic, unhappy eyes upon him. Of a sudden there enveloped him a great desire to take her in his arms and comfort her. He knew not why she was unhappy, but her sorrow cried aloud to him – as he thought simply to the protective instinct that was merely an attribute of his sex.

Nadara raised her hand slowly and pointed through the trees. It was as though she had torn her heart from her breast, so harrowing she felt the consequences of her act would be, but it was for his sake – for the sake of the man she loved.

As Waldo's eyes followed the direction of her pointing finger he came suddenly to his feet with a wild cry of joy; through the trees, out upon the shimmering surface of the placid sea, there lay a graceful, white yacht.

'Thank God!' cried the man fervently, and sinking to his knees he raised his hands aloft toward the author of joy and sorrow.

A moment later he sprang to his feet.

'Home! Nadara. Home!' he cried. 'Can't you realize it? I

99

am going home. I am saved! Oh, Nadara, child, can't you realize what it means to me? Home! Home! Home!'

He had been looking toward the yacht as he spoke, but now he turned toward the girl. She was crouching upon the ground, her face in her hands, her slender figure shaken by convulsive tears.

He came toward her and, kneeling, laid his hand upon her shoulder.

'Nadara!' he said gently. 'Why do you cry, child? What is the matter?' But she only shook her head, moaning.

He raised her to her feet, and as he supported her his arm circled her shoulders.

'Tell me, Nadara, why you are unhappy?' he urged.

But still she could not speak for sobbing, and only buried her face upon his breast.

He was holding her very close now, and with the pressure of her body against his a fire that, unknown, had been smoldering in his heart for months burst into sudden flame, and in the heat of it there were consumed the mists that had been before the eyes of his heart all that time.

'Nadara,' he asked in a very low voice, 'is it because I am going that you cry?'

But at that she pulled away from him, and through her tears her eyes blazed.

'No!' she cried. 'I shall be glad when you have gone. I wish that you had never come. I – I – hate you!' She turned and fled back up the valley, forgetful of the little packet Thandar had brought her, which lay forgotten upon the ground where she had dropped it.

Without so much as a backward glance toward the yacht Waldo was off in pursuit of her; but Nadara was as fleet as a hare, so that it was a much winded Waldo who finally overhauled her halfway up the face of a cliff two miles from the ocean.

'Go away!' cried the girl. 'Go back with your own kind, to your own home!'

Waldo did not answer.

Waldo was no more.

It was Thandar, the cave man, who took Nadara in his strong arms and crushed her to him.

'My girl!' he cried. 'My girl! I love you! And because I am a fool I did not learn until it was almost too late.'

He did not ask if she loved him, for he was Thandar, the cave man. Nor, a moment later, did he need to ask, since her strong, brown arms crept up about his neck and drew his lips down to hers.

It was quite half an hour later before either thought of the yacht again. From where they stood upon the cliff's face they could see the ocean and the beach.

Several boats were drawn up and a number of men were coming toward the forest. Presently they would discover the two upon the cliff.

'We shall go back together now,' said Thandar.

'I am afraid,' replied Nadara.

For a time the man stood gazing at the dainty yacht, and far beyond it into the civilization which it represented, and he saw there suave men and sneering women, and among them was a slender brown beauty who shrank from the cruel glances of the women – and Waldo writhed at this and at the greedy eyes of the suave men as they appraised the girl – and he, too, was afraid.

'Come,' he said, taking Nadara by the hand, 'let us hurry back into the hills before they discover us.'

Just as the men from the yacht, which Mr John Alden Smith-Jones had dispatched to the South Seas in search of his missing son, emerged from the forest into a view of the valley and the cliffs a cave man and his mate clambered over the brow of the latter and disappeared toward the hills beyond.

It was nearly dusk as the searchers from the yacht were returning toward the beach.

They had found no sign of human habitation in the little valley, nor anywhere along the coast that they had so carefully explored.

The commander of the expedition, Captain Cecil Burlinghame, a retired naval officer, was in advance.

They had penetrated the woods nearly to the beach when his foot struck against a package wrapped in the skin of a small rodent.

He stooped and picked it up.

'Here is the first evidence that another human being than ourselves has ever set foot upon this island,' he said as he cut the gut lacing with his pocket knife.

Within the first wrapping he found a chamois-bag such as women sometimes use to carry jewels about their persons.

From this he emptied into his palm a dozen priceless rings, a few old-fashioned brooches, bracelets, and lockets.

In one of the latter he discovered the ivory miniature of a woman – a very beautiful woman.

In the other side of the locket was engraved: 'To Eugénie Marie Céleste de la Valois, Countess of Crecy, from Henri, her husband. 17th January, 18—'

'Gad!' cried the old captain. 'Now what do you make of that?

'The Count and Countess of Crecy were returning to Paris from their honeymoon trip round the world in the steam yacht *Dolphin* nearly twenty years ago, and after they touched at Australia were never heard of again.

'What tragedy, what mystery, what romance might not these sparkling gems disclose had they but tongues!'

Part II

Note: *Part II of this book appeared serially under the title* 'The Cave Man'

CHAPTER ONE

KING BIG FIST

Waldo Emerson Smith-Jones, scion of the aristrocratic house of the John Alden Smith-Joneses of Boston, clambered up the rocky face of the precipitous cliff with the agility of a monkey.

His right hand clasped the slim fingers of his half-naked mate, assisting her over the more dangerous or difficult stretches.

At the summit the two turned their faces back toward the sea. Beyond the gently waving forest trees stretched the broad expanse of shimmering ocean. In the foreground, upon the bosom of a tiny harbor, lay a graceful yacht – a beautiful toy it looked from the distance of the cliff top.

For the first time the man obtained an unobstructed view of the craft. Before, when they first had discovered it, the boles of the forest trees had revealed it but in part.

Now he saw it fully from stem to stern with all its well-known graceful lines standing out distinctly against the deep blue of the water.

The shock of recognition brought an involuntary exclamation from his lips. The girl looked quickly up into his face.

'What is it, Thandar?' she asked. 'What do you see?'

'The yacht!' he whispered. 'It is the *Priscilla* – my father's. He is searching for me.'

'And you wish to go?'

For some time he did not speak – only stood there gazing at the distant yacht. And the young girl at his side remained quite motionless and silent, too, looking up at the man's profile, watching the expression upon his face with a look of dumb misery upon her own.

Quickly through the man's mind was running the gamut of his past. He recalled his careful and tender upbringing – the time, the money, the fond pride that had been expended upon his education. He thought of the result – the narrow-minded, weakling egoist; the pusillanimous coward that had been washed from the deck of a passing steamer upon the sandy beach of this savage, forgotten shore.

And yet it had been love, solicitous and tender, that had prompted his parents to their misguided efforts. He was their only son. They were doubtless grieving for him. They were no longer young, and in their declining years it appeared to him a pathetic thing that they should be robbed of the happiness which he might bring them by returning to the old life.

But could he ever return to the bookish existence that once had seemed so pleasant?

Had not this brief year into which had been crowded so much of wild, primitive life made impossible a return to the narrow, self-centered existence? Had it not taught him that there was infinitely more in life than ever had been written into the dry and musty pages of books?

It had taught him to want life at first hand – not through the proxy of the printed page. It and – Nadara. He glanced toward the girl.

Could he give her up? No! A thousand times, no!

He read in her face the fear that lurked in her heart. No, he could not give her up. He owed to her all that he possessed of which he was most proud – his mighty physique, his new found courage, his woodcraft, his ability to cope, primitively, with the primitive world, her savage world which he had learned to love.

No, he could not give her up; but – what? His gaze lingered upon her sweet face. Slowly there sank into his understanding something of the reason for his love of this wild, half-savage cave girl other than the primitive passion of the sexes.

He saw now not only the physical beauty of her face and figure, but the sweet, pure innocence of her girlishness, and, most of all, the wondrous tenderness of her love of him that was mirrored in her eyes.

To remain and take her as his mate after the manner and customs of her own people would reflect no shame upon himself or her; but was she not deserving of the highest honor that it lay within his power to offer at the altar of her love?

She -- his wonderful Nadara -- must become his through the most solemn and dignified ceremony that civilized man had devised. What the young women of his past life demanded was none too good for her.

Again the girl voiced her question.

'You wish to go?'

'Yes, Nadara,' he replied, 'I must go back to my own people – and you must go with me.'

Her face lighted with pleasure and happiness as she heard the last words; but the expression was quickly followed by one of doubt and fear.

'I am afraid,' she said; 'but if you wish it I will go.'

'You need not fear, Nadara. None will harm you by word or deed while Thandar is with you. Come, let us return to the sea and the yacht before she sails.'

Hand in hand they retraced their steps down the steep cliff, across the little valley toward the forest and the sea.

Nadara walked very close to Thandar, her hand snuggled in his and her shoulder pressed tightly against his side, for she was afraid of the new life among the strange creatures of civilization.

At the far side of the valley, just before one enters the forest, there grows a thick jungle of bamboo – really but a narrow strip, not more than a hundred feet through at its greatest width; but so dense as to quite shut out from view any creature even a few feet within its narrow, gloomy avenues.

Into this the two plunged, Thandar in the lead, Nadara

close behind him, stepping exactly in his footprints – an involuntary concession to training, for there was no need here either of deceiving a pursuer, or taking advantage of easier going. The trail was well-marked and smooth-beaten by many a padded paw.

It wound erratically, following the line of least resistance – it forked, and there were other trails which entered it from time to time, or crossed it. The hundred feet it traversed seemed much more when measured by the trail.

The two had come almost to the forest side of the jungle when a sharp turn in the path brought Thandar face to face with a huge, bear-like man.

The fellow wore a g-string of soft hide, and over one shoulder dangled an old and filthy leopard skin – otherwise, he was naked. His thick, coarse hair was matted low over his forehead. The balance of his face was covered by a bushy red beard.

At sight of Thandar his close set, little eyes burned with sudden rage and cunning. From his thick lips burst a savage yell – it was the preliminary challenge.

Ordinarily a certain amount of vituperation and coarse insults must pass between strangers meeting upon this inhospitable isle before they fly at one another's throat.

'I am Thurg,' bellowed the brute. 'I can kill you,' and then followed a volley of vulgar allusions to Thandar's possible origin, and the origin of his ancestors.

'The bad men,' whispered Nadara.

With her words there swept into the man's memory the scene upon the face of the cliff that night a year before when, even in the throes of cowardly terror, he had turned to do battle with a huge cave man that the fellow might not prevent the escape of Nadara.

He glanced at the right forearm of the creature who faced him. A smile touched Thandar's lips – the arm was crooked as from the knitting of a broken bone, poorly set.

'You would kill Thandar – again?' he asked tauntingly, pointing toward the deformed member.

Then came recognition to the red-rimmed eyes of Thurg, as, with another ferocious bellow, he launched himself toward the author of his old hurt.

Thandar met the charge with his short stick of pointed hard wood – his 'sword' he called it. It entered the fleshy part of Thurg's breast, calling forth a howl of pain and a trickling stream of crimson.

For several minutes he stood glaring at his foe, screaming hideous threats and insults at him. Then once more he charged.

Again the painful point entered his body, but this time he pressed in clutching madly at the goad and for a hold upon Thandar's body.

The latter held Thurg at arm's length, prodding him with the fire-hardened point of his wooden sword.

The cave man's little brain wondered at the skill and prowess of this stranger who had struck him a single blow with a cudgel many moons before and then run like a rabbit to escape his wrath.

Why was it that he did not run now? What strange change had taken place in him? He had expected an easy victim when he finally had recognized his foe; but instead he had met with brawn and ferocity equal to his own and with a strange weapon, the like of which he never before had seen.

Thandar was puncturing him rapidly now, and Thurg was screaming in rage and suffering. Presently he could endure it no longer. With a sudden wrench he tore himself loose and ran, bellowing, through the jungle.

Thandar did not pursue. It was enough that he had rid himself of his enemy. He turned toward Nadara, smiling.

'It will seem very tame in Boston,' he said; but though she gave him an answering smile, she did not understand, for to her Boston was but another land of primeval forests, and dense jungles; of hairy, battling men, and fierce beasts.

At the edge of the forest they came again upon Thurg, but this time he was surrounded by a score of his burly tribesmen. Thandar knew better than to pit himself against so many.

Thurg came rushing down upon them, his fellows at his heels. In loud tones he screamed anew his challenge, and the beasts behind him took it up until the forest echoed to their hideous bellowing.

He had seen Nadara as he had battled with Thandar, and recognized her as the girl he had desired a year before – the girl whom this stranger had robbed him of.

Now he was determined to wreak vengeance on the man and at the same time recapture the girl.

Thandar and Nadara turned back into the jungle where but a single enemy could attack them at a time in the narrow trails. Here they managed to elude pursuit for several hours, coming again into the forest nearly a mile below the beach where the *Priscilla* had lain at anchor.

Thurg and his fellows had apparently given up the chase – they had neither seen nor heard aught of them for some time. Now the two hastened back through the wood to reach a point on the shore opposite the yacht.

At last they came in sight of the harbor. Thandar halted. A look of horror and disappointment supplanted the expression of pleasurable anticipation that had lighted his countenance – the yacht was not there.

A mile out they discerned her, steaming rapidly north.

Thandar ran to the beach. He tore the black panther's hide from his shoulders, waving it frantically above his head, the while he shouted in futile endeavor to attract attention from the dwindling craft.

Then, quite suddenly, he collapsed upon the beach, burying his face in his hands.

Presently Nadara crept close to his side. Her soft arms encircled his shoulders as she drew his cheek close to hers in an attempt to comfort him.

'Is it so terrible,' she asked, 'to be left here alone with your Nadara?'

'It is not that,' he answered. 'If you were mine I should

109

not care so much, but you cannot be mine until we have reached civilization and you have been made mine in accordance with the laws and customs of civilized men. And now who knows when another ship may come – if ever another will come?'

'But I am yours, Thandar,' insisted the girl. 'You are my man – you have told me that you love me, and I have replied that I would be your mate – who can give us to each other better than we can give ourselves?'

He tried, as best he could, to explain to her the marriage customs and ceremonies of his own world, but she found it difficult to understand how it might be that a stranger whom neither might possibly ever have seen before could make it right for her to love her Thandar, or that it should be wrong for her to love him without the stranger's permission.

To Thandar the future looked most black and hopeless. With his sudden determination to take Nadara back to his own people he had been overwhelmed with a mad yearning for home.

He realized that his past apathy to the idea of returning to Boston had been due solely to recollection of Boston as he had known it – Boston without Nadara; but now that she was to have gone back with him Boston seemed the most desirable spot in the world.

As he sat pondering the unfortunate happenings that had so delayed them that the yacht had sailed before they reached the shore, he also cast about for some plan to mitigate their disappointment.

To live forever upon this savage island did not seem such an appalling thing as it had a year before – but then he had not realized this love for the wild young creature at his side. Ah, if she could but be made his wife then his exile here would be a happy rather than a doleful lot.

What if he had been born here too? With the thought came a new idea that seemed to offer an avenue from his dilemma. Had he, too, been native born how would he have wed Nadara?

Why through the ceremony of their own people, of course. And if men and women were thus wed here, living together in faithfulness throughout their lives, what more sacred a union could civilization offer?

He sprang to his feet.

'Come, Nadara!' he cried. 'We shall return to your people, and there you shall become my wife.'

Nadara was puzzled, but she made no comment; content simply to leave the future to her lord and master; to do whatever would bring Thandar the greatest happiness.

The return to the dwellings of Nadara's people occupied three never-to-be-forgotten days.

How different this journey by comparison with that of a year since, when the cave girl had been leading the terror-stricken Waldo Emerson in flight from the bad men toward, to him, an equally horrible fate at the hands of Korth and Flatfoot!

Then the forest glades echoed to the pads of fierce beasts and the stealthy passage of naked, human horrors. No twig snapped that did not portend instant and terrifying death.

Now Korth and Flatfoot were dead at the hands of the metamorphosed Waldo. The racking cough was gone. He had encountered the bad men and others like them and come away with honors. Even Nagoola, the sleek, black devil-cat of the hideous nights, no longer sent the slightest tremor through the rehabilitated nerves.

Did not Thandar wear Nagoola's pelt about his shoulder and loins – a pelt that he had taken in hand to hand encounter with the dread beast?

Slowly they walked beneath the shade of giant trees, beside pleasant streams, or, again, across open valleys where the grass grew knee high and countless, perfumed wild flowers opened a pathway before their naked feet.

At night they slept where night found them. Sometimes in the deserted lair of a wild beast, or again perched among the branches of a spreading tree where parallel branches permitted the construction of rude platforms.

And Thandar was always most solicitous to see that Nadara's couch was of the softest grasses and that his own lay at a little distance from hers and in a position where he might best protect her from prowling beasts.

Again was Nadara puzzled, but still she made no comment.

Finally they came to her village.

Several of the younger men came forth to meet them; but when they saw that the man was he who had slain Korth they bridled their truculence, all but one, Big Fist, who had assumed the role of King since Flatfoot had left.

'I can kill you,' he announced by way of greeting, 'for I am Big Fist, and until Flatfoot returns I am king – and maybe afterward, for some day I shall kill Flatfoot.'

'I do not wish to fight you,' replied Thandar. 'Already have I killed Korth, and Flatfoot will return no more, for Flatfoot I have killed also. And I can kill Big Fist, but what is the use? Why should we fight? Let us be friends, for we must live together, and if we do not kill one another there will be more of us to meet the bad men, should they come, and kill them.'

When Big Fist heard that Flatfoot was dead and by the hand of this stranger he pined less to measure his strength with that of the newcomer. He saw the knothole that the other offered, and promptly he sought to crawl through it, but with honor.

'Very well,' he said, 'I shall not kill you – you need not be afraid. But you must know that I am king, and do as I say that you shall do.'

' "Afraid".' Thandar laughed. 'You may be king,' he said, 'but as for doing what you say—' and again he laughed.

It was a very different Waldo Emerson Smith-Jones from the thing that the sea had spewed up twelve months before.

CHAPTER TWO

KING THANDAR

The first thing that Thandar did after he entered the village was to seek out Nadara's father.

They found the old man in the poorest and least protected cave in the cliff side, exposed to the attack of the first prowling carnivore, or skulking foeman.

He was sick, and there was none to care for him; but he did not complain. That was the way of his people. When a man became too old to be of service to the community it were better that he died, and so they did nothing to delay the inevitable. When one became an absolute burden upon his fellows it was customary to hasten the end – a carefully delivered blow with a heavy rock was calculated quickly to relieve the burdens of the community and the suffering of the invalid.

Thandar and Nadara came in and sat down beside him. The old fellow seemed glad to see them.

'I am Thandar,' said the young man. 'I wish to take your daughter as my mate.'

The old man looked at him questioningly for a moment.

'You have killed Korth and Flatfoot – who is to prevent you from taking Nadara?'

'I wish to be joined to her with your permission and in accordance with the marriage ceremonies of your people,' said Thandar.

The old man shook his head.

'I do not understand you,' he replied at last. 'There are several fine caves that are not occupied – if you wish a better one you have but to slay the present occupants if they do not get out when you tell them to – but I think they will get out when the slayer of Korth and Flatfoot tells them to.'

'I am not worried about a cave,' said Thandar. 'Tell me how men take their wives among you.'

'If they do not come with us willingly we take them by the hair and drag them with us,' replied Nadara's father. 'My mate would not come with me,' he continued, 'and even after I had caught her and dragged her to my cave she broke away and fled from me, but again I overhauled her, for when I was young none could run more swiftly, and this time I did what I should have done at first – I beat her upon the head until she went to sleep. When she awoke she was in my own cave, and it was night, and she did not try to run away any more.'

For a long time Thandar sat in thought. Presently he spoke addressing Nadara.

'In my country we do not take our wives in any such way, nor shall I take you thus. We must be married properly, according to the customs and laws of civilization.'

Nadara made no reply. To her it seemed that Thandar must care very little for her – that was about the only explanation she could put upon his strange behavior. It made her sad. And then the other women would laugh at her – of that she was quite certain, and that, too, made her feel very badly – they would see that Thandar did not want her.

The old man, lying upon his scant bed of matted, filthy grasses, had heard the conversation. He was as much at sea as Nadara. At last he spoke – very feebly now, for rapidly he was nearing dissolution.

'I am a very old man,' he said to Thandar. 'I have not long to live. Before I die I should like to know that Nadara has a mate who will protect her. I love her, though—' He hesitated.

'Though what?' asked Thandar.

'I have never told,' whispered the old fellow. 'My mate would not let me, but now that I am about to die it can do no harm. Nadara is not my daughter.'

The girl sprang to her feet.

'Not your daughter? Then who am I?'

'I do not know who you are, except that you are not even of my people. All that I know I will tell you now before I die. Come close, for my voice is dying faster than my body.'

The young man and the girl came nearer to his side, and squatting there leaned close that they might catch each faintly articulated syllable.

'My mate and I,' commenced the old man, 'were childless, though many moons had passed since I took her to my cave. She wanted a little one, for thus only may women have aught upon which to lavish their love.

'We had been hunting together for several days alone and far from the village for I was a great hunter when I was young – no greater ever lived among our people.

'And one day we came down to the great water, and there, a short distance from the shore we saw a strange thing that floated upon the surface of the water, and when it was blown closer to us we saw that it was hollow and that in it were two people – a man and a woman. Both appeared to be dead.

'Finally I waded out to meet the thing, dragging it to shore, and there sure enough was a man and a woman, and the man was dead – quite dead. He must have been dead for a long time; but the woman was not dead.

'She was very fair though her eyes and hair were black. We carried her ashore, and that night a little girl was born to her, but the woman died before morning.

'We put her back into the strange thing that had brought her – she and the dead man who had come with her – and shoved them off upon the great water, where the breeze, which runs away from the land twice each day carried them out of sight, nor ever did we see them again.

'But before we sent them off my mate took from the body of the woman her strange coverings and a little bag of skin which contained many sparkling stones of different colors and metals of yellow and white made into things the purposes of which we could not guess.

'It was evident that the woman had come from a strange land, for she and all her belongings were unlike anything that either of us ever had seen before. She herself was different as Nadara is different – Nadara looks as her mother looked, for Nadara is the little babe that was born that night.

'We brought her back to our people after another moon, saying that she was born to my mate; but there was one woman who knew better, for it seemed that she had seen us when we found the boat, having been running away from a man who wanted her as his mate.

'But my mate did not want anyone to say that Nadara was not hers, for it is a great disgrace, as you well know, for a woman to be barren, and so she several times nearly killed this woman, who knew the truth, to keep her from telling it to the whole village.

'But I love Nadara as well as though she had been my own, and so I should like to see her well mated before I die.'

Thandar had gone white during the narration of the story of Nadara's birth. He could scarce restrain an impulse to go upon his knees and thank his God that he had harked to the call of his civilized training rather than have given in to the easier way, the way these primitive, beast-like people offered. Providence, he thought, must indeed have sent him here to rescue her.

The old man, turning upon his rough pallet, fastened his sunken eyes questioningly upon Thandar. Nadara, too, with parted lips waited for him to speak. The old man gasped for breath – there was a strange rattling sound in his throat.

Thandar leaned above him, raising his head and shoulders slightly. The young man never had heard that sound before, but now that he heard it he needed no interpreter.

The locust, rubbing his legs along his wings, startles the uninitiated into the belief that a hidden rattler lurks in the pathway; but when the great diamond back breaks forth in warning none mistakes him for a locust.

And so is it with the death rattle in the human throat.

Thandar knew that it was the end. He saw the old man's

mighty effort to push back the grim reaper that he might speak once more. In the dying eyes were a question and a plea. Thandar could not misunderstand.

He reached forward and took Nadara's hand.

'In my own land we shall be mated,' he said. 'None other shall wed with Nadara, and as proof that she is Thandar's she shall wear this always,' and from his finger he slipped a splendid solitaire to the third finger of Nadara's left hand.

The old man saw. A look of relief and contentment that was almost a smile settled upon his features, as, with a gasping sigh, he sank limply into Thandar's arms, dead.

That afternoon several of the younger men carried the body of Nadara's foster father to the top of the cliff, depositing it about half a mile from the caves. There was no ceremony. In it, though, Waldo Emerson saw what might have been the first human funeral cortege – simple, sensible and utilitarian – from which the human race has retrograded to the ostentatious, ridiculous, pestilent burials of present day civilization.

The young men, acting under Big Fist's orders, carried the worthless husk to a safe distance from the caves, leaving it there to the rapid disintegration provided by the beasts and birds of prey.

Nadara wept, silently. An elderly lady with a single tooth, espying her, moaned in sympathy. Presently other females, attracted by the moaning, joined them, and, becoming affected by the strange hysteria to which womankind is heir, mingled their moans with those of the toothless one.

Excited by their own noise they soon were shrieking and screaming in hideous chorus. Then came Big Fist and others of the men. The din annoyed them. They set upon the mourners with their fists and teeth scattering them in all directions. Thus ended the festivities.

Or would have had not Big Fist made the fatal mistake of launching a blow on Nadara. Thandar had been standing nearby looking with wonder upon the strange scene.

He had noted the quiet grief of the young girl – real grief; and he had witnessed the hysterical variety of the 'mourners' – not sham grief. Precisely, because they made no pretense to grief – it was noise to which they aspired. And as the fiendish din had set his own nerves on edge he wondered not at all that Big Fist and the other men should take steps to quell the tumult.

The female half-brutes were theirs and Waldo Emerson had reverted sufficiently to the primitive to feel no incentive to interfere. But Nadara was not theirs – she was not of them, and even had she not belonged to him the American would have felt bound to stand between her and the savage creatures among whom fate had cast her.

That she did belong to him, however, sent him hot with the blood lust of the killer as she sprang to intercept the rush of Big Fist toward her.

Waldo Emerson Smith-Jones had learned nothing of the manly art of self-defense in that other life that had been so zealously guarded from the rude and vulgar. This was unfortunate since it would have given him a great advantage over the man-brute. A single well-timed swing to that unguarded chin would have ended hostilities at once; but of hooks and jabs and jolts, scientific, Thandar knew nothing.

Except for his crude weapons he was as primeval in battle as his original anthropoid progenitor, and quite as often as not he forgot all about his sword, his knife, his bow and arrows and his spear when, half stooped, he crouched to meet the charge of a foeman.

Now he sprang for Big Fist's hairy throat. There was a sullen thud as the two bodies met, and then, rolling, biting and tearing, they struggled hither and thither upon the rocky ground at the base of the cliff.

The other men desisted from their attack upon the women. The women ceased their vocal mourning. In a little circle they formed about the contestants – a circle which moved this way and that as the fighters moved, keeping them always in the center.

Nadara forced her way through them to the front. She wished to be near Thandar. In her hand she carried a jagged bit of granite – one could never tell.

Big Fist was burly – mountainous – but Thandar was muscled like Nagoola, the black panther. His movements were all grace and ease, but oh, so irresistible. A sudden and unexpected blow upon the side of Big Fist's head bent that bullet-shaped thing sidewards with a jerk that almost dislocated the neck.

Big Fist shrieked with the pain of it. Thandar, delighted by the result of the accidental blow, repeated it. Big Fist bellowed – agonized. He made a last supreme effort to close with his agile foeman, and succeeded. His teeth sought Thandar's throat, but the act brought his own jugular close to Thandar's jaws.

The strong white teeth of Waldo Emerson Smith-Jones closed upon it as naturally as though no countless ages had rolled their snail-like way between himself and the last of his progenitors to bury bloody fangs in the soft flesh of an antagonist.

Wasted ages! fleeing from the primitive and the brute toward the neoteric and the human – in a brief instant your labors are undone, the veneer of eons crumbles in the heat of some pristine passion revealing again naked and unashamed, the primitive and the brute.

Big Fist, white now from terror at impending death, struggled to be free. Thandar buried his teeth more deeply. There was a sudden rush of spurting blood that choked him. Big Fist relaxed, inert.

Thandar, drenched crimson, rose to his feet. The huge body on the ground before him floundered spasmodically once or twice as the life blood gushed from the severed jugular. The eyes rolled up and set, there was a final twitch and Big Fist was dead.

Thandar turned toward the circle of interested spectators. He singled out a burly quartet.

'Bear Big Fist to the cliff top,' he commanded. 'When you return we shall choose a king.'

The men did as they were bid. They did not at all understand what Thandar meant by choosing a king. Having slain Big Fist, Thandar was king, unless some ambitious one desired to dispute his right to reign. But all had seen him slay Big Fist, and all knew that he had killed Korth and Flatfoot, so who was there would dare question his kingship?

When they had come back to the village Thandar gathered them beneath a great tree that grew close to the base of the cliff. Here they squatted upon their haunches in a rough circle. Behind them stood the women and children, wide-eyed and curious.

'Let us choose a king,' said Thandar, when all had come.

There was a long silence, then one of the older men spoke.

'I am an old man. I have seen many kings. They come by killing. They go by killing. Thandar has killed two kings. Now he is king. Who wishes to kill Thandar and become king?'

There was no answer.

The old man arose.

'It was foolish to come here to choose a king,' he said, 'when a king we already have.'

'Wait,' commanded Thandar. 'Let us choose a king properly. Because I have killed Flatfoot and Big Fist does not prove that I can make a good king. Was Flatfoot a good king?'

'He was a bad man,' replied the ancient one.

'Has a good man ever been king?' asked Thandar.

The old fellow puckered his brow in thought.

'Not for a long time,' he said.

'That is because you always permit a bully and a brute to rule you,' said Thandar. 'That is not the proper way to choose a king. Rather you should come together as we are come, and among you talk over the needs of the tribe and when you are decided as to what measures are best for the welfare of the members of the tribe then should you select the man best fitted to carry out your plans. That is a better way to choose a king.'

The old man laughed.

'And then,' he said, 'would come a Big Fist or a Flatfoot and slay our king that he might be king in his place.'

'Have you ever seen a man who could slay all the other men of the tribe at the same time?'

The old man looked puzzled.

'That is my answer to your argument,' said Thandar. 'Those who choose the king can protect him from his enemies. So long as he is a good king they should do so, but when he becomes a bad king they can then select another, and if the bad king refuses to obey the new it would be an easy matter for several men to kill him or drive him away, no matter how mighty a fighter he might be.'

Several of the men nodded understandingly.

'We had not thought of that,' they said. 'Thandar is indeed wise.'

'So now,' continued the American, 'let us choose a king whom the majority of us want, and then so long as he is a good king the majority of us must fight for him and protect him. Let us choose a man whom we know to be a good man regardless of his ability to kill his fellows, for if he has the majority of the tribe to fight for him what need will he have to fight for himself? What we want is a wise man – one who can lead the tribe to fertile lands and good hunting, and in times of battle direct the fighting intelligently. Flatfoot and Big Fist had not brains enough between them to do aught but steal the mates of other men. Such should not be the business of kings. Your king should protect your mates from such as Flatfoot, and he should punish those who would steal them.'

'But how may he do these things?' asked a young man, 'if he is not the best fighter in the tribe?'

'Have I not shown you how?' asked Thandar. 'We who make him king shall be his fighters – he will not need to fight with his own hands.'

Again there was a long silence. Then the old man spoke again.

'There is wisdom in the talk of Thandar. Let us choose a king who will have to be good to us if he wishes to remain king. It is very bad for us to have a king whom we fear.'

'I, for one,' said the young man who had previously spoken, 'do not care to be ruled by a king unless he is able to defeat me in battle. If I can defeat him then I should be king.'

And so they took sides, but at last they compromised by selecting one whom they knew to be wise and a great fighter as well. Thus they chose Thandar king.

'Once each week,' said the new king, 'we shall gather here and talk among ourselves of the things which are for the best good of the tribe, and what seems best to the majority shall be done. The tribe will tell the king what to do – the king will carry out the work. And all must fight when the king says fight and all must work when the king says work, for we shall all be fighting or working for the whole tribe, and I, Thandar, your king, shall fight and work the hardest of you all.'

It was a new idea to them and placed the kingship in a totally different light from any by which they had previously viewed it. That it would take a long time for them to really absorb the idea Thandar knew, and he was glad that in the meantime they had a king who could command their respect according to their former standards.

And he smiled when he thought of the change that had taken place in him since first he had sat trembling, weeping and coughing upon the lonely shore before the terrifying forest.

CHAPTER THREE

THE GREAT NAGOOLA

Waldo Emerson Smith-Jones had gladly embraced the opportunity which chance had offered him to assume the kingship of the little tribe of troglodytes. First, because his position would assure Nadara greater safety, and, second, because of the opening it would give him for the exercise of his new-found initiative.

Where before he had shrunk from responsibility he now found himself anxious to assume it. He longed to do, where formerly he had been content to but read of the accomplishments of others.

To his chagrin, however, he soon discovered that the classical education to which his earlier life had been devoted under the guidance of a fond and ultra-cultured mother was to prove a most inadequate foundation upon which to build a practical scheme of life for himself and his people.

He wished to teach his tribe to construct permanent and comfortable houses, but he could not recollect any practical hints on carpentry that he had obtained from Ovid.

His people lived by hunting small rodents, robbing birds' nests, and gathering wild fruit and Thandar desired to institute a scheme of community farming, but the works of the Cyclic Poets, with which he was quite familiar, seemed to offer little of value along agricultural lines. He regretted that he had not matriculated at an agricultural college west of the Alleghanies rather than at Harvard.

However, he determined to do the best he could with the meager knowledge he possessed of things practical — a knowledge so meager that it consisted almost entirely of the bare definition of the word agriculture.

It was a germ, however, for it presupposed a knowledge of the results that might be obtained through agriculture.

So Thandar found himself a step ahead of the earliest of his progenitors who had thought to plant purposely the seeds that nature heretofore had distributed haphazard through the agencies of wind and bird and beast; but only a step ahead.

He realized that he occupied a very remarkable position in the march of ages. He had known and seen and benefited by all the accumulated knowledge of ages of progression from the stone age to the twentieth century, and now, suddenly, fate had snatched him back into the stone age, or possibly a few eons farther back, only to show him that all that he had from a knowledge of other men's knowledge was keen dissatisfaction with the stone age.

He had lived in houses of wood and brick and looked through windows of glass. He had read in the light of gas and electricity, and he even knew of candles; but he could not fashion the tools to build a house, he could not have made a brick to have saved his life, glass had suddenly become one of the wonders of the world to him, and as for gas and electricity and candles they had become one with the mystery of the Sphinx.

He could write verse in excellent Greek, but he was no longer proud of that fact. He would much rather that he had been able to tan a hide, or make fire without matches. Waldo Emerson Smith-Jones had a year ago been exceedingly proud of his intellect and his learning, but for a year his ego had been shrinking until now he felt himself the most pitiful ignoramus on earth. 'Criminally ignorant,' he said to Nadara, 'for I have thrown away the opportunities of a lifetime devoted to the accumulation of useless erudition when I might have been profiting by the practical knowledge which has dragged the world from the black bit of barbarism to the light of modern achievement – I might not only have done this but, myself, added something to the glory and welfare of mankind. I am no good, Nadara – worse than useless.'

The girl touched his strong brown hand caressingly, looking proudly into his eyes.

'To me you are very wonderful, Thandar,' she said. 'With your own hands you slew Nagoola, the most terrible beast in the world, and Korth, and Flatfoot, and Big Fist lie dead beneath the vultures because of your might – single-handed you killed them all; three awesome men. No, my Thandar is greater than all other men.'

Nor could Waldo Emerson repress the swelling tide of pride that surged through him as the girl he loved recounted his exploits. No longer did he think of his achievements as 'vulgar physical prowess'. The old Waldo Emerson, whose temperature had risen regularly at three o'clock each afternoon, whose pitifully skinny body had been racked by coughing continually, whose eyes had been terror filled by day and by night at the restling of dry leaves, was dead.

In his place stood a great, full blooded man, brown skinned and steel thewed; fearless, self-reliant, almost brutal in his pride of power – Thandar, the cave man.

The months that passed as Thandar led his people from one honeycombed cliff to another as he sought a fitting place for a permanent village were filled with happiness for Nadara and the king.

The girl's happiness was slightly alloyed by the fact that Thandar failed to claim her as his own. She could not yet quite understand the ethics which separated them. Thandar tried repeatedly to explain to her that some day they were to return to his own world, and that that world would not accept her unless she had been joined to him according to the rites and ceremonies which it had originated.

'Will this marriage ceremony of which you tell me make you love me more?' asked Nadara.

Thandar laughed and took her in his arms.

'I could not love you more,' he replied.

'Then of what good is it?'

Thandar shook his head.

'It is difficult to explain,' he said, 'especially to such a lovable little pagan as my Nadara. You must be satisfied to know – accept my word for it – that it is because I love you that we must wait.'

Now it was the girl's turn to shake her head.

'I cannot understand,' she said. 'My people take their mates as they will and they are satisfied and everybody is satisfied and all is well; but their king, who may mate as he chooses, waits until a man whom he does not know and who lives across the great water where we may never go, gives him permission to mate with one who loves him – with one whom he *says* he loves.'

Thandar noticed the emphasis which Nadara put upon the word 'says'.

'Some day,' he said, 'when we have reached my world you will know that I was right, and you will thank me. Until then, Nadara, you must trust me, and,' he added half to himself, 'God knows I have earned your trust even if you do not know it.'

And so Nadara made believe that she was satisfied but in her heart of hearts she still feared Thandar did not really love her, nor did the half-veiled comments of the women add at all to her peace of mind.

During all the time that Thandar was with her he had been teaching her his language for he had set his heart upon taking her home, and he wished her to be as well prepared for her introduction to Boston and civilization as he could make her.

Thandar's plan was to find a suitable location within sight of the sea that he might always be upon the lookout for a ship. At last he found such a place – a level meadow land upon a low plateau overlooking the ocean.

He had come upon it while he wandered alone several miles from the temporary cliff dwellings the tribe was occupying. The soil, when he dug into it, he found to be rich and black. There was timber upon one side and upon the other overhanging cliffs of soft limestone.

It was Thandar's plan to build a village partly of logs

against the face of the cliff, burrowing inward behind the dwellings for such additional apartments as each family might require.

The caves alone would have proved sufficient shelter, but the man hoped by compelling his people to construct a portion of each dwelling of logs to engender within each each family a certain feeling of ownership and pride in personal possession as would make it less easy for them to give up their abodes than in the past, when it had been necessary but to move to another cliff to find caves equally as comfortable as those which they so easily abandoned.

In other words he hoped to give them a word which their vocabulary had never held – home.

Whether or not he would have succeeded we may never know, for fate stepped in at the last moment to alter with a single stroke his every plan and aspiration.

As he returned to his people that afternoon filled with the enthusiasm of his hopes a burly, hairy figure crept warily after him. As Thandar emerged from the brush which reaches close to the cliffs where the temporary encampment had been made Nadara, watching for him, ran forward to meet him.

The creature upon Thandar's trail halted at the edge of the bush. As his close-set eyes fell upon the girl his flabby lips vibrated to the quick intaking of his breath and his red lids half closed in cunning and desire.

For a few moments he watched the man and the maid as they turned and walked slowly towards the cliffs, the arm of the former about the brown shoulders of the latter. Then he too turned and melted into the tangled branches behind him.

That evening Thandar gathered the members of the tribe about him at the foot of the cliff. They sat around a great fire while Thandar, their king, explained to them in minutest detail the future that he had mapped out for them.

Some of the old men shook their heads, for here was an unheard of thing – a change from the accustomed ordering of their lives – and they were loath to change regardless of the benefits which might accrue.

But for the most part the people welcomed the idea of comfortable and permanent habitations, though their anticipatory joy, Thandar reasoned, was due largely to a childish eagerness for something new and different – whether their enthusiasm would survive the additional labors which the new life was sure to entail was another question.

So Thandar laid down the new laws that were to guide his people thereafter. The men were to make all implements and weapons, for he had already taught them to use arrows and spears. The women were to keep all edged tools sharp. The men were to hew the logs and build the houses – the women make garments, cook and keep the houses in order.

The men were to turn up the soil, the women were to sow the seeds, and cultivate the growing crops, which, later, all hands must turn to and harvest.

The hunting and the fighting devolved upon the men, but the fighting must be confined to enemies of the tribe. A man who killed another member of the tribe except in defense of his home or his own person was to suffer death.

Other laws he made – good laws – which even these primitive people could see where good. It was quite late when the last of them crawled into his comfortless cave to dream of large, airy rooms built of the trees of the forest; of good food in plenty just before the rains as well as after; of security from the periodic raids of the 'bad men'.

Thandar and Nadara were the last to go. Together they sat upon a narrow ledge before Nadara's cave, the moonlight falling upon their glistening, naked shoulders, while they talked and dreamed together of the future.

Thandar had been talking of the wonderful plans which seemed to fill his whole mind – of the future of the tribe – of the great strides toward civilization they could make in a few brief years if they could but be made to follow the simple plans he had in mind.

'Why,' he said, 'in ten years they should have bridged a

gulf that it must have required ages for our ancestors to span.'

'And you are planning ten years ahead, Thandar,' she asked, 'when only yesterday you were saying that once beside the sea you hoped it would be but a short time before we might sight a passing vessel that would bear us away to your civilization? Must we wait ten years, Thandar?'

'I am planning for them,' he replied. 'We may not be here to witness the changes; but I wish to start them upon the road, and when we go I shall see to it that a king is chosen in my place who has the courage and the desire to carry out my plans.

'Yet,' he added, musingly, 'it would be splendid could we but return to complete our work. Never, Nadara, have I performed a single constructive act for the benefit of my fellow man, but now I see an opportunity to do something, however small it may seem, to – what was that?'

A low rumbling muttered threateningly out of the west. Deep and ominous it sounded, yet so low that it failed to awaken any member of the sleeping tribe.

Before either could again speak there came a slight trembling of the earth beneath them, scarcely sufficient to have been noticeable had it not been preceded by the distant grumbling of the earth's bowels.

The two upon the moonlit ledge came to their feet, and Nadara drew close to Thandar, the man's arm encircling her shoulders protectingly.

'The Great Nagoola,' she whispered. 'Again he seeks to escape.'

'What do you mean?' asked Thandar. 'It is an earthquake – distant and quite harmless to us.'

'No, it is The Great Nagoola,' insisted Nadara. 'Long time ago, when our fathers' fathers were yet unborn, The Great Nagoola roamed the land devouring all that chanced to come in his way – men, beasts, birds, everything.

'One day my people came upon him sleeping in a deep gorge between two mountains. They were mighty men in those days, and when they saw their great enemy asleep there in the gorge half of them went upon one side and half upon the other, and they pushed the two mountains over into the gorge upon the sleeping beast, imprisoning him there.

'It is all true, for my mother had it from her mother, who in turn was told it by her mother – thus has it been handed down truthfully since it happened long time ago.

'And even to this day is occasionally heard the growling of The Great Nagoola in his anger, and the earth shakes and trembles as he strives far, far beneath to shake the mountains from him and escape. Did you not hear his voice and feel the ground rock?'

Thandar laughed.

'Well, we are quite safe then,' he cried, 'for with two mountains piled upon him he cannot escape.'

'Who knows?' asked Nadara. 'He is huge – as huge, himself, as a small mountain. Some day, they say, he will escape, and then naught will pacify his rage until he has destroyed every living creature upon the land.'

'Do not worry, little one,' said Thandar. 'The Great Nagoola will have to grumble louder and struggle more fiercely before ever he may dislodge the two mountains. Even now he is quiet again, so run to your cave, sweetheart, nor bother your pretty head with useless worries – it is time that all good people were asleep,' and he stopped and kissed her as she turned to go.

For a moment she clung to him.

'I am afraid, Thandar,' she whispered. 'Why, I do not know. I only know that I am afraid, with a great fear that will not be quiet.'

CHAPTER FOUR

THE BATTLE

Early the following morning while several of the women and children were at the river drawing water the balance of the tribe of Thandar was startled into wakefulness by piercing shrieks from the direction the water carriers had taken.

Before the great, hairy men, led by the smooth-skinned Thandar, had reached the foot of the cliff in their rush to the rescue of the women several of the latter appeared at the edge of the forest, running swiftly toward the caves.

Mingled with their screams of terror were cries of: 'The bad men! The bad men!' But these were not needed to acquaint the rescuers with the cause of the commotion, for at the heels of the women came Thurg and a score of his vicious brutes. Little better than anthropoid apes were they. Long armed, hairy, skulking monsters, whose close-set eyes and retreating foreheads proclaimed more intimate propinquity to the higher orders of brutes than to civilized man.

Woe betide male or female who fell into their remorseless clutches, since to the base passions, unrestrained, that mark the primordial they were addicted to the foulest forms of cannibalism.

In the past their raids upon their neighbors for meat and women had met with but slight resistance – the terrified cave dwellers scampering to the safety of their dizzy ledges from whence they might hurl stones and roll boulders down to the confusion of any foe however ferocious.

Always the bad men caught a few unwary victims before the safety of the ledges could be attained, but this time there was a difference. Thurg was delighted. The men were rushing downward to meet him – great indeed would be the feast which should follow this day's fighting, for with the men disposed of there would be but little difficulty in storming the cliff and carrying off all the women and children, and as he thought upon these things there floated in his little brain the image of the beautiful girl he had watched come down the evening before from the caves to meet the smooth-skinned warrior who twice now had bested Thurg in battle.

That Thandar's men might turn the tables upon him never for a moment occurred to Thurg. Nor was there little wonder, since, mighty as were the muscles of the cave men, they were weaklings by comparison with the half-brutes of Thurg – only the smooth-skinned stranger troubled the muddy mind of the near-man.

It puzzled him a little, though, to see the long slim sticks that the enemy carried, and the little slivers in skin bags upon their backs, and the strange curved branches whose ends were connected by slender bits of gut. What were these things for!

Soon he was to know – this and other things.

Thandar's warriors did not rush upon Thurg and his brutes in a close packed, yelling mob. Instead they trotted slowly forward in a long thin line that stretched out parallel with the base of the cliff. In the center, directly in front of the charging bad men, was Thandar, calling directions to his people, first upon one hand and then upon the other.

And in accordance with his commands the ends of the line began to quicken the pace, so that quickly Thurg saw that there were men before him, and men upon either hand, and now, at fifty feet, while all were advancing cautiously, crouched for the final hand-to-hand encounter, he saw the enemy slip each sliver into the gut of the bent branches – there was a sudden chorus of twangs, and Thurg felt a sharp pain in his neck. Involuntarily he clapped his hand to the spot to find one of the slivers sticking there, scarce an inch from his jugular.

With a howl of rage he snatched the thing from him, and as he leaped to the charge to punish these audacious madmen he noted a dozen of his henchmen plucking slivers from various portions of their bodies, while two lay quite still upon the grass with just the ends of slivers protruding from their breasts.

The sight brought the beast-man to a momentary halt. He saw his fellows charging in upon the foe – he saw another volley of slivers speed from the bent branches. Down went another of his fighters, and then the enemy cast aside their strange weapons at a shouted command from the smooth-skinned one and grasping their long, slim sticks ran forward to meet Thurg's people.

Thurg smiled. It would soon be over now. He turned toward one who was bearing down upon him – it was Thandar. Thurg crouched to meet the charge. Rage, revenge, the lust for blood fired his bestial brain. With his huge paws he would tear the puny stick from this creature's grasp, and this time he would gain his hold upon that smooth throat. He licked his lips. And then out of the corner of his eye he glanced to the right.

What strange sight was this! His people flying? It was incredible! And yet it was true. Growling and raging in pain and anger they were running a gauntlet of fire-sharpened lances. Three lay dead. The others were streaming blood as they fled before the relentless prodding devils at their backs.

It was enough for Thurg. He did not wait to close with Thandar. A single howl of dismay broke from his flabby lips, and then he wheeled and dashed for the wood. He was the last to pass through the rapidly converging ends of Thandar's primitive battle line. He was running so fast that, afterward, Nadara who was watching the battle from the cliffside insisted that his feet flew higher than his head at each frantic leap.

Thandar and his victorious army pursued the enemy through the wood for a mile or more, then they returned, laughing and shouting, to receive the plaudits of the old men, the women and the children.

It was a happy day. There was feasting. And Thandar,

having in mind things he had read of savage races, improvised a dance in honor of the victory.

He knew little more of savage dances than his tribesmen did of the two-step and the waltz; but he knew that dancing and song and play marked in themselves a great step upward in the evolution of man from the lower orders, and so he meant to teach these things to his people.

A red flush spread to his temples as he thought of his dignified father and his stately mother and with what horrified emotions they would view him now could they but see him – naked but for a g-string and a panther skin, moving with leaps and bounds, and now stately waltz steps in a great circle, clapping his hands in time to his movements, while behind him strung a score of lusty, naked warriors, mimicking his every antic with the fidelity of apes.

About them squatted the balance of the tribe more intensely interested in this, the first ceremonial function of their lives, than with any other occurrence that had ever befallen them. They, too, now clapped their hands in time with the dancers.

Nadara stood with parted lips and wide eyes watching the strange scene. Within her it seemed that something was struggling for expression – something that she must have known long, long ago – something that she had forgotten but that she presently must recall. With it came an insistent urge – her feet could scarce remain quietly upon the ground, and great waves of melody and song welled into her heart and throat, though what they were and what they meant she did not know.

She only knew that she was intensely excited and happy and that her whole being seemed as light and airy as the soft wind that blew across the gently swaying treetops of the forest.

Now the dance was done. Thandar had led the warriors back to the feast. In the center of the circle where the naked bodies of the men had leaped and swirled to the clapping of many hands was an open space, deserted. Into it Nadara ran, drawn by some subtle excitement of the soul which she could not have fathomed had she tried — which she did not try to fathom.

Around her slim, graceful figure was draped the glossy, black pelt of Nagoola — another trophy of the prowess of her man. It half concealed but to accentuate the beauties of her form.

With eyes half-closed she took a half dozen graceful, tentative steps. Now the eyes of Thandar and several others were upon her, but she did not see them. Suddenly, with outthrown arms, she commenced to dance, bending her lithe body, swaying from side to side as she fell, with graceful abandon, into steps and poses that seemed as natural to her as repose.

About the little circle she wove her simple yet intricate way, and now every eye was upon her as every savage heart leaped in unison with her shapely feet, rising and falling in harmony with her lithe, brown limbs.

And of all the hearts that leaped, fastest leaped the heart of Thandar, for he saw in the poetry of motion of the untutored girl the proof of her birthright — the truth of all that he had guessed of her origin since her foster father had related the story of her birth upon his death bed. None but a child of an age-old culture could possess this inherent talent. Any moment he expected her lips to break forth in song, nor was he to be disappointed, for presently, as the circling cave folk commenced to clap their palms in time to her steps, Nadara lifted her voice in clear and bird-like notes — a worldless paean of love and life and happiness.

At last, exhausted, she paused, and as her eyes fell upon Thandar they broke into a merry laugh.

'The king is not the only one who can leap and play upon his feet,' she cried.

Thandar came to the center of the circle and kneeling at her feet took one of her hands in his and kissed it.

'The king is only mortal and a man,' he said. 'It is no

reproach that he cannot equal the divine grace of a goddess. You are very wonderful, my Nadara,' he continued, 'from loving you I am coming to worship you.'

And within the deep and silent wood another was stirred with mighty emotions by the sight of the half-naked, graceful girl. It was Thurg, the bad man, who had sneaked back alone to the edge of the forest that he might seek an opportunity to be revenged upon Thandar and his people.

Half formed in his evil brain had been a certain plan, which the sight of Nadara, dancing in the firelight, had turned to concrete resolution.

With the dancing and the feasting over, the tribe of Thandar betook itself by ones and twos to the rocky caves that they expected so soon to desert for the more comfortable village which they were to build under the direction of their king, to the east, beside the great water.

At last all was still – the village slept. No sentry guarded their slumbers, for Thandar, steeped in book learning, must needs add to his stock of practical knowledge by bitter experience, and never yet had the cause arisen for a night guard about his village.

Having defeated Thurg and his people he thought that they would not return again, and certainly not by night, for the people of this wild island roamed seldom by night, having too much respect for the teeth and talons of Nagoola to venture forth after darkness had settled upon the grim forests and the lonely plains.

But a tempest of uncontrolled emotions surged through the hairy breast of Thurg. He forgot Nagoola. He thought only of revenge – revenge and the black haired beauty who had so many times eluded him.

And as he saw her dancing in the circle of hand-clapping tribesmen, in the light of the brush wood fire, his desire for her became a veritable frenzy.

He could scarce restrain himself from rushing single-handed among his foes and snatching the girl before their faces. However, caution came to his rescue, and so he waited, albeit impatiently, until the last of the cave folk had retired to his cavern.

He had seen into which Nadara had withdrawn – one that lay far up the face of the steep cliff and directly above the cave occupied by Thandar. The moon was overcast, the fire at the foot of the cliff had died to glowing embers, all was wrapped in darkness and in shadow. Far in the depths of the wood Nagoola coughed and cried. The weird sound raised the coarse hair at the nape of Thurg's bull neck. He cast an apprehensive backward glance, then, crouching low, he moved quickly and silently across the clearing toward the base of the cliff.

Flattened against a protruding boulder there he waited, listening, for a moment. No sound broke the stillness of the sleeping village. None had seen his approach – of that he was convinced.

Carefully he began the ascent of the cliff face, made difficult by the removal of the rough ladders that led from ledge to ledge by day, but which were withdrawn with the retiring of the community to their dark holes.

But Thurg had dragged with him from the forest a slim sapling. This he leaned against the face of the cliff. Its uptilted end just topped the lowest ledge.

Thurg was almost as large and quite as clumsy in appearance as a gorilla, yet he was not as far removed from his true arboreal ancestors as is the great simian, and so he accomplished in silence and with evident ease what his great bulk might have seemed to have relegated to the impossible.

Like a huge cat he scrambled up the frail pole until his fingers clutched the ledge edge above him. Ape-like he drew himself to a squatting position there. Then he groped for the ladder that the cave folk had drawn up from below.

This he erected to the next ledge above. Thereafter the way was easy, for the balance of the ledges were connected by steeply inclined trails cut into the cliff face. This had been an innovation of Thandar's who considered the rickety ladders not only a nuisance, but extremely dangerous to life and limb, for scarce a day passed that some child or woman did not receive a bad fall because of them.

So Thurg, with Thandar's unintentional aid, came easily to the mouth of Nadara's cave.

Great had been the temptation as he passed the cave below to enter and slay his enemy. Never had Thurg so hated any creature as he hated this smooth-skinned interloper – with all the venom of his mean soul he hated him.

Now he stooped, listening, just beside the entrance to the cave. He could hear the regular breathing of the girl within. The hot blood surged through his brute veins. His huge paws opened and closed spasmodically. His breath sucked hot between his flabby lips.

Just beneath him Thandar lay dreaming. He saw a wonderful vision of a beautiful nymph dancing in the firelight. In a circle about her sat the Smith-Joneses, the Percy Standishes, the Livingston-Brownes, the Quincy Adams-Cootses, and a hundred more equally aristocratic families of Boston.

It did not seem strange to Thandar that there was not enough clothing among the entire assemblage to have recently draped the Laocoön. His father wore a becoming loin cloth, while the stately Mrs John Alden Smith-Jones, his mother, was tastefully arrayed in a scant robe of the skins of small rodents sewn together with bits of gut.

As the nymph danced the audience kept time to her steps with loudly clapping palms, and when she was done they approached her one by one, crawling upon their hands and knees, and kissed her hand.

Suddenly he saw that the nymph was Nadara, and as he sprang forward to claim her a large man with a coarse matted beard, a slanted forehead, and close-set eyes, leaped out from among the others, seized Nadara and fled with her toward a waiting trolley car.

He recognized the man as Thurg, and even in his dream it seemed rather incongruous that he should be clothed in well-fitting evening clothes.

Nadara screamed once, and the scream roused Thandar

from his dream. Raising upon one elbow he looked toward the entrance of his cave. The recollection of the dream swept back into his memory. With a little sigh of relief that it had been but a dream, he settled back once more upon his bed of grasses, and soon was wrapped in dreamless slumber.

CHAPTER FIVE

THE ABDUCTION OF NADARA

Cautiously Thurg crawled into the cave where Nadara slept upon her couch of soft grasses, wrapped in the glossy pelt of Nagoola, the black panther.

The hulking form of the beast man blotted out the faint light that filtered from the lesser darkness of the night without through the jagged entrance to the cave.

All within was Stygian gloom.

Groping with his hands Thurg came at last upon a corner of the grassy pallet. Softly he wormed inch by inch closer to the sleeper. Now his fingers felt the thick fur of the panther skin.

Lightly, for so gross a thing, his touch followed the recumbent figure of the girl until his giant paws felt the silky luxuriance of her raven hair.

For an instant he paused. Then, quickly and silently, one great palm clapped roughly over Nadara's mouth, while the other arm encircled her waist, lifting her from her bed.

Awakened and terrified, Nadara struggled to free herself and to scream; but the giant hand across her mouth effectively sealed her lips, while the arm about her waist held her as firmly as might iron bands.

Thurg spoke no word, but as Nadara's hands came in contact with his hairy breast and matted beard as she fought for freedom she guessed the identity of her abductor, and shuddered.

Waiting only to assure himself that his hold upon his prisoner was secure and that no trailing end of her robe might trip him in his flight down the cliff face, Thurg commenced the descent.

Opposite the entrance to Thandar's cave Nadara redoubled her efforts to free her mouth that she might scream aloud but once. Thurg, guessing her desire, pressed his palm the tighter, and in a moment the two had passed unnoticed to the ledge below.

Down the winding trail of the upper ledges Thurg's task was comparatively easy – thanks to Thandar, but at the second ledge from the bottom of the cliff he was compelled to take to the upper of the two ladders which completed the way to the ground below.

And here it was necessary to remove his hand from Nadara's mouth. In a low growl he warned her to silence with threats of instant death, then he removed his hand from across her face, grasped the top of the ladder and swung over the dangerous height with his burden under his arm.

For an instant Nadara was too paralyzed with terror to take advantage of her opportunity, but just as Thurg set foot upon the ledge at the bottom of the ladder she screamed aloud once.

Instantly Thurg's hand fell roughly across her lips. Brutally he shook her, squeezing her body in his mighty grip until she gasped for breath, and each minute expected to feel her ribs snap to the terrific strain.

For a moment Thurg stood silently upon the ledge, compressing the tortured body of his victim and listening for signs of pursuit from above.

Presently the agony of her suffering overcome Nadara – she swooned. Thurg felt her form relax, and his flabby lips twisted to a hideous grin.

The cliff was quiet – the girl's scream had not disturbed the slumbers of her tribesmen. Thurg swung the ladder he had just descended over the edge of the cliff below, and a moment later he stood at the bottom with his burden.

Without noise he removed the ladder and the sapling that he had used in his ascent, laying them upon the ground at the foot of the cliff. This would halt, temporarily, any pursuit until the cave men could bring other ladders from the higher levels, where they doubtless had them hidden.

But no pursuit developed, and Thurg disappeared into the dark forest with his prize.

For a long distance he carried her, his little pig eyes searching and straining to right and left into the black night for the first sign of savage beast. The half atrophied muscles of his little ears, still responding to an almost dead instinct, strove to prick those misshapen members forward that they might catch the first crackling of dead leaves beneath the padded paw of the fanged night prowlers.

But the wood seemed dead. No living creature appeared to thwart the beast-man's evil intent. Far behind him Thandar slept. Thurg grinned.

The moon broke through the clouds, splotching the ground all silver green beneath the forest trees. Nadara awoke from her swoon. They were in a little open glade. Instantly she recalled the happenings that had immediately preceded her unconsciousness. In the moonlight she recognized Thurg. He was smirking horribly down into her up-turned face.

Thandar had often talked with her of religion. He had taught her of his God, and now the girl thanked Him that Thurg was still too low in the scale of evolution to have learned to kiss. To have had that matted beard, those flabby, pendulous lips pressed to hers! It was too horrible – she closed her eyes in disgust.

Thurg lowered her to her feet. With one hand he still clutched her shoulder. She saw him standing there before her – his greedy, blood-shot eyes devouring her. His awful lips shook and trembled as his hot breath sucked quickly in and out in excited gasps.

She knew that the end was coming. Frantically she cast about her for some means of defense or escape. Thurg was drawing her toward him.

Suddenly she drew back her clenched fist and struck him

full in the mouth, then, tearing herself from his grasp, she turned and fled.

But in a moment he was upon her. Seizing her roughly by the shoulders he shook her viciously, hurling her to the ground.

The blood from his wounded lips dropped upon her face and throat.

From the distance came a deep toned, thunderous rumbling. Thurg raised his head and listened. Again and again came that awesome sound.

'The Great Nagoola is coming to punish you,' whispered Nadara.

Thurg still remained squatting beside her. She had ceased to fight, for now she felt that a greater power than hers was intervening to save her.

The ground beneath them trembled, shook and then tossed frightfully. The rumbling and the roaring became deafening. Thurg, his passion frozen in the face of this new terror, rose to his feet. For a moment there was a lull, then came another and more terrific shock.

The earth rose and fell sickeningly. Fissures opened, engulfing trees, and then closed like hungry mouths gulping food long denied.

Thurg was thrown to the ground. Now he was terror stricken. He screamed aloud in his fear.

Again there came a lull, and this time the beast-man leaped to his feet and dashed away into the forest. Nadara was alone.

Presently the earth commenced to tremble again, and the voice of The Great Nagoola rumbled across the world. Frightened animals scampered past Nadara, fleeing in all directions. Little deer, foxes, squirrels and other rodents in countless numbers scurried, terrified, about.

A great black panther and his mate trotted shoulder to shoulder into the glade where Nadara still stood too bewildered to know which way to fly.

They eyed her for a moment, as they paused in the moonlight, then without a second glance they loped away into the brush. Directly behind them came three deer.

Nadara realized that she had felt no fear of the panthers as she would have under ordinary circumstances. Even the little deer ran with their natural enemies. Every lesser fear was submerged in the overwhelming terror of the earthquake.

Dawn was breaking in the east. The rumblings were diminishing, the tremors at greater intervals and of lessening violence.

Nadara started to retrace her steps toward the village. Momentarily she looked to see Thandar coming in search of her, but she came to the edge of the forest and no sign of Thandar or another of her tribesmen had come to cheer her.

At last she stepped into the open. Before her was the cliff. A cry of anguish broke from her lips at the sight that met her eyes. Torn, tortured and crumpled were the lofty crags that had been her home – the home of the tribe of Thandar.

The overhanging cliff top had broken away and lay piled in a jagged heap at the foot of the cliff. The caves had disappeared. The ledges had crumbled before the titanic struggles of The Great Nagoola. All was desolation and ruin.

She approached more closely. Here and there in the awful jumble of shattered rock were wedged the crushed and mangled forms of men, women and children.

Tears coursed down Nadara's cheeks. Sobs wracked her slender figure. And Thandar! Where was he?

With utmost difficulty the girl picked her way aloft over the tumbled debris. She could only guess at the former location of Thandar's cave, but now no sign of cave remained – only the same blank waste of silent stone.

Frantically she tugged and tore at massive heaps of sharp edged rock. Her fingers were cut and bruised and bleeding. She called aloud the name of her man, but there was no response.

It was late in the afternoon before, weak and exhausted, she gave up her futile search of a cave where she might live out the remainder of her lonely life in what safety and meager comfort a lone girl could wring from this savage world.

For a week she wandered hither and thither only to find most of the caves she had known in the past demolished as had been those of her people.

At last she stumbled upon the very cliff which Thandar had chosen as the permanent home of his people. Here the wrath of the earthquake seemed to have been less severe, and Nadara found, high in the cliff's face, a safe and comfortable cavern.

The last span to it required the use of a slender sapling, which she could draw up after her, effectually barring the approach of Nagoola and his people. To further protect herself against the chance of wandering men the girl carried a quantity of small bits of rock to the ledge beside the entrance to her cave.

Fruit and nuts and vegetables she took there too, and a great gourd of water from the spring below. As she completed her last trip, and sat resting upon the ledge, her eyes wandering over the landscape and out across the distant ocean, she thought she saw something move in the shadow of the trees across the open plain beneath her.

Could it have been a man? Nadara drew her sapling ladder to the ledge beside her.

Thurg, fleeing from the wrath of The Great Nagoola, had come at daybreak to the spot where his people had been camped, but there he found no sign of them, only the ragged edges of a great fissure, half-closed, that might have swallowed his entire tribe as he had seen the fissures in the forest swallow many, many trees at a single bite.

For some time he sought for signs of his tribesmen, but without success. Then, his fear of the earthquake allayed, he sought her. He came to the ruins of the cliff that had housed her people, and there he discovered signs that the girl had been there since the demolition of the cliff.

He saw the print of her dainty feet in the soft earth at the base of the rocks – he saw how she had searched the debris for Thandar – he saw her bed of grasses in the crevice between the two boulders, and then, after diligent search, he found her spoor leading away to the east.

For many days he followed her until, at last, close by the sea, he came to a level plain at the edge of a forest. Across the narrow plain rose lofty cliffs – and what was that clambering aloft toward the dark mouth of a cave?

Could it be a woman? Thurg's eyes narrowed as he peered intently toward the cliff. Yes, it was a woman – it was *the* woman – it was she he sought, and she was alone.

With a whoop of exultation Thurg broke from the forest into the plain, running swiftly toward the cliff where Nadara crouched beside her little pile of jagged missiles, prepared to once more battle with this hideous monster for more than life.

CHAPTER SIX

THE SEARCH

A year had elapsed since Waldo Emerson Smith-Jones had departed from the Back Bay home of his aristocratic parents to seek in a long sea voyage a cure for the hacking cough and hectic cheeks which had in themselves proclaimed the almost incurable.

Two months later had come the first meager press notices of the narrow escape of the steamer, upon which Waldo Emerson had been touring the south seas, from utter destruction by a huge tidal wave. The dispatch read:

The captain reports that the great wave swept entirely over the steamer, momentarily submerging her. Two members of the crew, the officer upon the bridge, and one passenger were washed away.

The latter was an American traveling for his health, Waldo E. Smith-Jones, son of John Alden Smith-Jones of Boston.

The steamer came about, cruising back and forth for some time, but as the wave had washed her perilously close to a dangerous shore, it seemed unsafe to remain longer in the vicinity, for fear of a recurrence of the tidal wave which would have meant the utter annihilation of the vessel upon the nearby beach.

No sign of any of the poor unfortunates was seen.

Mrs Smith-Jones is prostrated.

Immediately John Alden Smith-Jones had fitted out his yacht, *Priscilla*, dispatching her under Captain Burlinghame, a retired naval officer, and an old friend of Mr Smith-Jones, to the far distant coast in search of the body of his son, which the captain of the steamer was of the opinion might very possibly have been washed upon the beach.

And now Burlinghame was back to report the failure of his mission. The two men were sitting in the John Alden Smith-Jones library. Mrs Smith-Jones was with them.

'We searched the beach diligently at the point opposite which the tidal wave struck the steamer,' Captain Burlinghame was saying. 'For miles up and down the coast we patrolled every inch of the sand.

'We found, at one spot upon the edge of the jungle and above the beach, the body of one of the sailors. It was not and could not have been Waldo's. The clothing was that of a seaman, the frame was much shorter and stockier than your son's. There was no sign of any other body along that entire coast.

'Thinking it possible one of the men might have been washed ashore alive we sent parties into the interior. Here we found a wild and savage country, and on two occasions met with fierce, white savages, who hurled rocks at us and fled at the first report of our firearms.

'We continued our search all around the island, which is of considerable extent. Upon the east coast I found this,' and here the captain handed Mr Smith-Jones the bag of jewels which Nadara had forgotten as she fled from Thandar.

Briefly he narrated what he knew of the history of the poor woman to whom it had belonged.

'I recall the incident well,' said Mrs Smith-Jones, 'I had the pleasure of entertaining the count and countess when they stopped here upon their honeymoon. They were lovely people, and to think that they met so tragic an end!'

The three lapsed into silence. Burlinghame did not know whether he was glad or sorry that he had not found the bones of Waldo Emerson – that would have meant the end of hope for his parents. Perhaps much the same thoughts were running through the minds of the others.

Somewhere in the nether regions of the great house an electric bell sounded. Still the three sat on in silence. They heard the houseman open the front door. They heard low voices, and presently there came a deferential tap upon the door of the library.

Mr Smith-Jones looked up and nodded. It was the houseman. He held a letter in his hand.

'What is it Krutz?' asked the master in a tired voice. It seemed that nothing ever again would interest him.

'A special delivery letter, sir,' replied the servant. 'The boy says you must sign for it yourself, sir.'

'Ah, yes,' replied Mr Smith-Jones, as he reached for the letter and the receipt blank.

He glanced at the post mark – San Francisco.

Idly he cut the envelope.

'Pardon me?' He glanced first at his wife and then at Captain Burlinghame.

The two nodded.

Mr John Alden Smith-Jones opened the letter. There was a single written sheet and an enclosure in another envelope. He had read but a couple of lines when he came suddenly upright in his chair.

Captain Burlinghame and Mrs Smith-Jones looked at him in polite and surprised questioning.

'My God!' exclaimed Mr Smith-Jones. 'He is alive – Waldo is alive!'

Mrs Smith-Jones and Captain Burlinghame sprang from their chairs and ran toward the speaker.

With trembling hands that made it difficult to read the words that his trembling voice could scarce utter John Alden Smith-Jones read aloud:

> *On board the* Sally Corwith,
> *San Francisco, California.*

Mr John Alden Smith-Jones,
Boston, Mass.
   Dear Sir: Just reached port and hasten to foward letter your son gave me for his mother. He wouldn't come with

149

us. We found him on   Island, Lat. 10°–'' South, Long. 150°–'' West. He seemed in good health and able to look out for himself. Didn't want anything, he said, except a razor, so we gave him that and one of the men gave him a plug of chewing tobacco. Urged him to come, but he wouldn't. The enclosed letter will doubtless tell you all about him.

Yours truly,
Henry Dobbs, Master.

'Ten south, a hundred and fifty west,' mused Captain Burlinghame. 'That's the same island we searched. Where could he have been!'

Mrs Smith-Jones had opened the letter addressed to her, and was reading it breathlessly.

My dear Mother: I feel rather selfish in remaining and possibly causing you further anxiety, but I have certain duties to perform to several of the inhabitants which I feel obligated to fulfill before I depart.

My treatment here has been all that anyone might desire – even more, I might say.

The climate is delightful. My cough has left me, and I am entirely a well man – more robust than I ever recall having been in the past.

At present I am sojourning in the mountains, having but run down to the sea shore today, where, happily, I chanced to find the Sally Corwith *in the harbor, and am taking advantage of Captain Dobbs' kindness to forward this letter to you.*

Do not worry, dearest mother; my obligations will soon be fulfilled and then I shall hasten to take the first steamer for Boston.

I have met a number of interesting people here – the most interesting people I have ever met. They quite overwhelm one with their attentions.

And now, as Captain Dobbs is anxious to be away, I will

close, with every assurance of my deepest love for you and father.

Ever affectionately your son,

Waldo.

Mrs Smith-Jones' eyes were dim with tears – tears of thanksgiving and happiness.

'And to think,' she exclaimed, 'that after all he is alive and well – quite well. His cough has left him – that is the best part of it, and he is surrounded by interesting people – just what Waldo needed. For some time I feared, before he sailed, that he was devoting himself too closely to his studies and to the little coterie of our own set which surrounded him. This experience will be broadening. Of course these people may be slightly provincial, but it is evident that they possess a certain culture and refinement – otherwise my Waldo would never have described them as "interesting". The coarse, illiterate, or vulgar could never prove "interesting" to a Smith-Jones.'

Captain Cecil Burlinghame nodded politely – he was thinking of the naked, hairy man-brutes he had seen within the interior of the island.

'It is evident, Burlinghame,' said Mr Smith-Jones, 'that you overlooked a portion of this island. It would seem, from Waldo's letter, that there must be a colony of civilized men and women somewhere upon it. Of course it is possible that it may be further inland than you penetrated.'

Burlinghame shook his head.

'I am puzzled,' he said. 'We circled the entire coast, yet nowhere did we see any evidence of a man-improved harbor, such as one might have reason to expect were there really a colony of advanced humans in the interior. There would have been at least a shack near the beach in one of the several natural harbors which indent the coast line was there even an occasional steamer touching for purposes of commerce with the colonists.

'No, my friends,' he continued, 'as much as I should like

to believe it my judgment will not permit me to place any such translation upon Waldo's letter.

'That he is safe and happy seems evident, and that is enough for us to know. Now it should be a simple matter for us to find him – if it is still your desire to send for him.'

'He may already have left for Boston,' said Mrs Smith-Jones; 'his letter was written several months ago.'

Again Burlinghame shook his head.

'Do not bank on that, my dear madam,' he said kindly. 'It may be fifty years before another vessel touches that forgotten shore – unless it be one which you yourselves send.'

John Alden Smith-Jones sprang to his feet, and commenced pacing up and down the library.

'How soon can the *Priscilla* be put in shape to make the return voyage to the island?' he asked.

'It *can* be done in a week, if necessary,' replied Burlinghame.

'And you will accompany her, in command?'

'Gladly.'

'Good!' exclaimed Mr Smith-Jones. 'And now, my friend, let us lose no time in starting our preparations. I intend accompanying you.'

'And I shall go too,' said Mrs Smith-Jones.

The two men looked at her in surprise.

'But my dear!' cried her husband, 'there is no telling what hardships and dangers we may encounter – you could never stand such a trip.'

'I am going,' said Mrs Smith-Jones, firmly. 'I know my Waldo. I know his refined and sensitive nature. I know that I am fully capable of enduring whatever he may have endured. He tells me that he is among interesting people. Evidently there is nothing to fear, then, from the inhabitants of the island, and furthermore I wish personally to meet the people he has been living with. I have always been careful to surround Waldo with only the nicest people, and if any vulgarizing influences have been brought to bear upon him since he has been beyond my mature guidance I wish to know it, that I may determine how to combat their results.'

That was the end of it. If Mrs Smith-Jones knew her son, Mr Smith-Jones certainly knew his wife.

A week later the *Priscilla* sailed from Boston harbor on her long journey around the Horn to the south seas.

Most of the old crew had been retained. The first and second officers were new men. The former, William Stark, had come to Burlinghame well recommended. From the first he seemed an intelligent and experienced officer. That he was inclined to taciturnity but enhanced his value in the eyes of Burlinghame. Stark was inclined to be something of a martinet, so that the crew soon took to hating him cordially, but as his display of this unpleasant trait was confined wholly to trivial acts the men contented themselves with grumbling among themselves, which is the prerogative and pleasure of every good sailorman. Their loyalty to the splendid Burlinghame, however, was not to be shaken by even a dozen Starks.

The monotonous and uneventful journey to the vicinity of ten south and a hundred and fifty west was finally terminated. At last land showed on the starboard bow. Excitement reigned supreme throughout the trim, white *Priscilla*. Mrs Smith-Jones peered anxiously and almost constantly through her binoculars, momentarily expecting to see the well-known thin and emaciated figure of her Waldo Emerson standing upon the beach awaiting them.

For two weeks they sailed along the coast, stopping here and there for a day while parties tramped inland in search of signs of civilized habitation. They lay two days in the harbor where the *Sally Corwith* had lain. There they pressed farther inland than at any other point, but all without avail. It was Burlinghame's plan to first make a cursory survey of the entire coast, with only short incursions toward the center of the island. Should this fail to discover the missing Waldo the party was then to go over the ground once more, remaining weeks or months as might be required to thoroughly explore every foot of the island.

It was during the pursuit of the initial portion of the program that they dropped anchor in the self-same harbor upon whose waters Waldo Emerson and Nadara had seen the *Priscilla* lying, only to fly from her.

Burlinghame recalled it as the spot at which the bag of jewels had been picked up. Next to the *Sally Corwith* harbor, as they had come to call the other anchorage, this seemed most fraught with possibilities of success. They christened it Eugenie Bay, after that poor, unfortunate lady, Eugenie Marie Celeste de la Valois, Countess of Crecy, whose jewels had been recovered upon its shore.

Burlinghame and Waldo's father with half a dozen officers and men of the *Priscilla* had spent the day searching the woods, the plain and the hills for some slight sign of human habitation. Shortly after noon First Officer Stark stumbled upon the whitened skeleton of a man. In answer to his shouts the other members of the party hastened to his side. They found the grim thing lying in a little barren spot among the tall grasses. About it the liquids of decomposition had killed vegetation leaving the thing alone in all its grisly repulsiveness as though shocked, nature had withdrawn in terror.

Stark stood pointing toward it without a word as the others came up. Burlinghame was the first to reach Stark's side. He bent low over the bones examining the skull carefully. John Alden Smith-Jones came panting up. Instantly he saw what Burlinghame was examining he turned deathly white. Burlinghame looked up at him.

'It's not,' he said. 'Look at that skull – either a gorilla or some very low type of man.'

Mr Smith-Jones breathed a sigh of relief.

'What an awful creature it must have been,' he said, when he had fully taken in the immense breadth of the squat skeleton. 'It cannot be that Waldo has survived in a wilderness peopled by such creatures as this. Imagine him confronted by such a beast. Timid by nature and never robust he would have perished of fright at the very sight of this thing charging down upon him.'

Captain Cecil Burlinghame acquiesced with a nod. He knew Waldo Emerson well, and so he could not even imagine a meeting between the frail and cowardly youth and such a beast as this bleaching frame must once have supported. And at their feet the bones of Flatfoot lay mute witnesses to the impossible.

Presently a shout from one of the sailors attracted their attention toward the far side of the valley. The man was standing upon a rise of ground waving his arms and gesticulating violently toward the lofty cliffs which rose sheer from the rank jungle grasses. All eyes turned in the direction indicated by the excited sailor. At first they saw nothing, but presently a figure came in sight upon a little elevation. It was the figure of a human being, and even at the distance they were from it all were assured that it was the figure of a female. She was running toward the cliffs with the speed of a deer. And now behind her, came another figure. Thick set and squat was the thing that pursued the woman. It might have been the reanimated skeleton that they had just discovered.

Would the creature catch her before she reached the cliff? Would she find sanctuary even there? Already Burlinghame and Stark had started toward the cliff on a run. John Alden Smith-Jones followed more slowly. The men raced after their officers.

The girl had reached the rocks and was scampering up their precipitous face like a squirrel. Close behind her came the man. They saw the girl reach a ledge just below the mouth of a cave in which she evidently expected to find safety. They saw her clambering up the rickety sapling that answered for a ladder. They breathed sighs of relief, for it seemed that she was now quite safe – the man was still one ledge below her.

But in another moment the watchers were filled with horror. The brute pursuing her had reached forth a giant hand and seized the base of the sapling. He was dragging it over the edge of the cliff. In another moment the girl

CHAPTER SEVEN

FIRST MATE STARK

Upon the day that Thurg discovered Nadara he had come racing to the foot of the cliff, roaring and bellowing like a mad bull. Upward he clambered half the distance to the girl's lofty perch. Then a bit of jagged rock, well aimed, had brought him to a sudden halt, spitting blood and teeth from his injured mouth. He looked up at Nadara and shrieked out his rage and his threats of vengeance. Nadara launched another missile at him that caught him full upon one eye, dropping him like a stone to the narrow ledge upon which he had been standing. Quickly the girl started to descend to his side to finish the work she had commenced, for she knew that there could be no peace or safety for her, now that Thurg had discovered her hiding place, while the monster lived.

But she had scarce more than lowered her sapling to the ledge beneath her when the giant form of the man moved and Thurg sat up. Quickly Nadara clambered back to her ledge, again drawing her sapling after her. She was about to hurl another missile at the man when he spoke to her.

'We are alone in the world,' he said. 'All your people and all my people have been slain by the Great Nagoola. Come down. Let us live together in peace. There is no other left in all the world.'

Nadara laughed at him.

'Come down to you!' she cried, mockingly. 'Live with you! I would rather live with the pigs that root in the forest. Go away, or I will finish what I have commenced, and kill you. I would not live with you though I knew that you were the last human being on earth.'

Thurg pleaded and threatened, but all to no avail. Again he tried to clamber to her side, but again he was repulsed with well-aimed missiles. At last he withdrew, growling and threatening.

For weeks he haunted the vicinity of the cliff. Nadara's meager food supply was soon exhausted. She was forced to descend to replenish her larder and fill her gourd, or die of starvation and thirst. She made her trips to the forest at night, though black Nagoola prowled and the menace of Thurg loomed through the darkness. At last the man discovered her in one of these nocturnal expeditions and almost caught her before she reached her ledge of safety.

For three days he kept her a close prisoner. Again her stock of provisions were exhausted. She was desperate. Twice had Nagoola nearly trapped her in the forest. She dared not again tempt fate in the gloomy wood by night. There was nothing left but to risk all in one last effort to elude Thurg by day and find another asylum in some far distant corner of the island.

Carefully she watched her opportunity, and while the beast-man was temporarily absent seeking food for himself the girl slid swiftly to the base of the cliff and started through the tall grasses for the opposite side of the valley.

Upon this day Thurg had fallen upon the spoor of deer as he had searched the forest for certain berries that were in season and which he particularly enjoyed. The trail led along the edge of the wood to the opposite side of the valley, and over the hills into the region beyond. All day Thurg followed the fleet animals, until at last not having come up with them he was forced to give up the pursuit and return to the cliffs, lest his more valuable quarry should escape.

Halfway between the hills and the cliff he came suddenly face to face with Nadara. Not twenty paces separated them. With a howl of satisfaction Thurg leaped to seize her, but she turned and fled before he could lay his hand upon her. If Thurg had found his other quarry of that day swift, so, too, he now found Nadara, for terror gave wings to her flying feet. Lumbering after her came Thurg, and had the distance been less he would have been left far behind, but it was a long distance from the spot, where they had met, to Nadara's cliffs. The girl could out-run the man for a short distance, but when victory depended upon endurance the advantage was all upon the side of the brute.

As they neared the goal Nadara realized that the lead she had gained at first was rapidly being overcome by the horrid creature panting so close behind her. She strained every nerve and muscle in a last mad effort to distance the fate that was closing upon her. She reached the cliff. Thurg was just behind her. Half spent, she stumbled upward in what seemed to her, pitiful slowness. At last her hand grasped the sapling that led to the mouth of her cave – in another instant she would be safe. But her new-born hope went out as she felt the sapling slipping and glanced downward to see Thurg dragging it from its position.

She shut her eyes that she might not see the depths below into which she was about to be hurled, and then there smote upon her ears the most terrific burst of sound that had ever assailed them, other than the thunders that rolled down out of the heavens when the rains came. But this sound did not come from above – it came from the valley beneath.

The ladder ceased to slip. She opened her eyes and glanced downward. Far below her lay the body of Thurg. She could see that he was quite dead. He lay upon his face and from his back trickled two tiny streams of blood from little holes.

Nadara clambered upward to her ledge, drawing her sapling after her, and then she looked about for an explanation of the strange noise and the sudden death of Thurg, for she could not but connect the one with the other. Below, in the valley, she saw a number of men strangely garbed. They were coming toward her cliff. She gathered her missiles closely about her, ready to her hand. Now they were below and calling up to her. Her eyes dilated in wonder – they spoke the strange tongue that Thandar had tried to teach

159

her. She called down to them in her own tongue, but they shook their heads, motioning her to descend. She was afraid. All her life she had been afraid of men, and with reason – of all except her old foster father and Thandar. These, evidently, were men. She could only expect from them the same treatment that Thurg would have accorded her.

One of them had started up the face of the cliff. It was Stark. Nadara seized a bit of rock and hurled it down upon him. He barely dodged the missile, but he desisted in his attempt to ascend to her. Now Burlinghame advanced, raising his hand, palm toward her in sign that she should not assault him. She recalled some of the language that Thandar had taught her – maybe they would understand it.

'Go-away!' she cried. 'Go-away! Nadara kill bad-men.'

A look of pleasure overspread Burlinghame's face – the girl spoke English.

'We are not bad men,' he called up to her. 'We will not harm you.'

'What you want?' asked Nadara, still unconvinced by mere words.

'We want to talk with you,' replied Burlinghame. 'We are looking for a friend who was ship-wrecked upon this island. Come down. We will not harm you. Have we not already proved our friendship by killing this fellow who pursued you?'

This man spoke precisely the tongue of Thandar. Nadara could understand every word, for Thandar had talked to her much in English. She could understand it better than she could speak it. If they talked the same tongue as Thandar they must be from the same country. Maybe they were Thandar's friends. Anyway they were like him, and Thandar never harmed women. She could trust them. Slowly she lowered her sapling and began the descent. Several times she hesitated as though minded to return to her ledge, but Burlinghame's kindly voice and encouragement at last prevailed, and presently Nadara stood before them.

The officers and men of the *Priscilla* crowded around the

girl. They were struck with her beauty, and the simple dignity of her manner and her carriage. The great black panther skin that fell from her left shoulder she wore with the majesty of a queen and with a naturalness that cast no reflection upon her modesty, though it revealed quite as much of her figure as it hid. William Stark, first officer of the *Priscilla*, caught his breath – never, he was positive, had God made a more lovely creature.

From the top of the cliff a shaggy man peered down upon the strange scene. He blinked his little eyes, scratched his matted head, and once he picked up a large stone that lay near him; but he did not hurl it upon those below, for he had heard the loud report of the rifles, seen the smoke belch from the muzzles, and witnessed the sudden and miraculous collapse of Thurg.

Burlinghame was speaking to Nadara.

'Who are you?' he asked.

'Nadara,' replied the girl.

'Where do you live?'

Nadara jerked her thumb over her shoulder toward the cliff at her back. Burlinghame searched the rocky escarpment with his eyes, but saw no sign of another living being there.

'Where are your people?'

'Dead.'

'All of them?'

Nadara nodded affirmatively.

'How long have they been dead and what killed them?' continued Burlinghame.

'Almost a moon. The Great Nagoola killed them.'

In answer to other questions Nadara related all that had transpired since the night of the earthquake. Her description of the catastrophe convinced the Americans that a violent quake had recently occurred to shake the island to its foundations.

'Ask her about Waldo,' whispered Mr Smith-Jones, himself dreading to put the question.

'We are looking for a young man,' said Burlinghame, 'who was lost overboard from a steamer on the west coast of this island. We know that he reached the shore alive, for we have heard from him. Have you ever seen or heard of this stranger? His name is Waldo Emerson Smith-Jones – this gentleman is his father,' indicating Mr Smith-Jones.

Nadara looked with wide eyes at John Alden Smith-Jones. So this man was Thandar's father. She felt very sorry for him, for she knew that he loved Thandar – Thandar had often told her so. She did not know how to tell him – she shrank from causing another the anguish and misery that she had endured.

'Did you know of him?' asked Burlinghame.

Nadara nodded her head.

'Where is he?' cried Waldo's father. 'Where are the people with whom he lived here?'

Nadara came close to John Alden Smith-Jones. There was no fear in her innocent young heart for this man who was Thandar's father – who loved Thandar – only a great compassion for him in the sorrow that she was about to inflict. Gently she took his hand in hers, raising her sad eyes to his.

'Where is he? Where is my boy?' whispered Mr Smith-Jones.

'He is with his people, who were my people – the people of whom I have just told you,' replied Nadara softly – 'He is dead.' And then she dropped her face upon the man's hand and wept.

The shock staggered John Alden Smith-Jones. It seemed incredible – impossible – that Waldo could have lived through all that he must have lived through to perish at last but a few short weeks before succor reached him. For a moment he forgot the girl. It was her hot tears upon his hand that aroused him to a consciousness of the present.

'Why do you weep?' he cried almost roughly.

'For you,' she replied, 'who loved him, too.'

'You loved Waldo?' asked the boy's father.

Nadara nodded her tumbled mass of raven hair. John

162

Alden Smith-Jones looked down upon the bent head of the sobbing girl in silence for several minutes. Many things were racing through his patrician brain. He was by training, environment and heredity narrow and Puritanical. He saw the meager apparel of the girl – he saw her nut brown skin; but he did not see her nakedness, for something in his heart told him that sweet virtue clothed her more effectually than could silks and satins without virtue. Gently he placed an arm about her, drawing her to him.

'My daughter,' he said, and pressed his lips to her forehead.

It was a solemn and sorrow-ridden party that boarded the *Priscilla* an hour later. Mrs Smith-Jones had seen them coming. Some intuitive sense may have warned her of the sorrow that lay in store for her upon their return. At any rate she did not meet them at the rail as in the past, instead she retired to her cabin to await her husband there. When he joined her he brought with him a half-naked young woman. Mrs Smith-Jones looked upon the girl with ill concealed horror.

Waldo's mother met the shock of her husband's news with much greater fortitude than he had expected. As a matter of fact she had been prepared for this from the first. She had never really believed that Waldo could survive for any considerable time far from the comforts and luxuries of his Boston home and the watchful care of herself.

'And who is this – ah – person?' she asked coldly at last, holding her pince-nez before her eyes as with elevated brows she cast a look of disapproval upon Nadara.

The girl, reading more in the older woman's manner than her words, drew herself up proudly. Mr Smith-Jones coughed and colored. He stepped to Nadara's side, placing his arm about her shoulders.

'She loved Waldo,' he said simply.

'The brazen huzzy!' exclaimed Mrs Smith-Jones. 'To dare to love a Smith-Jones!'

'Come, come, Louisa!' ejaculated her husband. 'Remember

163

that she too is suffering – do not add to her sorrow. She loved our boy, and he returned her love.'

'How do you know that?'

'She has told me,' replied the man.

'It is not true,' cried Mrs Smith-Jones. 'It is not true! Waldo Emerson would never stoop to love one out of his own high class. Who is she, and what proof have you that Waldo loved her?'

'I am Nadara,' said the girl proudly, answering for herself. 'And this is the proof that he loved me. He told me that this was the pledge token between us until we could come to his land and be mated according to the customs there.' She held out her left hand, upon the third finger of which sparkled a great solitaire – a solitaire which Mrs John Alden Smith-Jones recognized instantly.

'He gave you that?' she asked.

Then she turned toward her husband.

'What do you intend doing with this girl?' she asked.

'I shall take her back home,' replied he. 'She should be as a daughter to us, for Waldo would have made her such had he lived. She cannot remain upon the island. All her people were killed by the earthquake that destroyed Waldo. She is in constant danger of attack by wild beasts and wilder men. We cannot leave her here, and even if we could I should not do so, for we owe a duty to our dead boy to care for her as he would have cared for her – and we owe a greater duty to her.'

'I must be alone,' was all that Mrs Smith-Jones replied. 'Please take her away, John. Give her the cabin next to this, and have Marie clothe her properly – Marie's clothes should about fit her.' There was more of tired anguish in her voice now than of anger.

Mr Smith-Jones led Nadara out and summoned Marie, but Nadara upset his plans by announcing that she wished to return ashore.

'She does not like me,' she said, nodding toward Mrs Smith-Jones's cabin, 'and I will not stay.'

It took John Alden Smith-Jones a long time to persuade the girl to change her mind. He pointed out that his wife was greatly overwrought by the shock of the news of Waldo's death. He assured Nadara that at heart she was a kindly woman, and that eventually she would regret her attitude toward the girl. And at last Nadara consented to remain aboard the *Priscilla*. But when Marie would have clothed her in the garments of civilization she absolutely refused — scorning the hideous and uncomfortable clothing.

It was two days before Mrs Smith-Jones sent for her. When she entered that lady's cabin the latter exclaimed at once against her barbarous attire.

'I gave instructions that Marie should dress you properly,' she said. 'You are not decently clothed — that bear skin is shocking.'

Nadara tossed her head, and her eyes flashed fire.

'I shall never wear your silly clothes,' she cried. 'This, Thandar gave me — he slew Nagoola, the black panther, with his own hands, and gave the skin to me who was to be his mate — do you think I would exchange it for such foolish garments as those?' and she waved a contemptuous gesture toward Mrs Smith-Jones's expensive morning gown.

The elder woman forgot her outraged dignity in the suggestion the girl had given her for an excuse to be rid of her at the first opportunity. She had mentioned a party named Thandar. She had brazenly boasted that this Thandar had killed the beast whose pelt she wore and given her the thing for a garment. She had admitted that she was to become this person's 'mate'. Mrs Smith-Jones shuddered at the primitive word. At this moment Mr Smith-Jones entered the cabin. He smiled pleasantly at Nadara, and then, seeing in the attitudes of the two women that he had stepped within a theater of war, he looked questioningly at his wife.

'Now what, Louisa?' he asked, somewhat sharply.

'Sufficient, John,' exclaimed that lady, 'to bear out my original contention that it was a very unwise move to bring this woman with us — she has just admitted that she was the promised "mate" of a person she calls Thandar. She is brazen – I refuse to permit her to enter my home; nor shall she remain upon the *Priscilla* longer than is necessary to land her at the first civilized port.'

Mr Smith-Jones looked questioningly at Nadara. The girl had guessed the erroneous reasoning that had caused Mrs Smith-Jones's excitement. She had forgotten that they did not know that Waldo and Thandar were one. Now she could scarce repress a smile of amusement nor resist the temptation to take advantage of Mrs Smith-Jones's ignorance to bait her further.

'You had another lover beside Waldo?' asked Mr Smith-Jones.

'I loved Thandar,' she replied. 'Thandar was king of my people. He loved me. He slew Nagoola for me and gave me his skin. He slew Korth and Flatfoot, also. They wanted me, but Thandar slew them. And Big Fist he slew, and Sag the Killer – oh, Thandar was a mighty fighter. Can you wonder that I loved him?'

'He was a hideous murderer!' cried Mrs Smith-Jones, 'and to think that my poor Waldo; poor, timid, gentle Waldo, was condemned to live among such savage brutes. Oh, it is too terrible!'

Nadara's eyes went wide. It was her turn to suffer a shock. 'Poor, timid, gentle Waldo!' Had she heard aright? Could it be that they were describing the same man? There must be some mistake.

'Did Waldo know that you loved Thandar?' asked Mr Smith-Jones.

'Thandar was Waldo,' she replied. 'Thandar is the name I gave him – it means the Brave One. He was very brave,' she cried. 'He was not "timid", and he was only "gentle" with women and children.'

Mrs Smith-Jones had never been so shocked in all her life. She sprang to her feet.

'Leave my cabin!' she cried. 'I see through your shallow deception. You thoughtlessly betrayed yourself and your vulgar immoralities, and now you try to hide behind a base calumny that pictures my dear, dead boy as one with your hideous, brutal chief. You shall not deceive me longer. Leave my cabin, please!'

Mr Smith-Jones stood as one paralyzed. He could not believe in the perfidy of the girl – it seemed impossible that she could have so deceived him – nor yet could he question the integrity of his own ears. It was, of course, too far beyond the pale of reason to attempt to believe that Waldo Emerson and the terrible Thandar were one and the same. The girl had gone too far, and yet he could not believe that she was bad. There must be some explanation.

In the meantime Nadara had left the room, her little chin high in air. Never again, she determined, would she subject herself to the insults of Thandar's mother. She went on deck. She had found it difficult to remain below during the day. She craved the fresh air, and the excitement to be found above. The officers had been very nice to her. Stark was much with her. The man had fallen desperately in love with the half-savage girl. As she reached the deck after leaving Mrs Smith-Jones's cabin Stark was the first she chanced to meet. She would have preferred being alone with her sorrow and her anger, but the man joined her. Together they stood by the rail watching the approach of heavy clouds. A storm was about to break over them that had been brewing for several days.

Stark knew nothing of what had taken place below, but he saw that the girl was unhappy. He attempted to cheer her. At last he took her hand and stroked it caressingly as he talked with her. Before she could guess his intention he was pouring words of love and passion into her ears. Nadara drew away. A puzzled frown contracted her brows.

'Do not talk so to Nadara,' she said. 'She does not love you.' And then she moved away and went to her cabin.

Stark looked after her as she departed. He was thoroughly aroused. Who was this savage girl, to repulse him? What would have been her fate but for his well-directed shot? Was not the man who had been pursuing her but acting after the customs of her wild people? He would have taken her by force. That was the only way she would have been taken had she been left upon her own island. That was the only kind of betrothal she knew. It was what she expected. He had been a fool to approach her with the soft words of civilization. They had made her despise him. She would have understood force, and loved him for it. Well, he would show her that he could be as primitive as any of her savage lovers.

The storm broke. The wind became a hurricane. The *Priscilla* was forced to turn and flee before the anger of the elements, so that she retraced her course of the past two days and then was blown to the north.

Stark saw nothing of Nadara during this period. At the end of thirty-six hours the wind had died and the sea was settling to its normal quiet. It was the first evening after the storm. The deck of the *Priscilla* was almost deserted. The yacht was moving slowly along not far off the shore of one of the many islands that dot that part of the south seas.

Nadara came on deck for a walk before retiring. Stark and two sailors were on watch. At sight of the girl the first officer approached her. He spoke pleasantly as though nothing had occurred to mar their friendly relations. He talked of the storm and pointed out the black outlines of the nearby shore, and as he talked he led her toward the stern, out of sight of the sailors forward.

Suddenly he turned upon her and grasped her in his arms. With brutal force he crushed her to him, covering her face with kisses. She fought to free herself, but Stark was a strong man. Slowly he forced her to the deck. She beat him in the face and upon the breast, and at last, in the extreme of desperation, she screamed for help. Instantly he struck her a heavy blow upon the jaw. The slender form of the girl relaxed upon the deck in unconsciousness.

Now Stark came to a sudden realization of the gravity of the thing he had done. He knew that when Nadara regained consciousness his perfidy would come to the attention of

Captain Burlinghame, and he feared the quiet, ex-naval officer more than he did the devil. He looked over the rail. It would be an easy thing to dispose of the girl. He had only to drop her unconscious body into the still waters below. He raised her in his arms and bore her to the rail. The moon shone down upon her face. He looked out over the water and saw the shore so close at hand.

There would be a thorough investigation and the sailors, who had no love for him, as he well knew, would lose no time in reporting that he had been the last to be seen with the girl. Evidently he was in for it, one way or the other.

Again he looked down into Nadara's face. She was very beautiful. He wanted her badly. Slowly his glance wandered to the calm waters of the ocean and on to the quiet shore line. Then back to the girl. For a moment he stood irresolute. Then he stepped to the side of the cabin where hung a life preserver to which was attached a long line.

He put his life preserver about Nadara. Then he lowered her into the ocean. The moment he felt her weight transferred from the lowering rope to the life preserver he vaulted over the yacht's rail into the dark waters beneath her stern.

CHAPTER EIGHT

THE WILD MEN

Nadara did not regain consciousness until Stark had reached shore and was dragging her out upon the beach above the surf. For several minutes after she had opened her eyes she had difficulty in recalling the events that had immediately preceded Stark's attack upon her. She felt the life belt still about her, and as Stark stooped above her to remove it she knew that it was he though she could not distinguish his features.

What had happened? Slowly a realization of the man's bold act forced itself upon her – he had leaped overboard from the *Priscilla* and swam ashore with her rather than face the consequences of his brutal conduct toward her.

To the girl reared within the protective influences of civilization Nadara's position would have seemed hopeless; but Nadara knew naught of other protection than that afforded by her own quick wits and the agility of her swift young muscles. To her it would have seemed infinitely more appalling to have been confined within the narrow limits of the yacht with this man, for there all was strange and new. She still had half feared and mistrusted all aboard the *Priscilla* except Thandar's father and Captain Burlinghame; but would they have protected her from Stark? She did not know. Among her own people only a father, brother or mate protected a woman from one who sought her against her will, and of these she had none upon the little vessel.

But now it was different. Intuitively she knew that upon a savage shore, however strange and unfamiliar it might be, she would have every advantage over the first officer of the *Priscilla*. His life had been spent close to the haunts of civilization; he knew nothing of the woodcraft that was second nature to her; he might perish in a land of plenty through ignorance of where to search for food, and of what was edible and what was not. This much her early experience with Waldo Emerson had taught her. When their paths first had crossed Waldo had been as ignorant as a new-born babe in the craft of life primeval – Nadara had had to teach him everything.

Behind them Nadara heard the gentle soughing of trees – the myriad noises of the teeming jungle night – and she smiled. It was inky black about them. Stark had removed the life belt and placed it beneath the girl's head. He thought her still unconscious – perhaps dead. Now he was wringing the water from his clothes; his back toward her.

Nadara rose to her feet – noiseless as Nagoola. Like a shadow she melted into the blackness of the jungle that fringed the shore. Careful and alert, she picked her way within the tangled mass for a few yards. At the bole of a large tree she halted, listening. Then she made a low, weird sound with her lips, listening again for a moment after. This she repeated thrice, and then, seemingly satisfied that no danger lurked above she swung herself into the low-hanging branches, quickly ascending until she found a comfortable seat where she might rest in ease.

Down upon the beach Stark, having wrung the surplus water from his garments, turned to examine and revive the girl, if she still lived. Even in the darkness her form had been plainly visible against the yellow sand, but now she was not there. Stark was dumbfounded. His eyes leaped quickly from one point to another, yet nowhere could they discover the girl. There was the beach, the sea and the jungle. Which had she chosen for her flight? It did not take Stark long to guess, and immediately he turned his steps toward the shapeless, gloomy mass that marked the forest's fringe.

As he approached he went more slowly. The thought of entering that forbidding wood sent cold shivers creeping through him. Could a mere girl have dared its nameless horrors? She must have, and with the decision came new resolution. What a girl had dared certainly he might dare. Again he strode briskly toward the jungle.

Just at its verge he heard a low, weird sound not a dozen paces within the black, hideous tangle. It was Nadara voicing the two notes which some ancient forbear of her tribe had discovered would wring an answering growl from Nagoola, and an uneasy hiss from that other arch enemy of man – the great, slimy serpent whose sinuous coils twined threateningly above them in the branches of the trees. Only these Nadara feared – these and man. So, before entering a tree at night it was her custom to assure herself that neither Nagoola nor Coovra lurked in the branches of the tree she had chosen for sanctuary. Stark beat a hasty retreat, nor did he again venture from the beach during the balance of the long, dismal night.

When dawn broke it found Nadara much refreshed by the sleep she had enjoyed within the comparative safety of the great tree, and Stark haggard and exhausted by a sleepless night of terror and regret. He cursed himself, the girl and his bestial passion, and then as his thoughts conjured her lovely face and perfect figure before his mind's eye, he leaped to his feet and swung briskly toward the jungle. He would find her. All that he had sacrificed should not be in vain. He would find her and keep her. Together they would make a home upon this tropical shore. He would get everything out of life that there was to get.

He had taken but a few steps before he discovered, plain in the damp sand before him, the prints of Nadara's naked feet in a well defined trail leading toward the wood. With a smile of satisfaction and victory the man followed it into the maze of vegetation, dank and gloomy even beneath the warm light of the morning sun.

By chance he stumbled directly upon Nadara. She had descended from her tree to search for water. They saw each other simultaneously. The girl turned and fled farther into the forest. Close behind her came the man. For several hundred yards the chase led through the thick jungle which terminated abruptly at the edge of a narrow, rock-covered clearing behind which loomed sheer, precipitous cliffs, raising their lofty heads three hundred feet above the forest.

A half smile touched Stark's lips as he saw the barrier that nature had placed in the path of his quarry; but almost instantly it froze into an expression of horror as a slight noise to his right attracted his attention from the girl fleeing before him. For an instant he stood bewildered, then a quick glance toward the girl revealed her scaling the steep cliff with the agility of a monkey, and with a cry to attract her attention he leaped after her once more, but this time himself the quarry — the hunter become the hunted, for after him raced a score of painted savages, brandishing long, slim spears, or waving keen edged parangs.

Nadara had not needed Stark's warning cry to apprise her of the proximity of the wild men. She had seen them the instant that she cleared the jungle, and with the sight of them she knew that she need no longer harbor fear of the white man. In them, though, she saw a graver danger for herself, since they, doubtless, would have little difficulty in overhauling her in their own haunts, while she had not had much cause for worry as to her ability to elude the white man indefinitely.

Part way up the cliffs she paused to look back. Stark had reached the foot of the lowering escarpment a short distance ahead of his pursuers. He had chosen this route because of the ease with which the girl had clambered up the rocky barrier, but he had reckoned without taking into consideration the lifetime of practice which lay back of Nadara's agility. From earliest infancy she had lived upon the face and within the caves of steep cliffs. Her first toddling, baby footsteps had been along the edge of narrow shelving ledges.

When the man reached the cliff, however, he found confronting him an apparently unscalable wall. He cast a frightened, appealing glance at the girl far above him. Twice he essayed to scramble out of reach of the advancing savages, whose tattooed faces, pendulous slit ears, and sharp filed, blackened teeth lent to them a more horrid aspect than even that imparted by their murderous weapons or warlike whoops and actions. Each time he slipped back, clutching frantically at rocky projections and such hardy vegetation as had found foothold in the crevices of the granite. His hands were torn and bleeding, his face scratched and his clothing rent. And now the savages were upon him. They had seen that he was unarmed. No need as yet for spear or parang — they would take him alive.

And the girl. They had watched her in amazement as she clambered swiftly up the steep ascent. With all their primitive accomplishments this was beyond even them. They were a forest people and a river people. They dwelt in thatched houses raised high upon long piles. They knew little or nothing of the arts of the cliff dwellers. To them the feat of this strange, white girl was little short of miraculous.

Nadara saw them seize roughly upon the terror-stricken Stark. She saw them bind his hands behind his back, and then she saw them turn their attention once more toward herself.

Three of the warriors attempted to scale the cliff after her. Slowly they ascended. She smiled at their manifest fear and their awkwardness — she need have no fear of these, they never could reach her. She permitted them to approach within a dozen feet of her and then, loosening a bit of the crumbling granite, she hurled it full at the head of the foremost. With a yell of pain and terror he toppled backward upon those below him, the three tumbling, screaming and pawing to the rocks at the base of the cliff.

None of them was killed, though all were badly bruised, and he who had received her missile bled profusely from a wound upon his forehead. Their fellows laughed at them — it was scant comfort they received for being bested by a girl. Then they withdrew a short distance, and squatting in a circle commenced a lengthy palaver. Their repeated gestures in her direction convinced Nadara that she was the subject of their debate.

Presently one of their number arose and approached the foot of the cliff. There he harangued the girl for several minutes. When he was done he awaited, evidently for a reply from her; but as Nadara had not been able to understand a word of the fellow's language she could but shake her head.

The spokesman returned to his fellows and once again a lengthy council was held. During it Nadara climbed farther aloft, that she might be out of range of the slender spears. Upon a narrow ledge she halted, gathering about her such loose bits of rock as she could dislodge from the face of the cliff – she would be prepared for a sudden onslaught, nor for a moment did she doubt the outcome of the battle. She felt that but for the lack of food and water she could hold this cliff face forever against innumerable savages – could they climb no better than these.

But the wild men did not again attempt to storm her citadel. Instead they leaped suddenly from their council, and without a glance toward her disappeared in the forest, taking their prisoner with them. Out of sight of the girl, they stationed two of their number just within the screening verdure to capture the girl should she descend. The others hastened parallel with the cliff until a sudden turn inland took them to a point from which they could again emerge into the clearing out of the sight of Nadara.

Here they took immediately to a well-worn path that led back and forth upward across the face of the cliff. Stark was dragged and prodded forward with them in their ascent. Sharp spears and the points of keen parangs urged him to haste. By the time the party reached the summit the white man was bleeding from a score of superficial wounds.

Now the party turned back along the top of the bluff in the direction from which they had come.

Nadara, unable to fathom their reason for having abandoned the attempt to capture her, was, however, not lulled into any feeling of false security. She knew the cliff was the safest place for her, and yet the pangs of thirst and hunger warned her that she must soon leave it to seek sustenance. She was about to descend to the jungle below in search of food and water, when the faintest of movements of the earth sweeping creepers depending from a giant buttress tree below her and just within the verge of the forest arrested her acute attention. She knew that the movement had been caused by some animal beneath the tree, and finally, as she watched intently for a moment or two, she descried through an opening in the wall of verdure the long feathers of an Argus pheasant with which the war caps of the savages had been adorned.

Though she knew now that she was watched, she also knew that she could reach the top of the cliff and possibly find both food and drink, if it chanced to be near, before the savages could overtake her. Then she must depend upon her wits and her speed to regain the safety of the cliff ahead of them. That they would attempt to scale the barrier at the same point at which she had climbed it she doubted, for she had seen that they were comparatively unaccustomed to this sort of going, and so she guessed that if they followed her upward at all it would be by means of some beaten trail of which they had knowledge.

And so Nadara scaled the heights, passing over and around obstacles that would have blanched the cheek of the hardiest mountain climber, with the ease and speed of the chamois. At the summit she found an open, park-like forest, and into this she plunged, running forward in quest of food and drink. A few familiar fruits and nuts assuaged the keenest pangs of hunger, but nowhere could she find water or signs of water.

She had traveled for almost a mile, directly inland from the coast, when she stumbled, purely by chance, upon a little spring hidden in a leafy bower. The cool, clear water refreshed her, imparting to her new life and energy. After drinking her fill she sought some means of carrying a little supply of the priceless liquid back to her cliff side refuge, but though she searched diligently she could discover no growing thing which might be transformed into a vessel.

There was nothing for it then other than to return without the water, trusting to her wits to find the means of eluding the savages from time to time as it became necessary for her to quench her thirst. Later, she was sure, she should discover some form of gourd, or the bladder of an animal in which she could hoard a few precious drops.

Her woodcraft, combined with her almost uncanny sense of direction, led her directly back to the spot at which she had topped the cliff. There was no sign of the savages. She breathed a sigh of relief as she stepped to the edge of the forest, and then, all about her, from behind trees and bushes, rose the main body of the wild men. With shouts of savage glee they leaped upon her. There was no chance for flight — in every direction brutal faces and murderous weapons barred her way.

With greater consideration than she had looked forward to they signaled her to accompany them. Stark was with them. To him slight humanity was shown. If he lagged, a spear point, already red with his blood, urged him to greater speed; but to the girl no cruelty nor indignity was shown.

In single file, the prisoners in the center of the column, the party made its way inland. All day they marched, until Stark, unused to this form of exertion, staggered and fell a dozen times in each mile.

Nadara could almost have found it in her heart to be sorry for him, had it not been for the fact that she realized all too keenly that but for his own bestial brutality neither of them need have been there to be subjected to the present torture, and to be tortured by anticipation of the horrors to come.

To the girl it seemed that her fate must be a thousand fold more terrible than the mere death the man was to suffer, for that these degraded savages would let him live seemed beyond the pale of reason. She prayed to the God of which her Thandar had taught her for a quick and merciful death, yet while she prayed she well knew that no such boon could be expected.

She compared her captors with Korth and Flatfoot, with Big Fist and Thurg, nor did she look for greater compassion in them than in the men she had known best.

Late in the afternoon it became evident that Stark could proceed no farther unless the savages carried him. That they had any intention of so doing was soon disproved. The first officer of the *Priscilla* had fallen for the twentieth time. A dozen vicious spear thrusts had failed to bring him, staggering and tottering, to his feet as in the past.

The chief of the party approached the fallen white, kicking him in the sides and face, and at last pricking him with the sharp point of his parang. Stark but lay an inert mass of suffering flesh, and groaned. The chief grew angry. He grasped the white man around the body and raised him to his feet, but the moment that he released him Stark fell to earth once more.

At last the warrior could evidently control his rage no further. With a savage whoop he swung his parang aloft, bringing it down full upon the neck of the prostrate white. The head, grinning horribly, rolled to Nadara's feet. She looked at it, lying there staring up at her out of its blank and sightless eyes, without the slightest trace of emotion.

Nadara, the cave girl, was accustomed to death in all its most horrible and sudden forms. She saw before her but the head of an enemy. It was nothing to her – Stark had only himself to thank.

The chief gathered the severed head into a bit of bark cloth, and fastening it to the end of his spear, signaled his followers to resume the journey.

On and on they went, farther into the interior, and with them went Nadara, borne to what nameless fate she could but guess.

CHAPTER NINE

BUILDING THE BOAT

Two days after the earthquake that had saved Nadara from Thurg and wiped out the people of the girl's tribe, a man moved feebly beneath the tumbled debris from the roof top of his clogged cavern. It was Thandar. The tons of rock that had toppled from above and buried the entrance to his cave had passed him by unscathed, while the few pounds shaken from the ceiling had stunned him into a long enduring insensibility.

Slowly he regained consciousness, but it was a long time before he could marshal his faculties to even a slight appreciation of the catastrophe that had overwhelmed him. Then his first thought was of Nadara. He crawled to what had once been the entrance of his cave. He had not as yet linked the darkness to its real cause – he thought it night. It had been night when he closed his eyes. How could he guess that that had been three nights before, or all the cruel blows that fate had struck him since he slept!

At the opening from the cave he met his first surprise and setback – the way was blocked! What was the meaning of it? He tugged and pushed weakly upon the mass that barred him from escape. Who had imprisoned him? He recalled the vivid dream in which he had seen Nadara stolen away by Thurg. The recollection sent him frantically at the pile of shattered rock and loose debris which choked the doorway.

To his chagrin he found himself too weak to direct any long sustained effort against the obstacle. It occurred to him that he must have been injured. Whoever imprisoned him must first have beaten him. He felt of his head. Yes, there was a great gash, but his touch told him that it was not a new one. How long, then, had he been imprisoned? As he sat pondering this thing he became aware of the gnawing of hunger and the craving of thirst within his slowly awakening body. The sensations were almost painful. So much so that they forced him to a realization of the fact that he must have been without food or water for a considerable time.

Again he assailed the mass that held him prisoner, and as he burrowed slowly into it the truth dawned upon him. He recalled the rumblings of the great Nagoola that had frightened Nadara the night of the council. A terrific quake had done this thing. Thandar shuddered as he thought of Nadara. Was she, too, imprisoned in her cave, or had the worst happened to her? Frantically, now, he tore at the close-packed rubble. But he soon discovered that not in ill-directed haste lay his means of escape. Slowly and carefully, piece by piece he must remove the broken rock until he had tunneled through to the outer world.

Reason told him that he was not deeply buried, for the fact that he lived and could breathe was sufficient proof that fresh air was finding its way through the debris, which it could not have done did the stuff lie before the cave in any considerable thickness.

Weak as he was he could work but slowly, so that it was several hours later before he caught the first glimpse of daylight beyond the obstacle. After that he progressed more rapidly, and presently he crawled through a small opening to view the wreckage of the shattered cliff.

A flock of vultures rose from their hideous feast as the sight of Thandar disturbed them. The man shuddered as he looked down upon the grisly things from which they had risen. Forgetting his hunger and his thirst he scrambled up over the tortured cliff face to where Nadara's cave had been. Its mouth was buried as his had been. Again he set to work, but this time it was easier. When at last he had opened a way within he hesitated for fear of the blighting sorrow that awaited him.

At last, nerving himself to the ordeal, he crawled within the cave that had been Nadara's. Groping about in the darkness, expecting each moment to feel the body of his loved one cold in death, he at last covered the entire floor – there was no body within.

Hastily he made his way to the face of the cliff again, and then commenced a horrible and pitiful search among the ghastly remnants of men and women that lay scattered about among the tumbled rocks. But even here his search was vain, for the ghoulish scavengers had torn from their prey every shred of their former likenesses.

Weak, exhausted, sorrow ridden and broken, Thandar dragged himself painfully to the little river. Here he quenched his thirst and bathed his body. After, he sought food, and then he crawled to a hole he knew of in the river bank, and curling up upon the dead grasses within, slept the sun around.

Refreshed and strengthened by his sleep and the food that he had taken. Thandar emerged from his dark warren with renewed hope. Nadara could not be dead! It was impossible. She must have escaped and be wandering about the island. He would search for her until he found her. But as day followed day and still no sign of Nadara, or any other living human being he became painfully convinced that he alone of the inhabitants of the island had survived the cataclysm.

The thought of living on through a long life without her cast him into the blackest pit of despair. He reproached heaven for not having taken him as well, for without Nadara life was not worth the living. With the passage of time his grief grew more rather than less acute. As it increased so too increased the horror of his loneliness. The island became a hated thing – life a mockery. The chances that a vessel would touch the shore again during his lifetime seemed remote indeed, unless his father sent out a relief party, but in his despair he did not even hope for such a contingency.

He could not take his own life, though the temptation was great, but he courted death in every form that the savage island owned. He slept out upon the ground at night. He sought Nagoola in his lair, and armed only with his light lance he leaped to close quarters with every one of the great cats he could find.

The wild boars, often as formidable as Nagoola himself, were hunted now as they never had been hunted before. Thandar lived high those days, and many were the panther pelts that lined his new-found cave in the cliff beside the sea – the same cliff in which Nadara had found shelter, and from whence she had gone away with the search party from the *Priscilla*.

One day as Thandar was returning from the beach where he often went to scan the horizon for a sail, he saw something moving at the foot of his cliff. Thandar dropped behind a bush, watching. A moment later the thing moved again, and Thandar saw that it was a man. Instantly he sprang to his feet and ran forward. The days that he had been without human companionship had seemed to drag themselves into as many weary months. Now he had reached the pinnacle of loneliness from which he would gladly have embraced the devil had he come in human guise.

Thandar ran noiselessly. He was almost upon the man, a great, hairy brute, before the fellow was aware of his presence. At first the fellow turned to run, but when he saw that Thandar was alone he remained to fight.

'I am Roof,' he cried, 'and I can kill you!'

The familiar primitive greeting no longer raised Thandar's temperature or filled him with the fire of battle. He wanted companionship now, not a quarrel.

'I am Thandar,' he replied.

The slow-witted, hulking brute recognized him, and stepped back a pace. He was not so keen to fight now that he had learned the identity of the man who faced him. He had seen Thandar in battle. He had witnessed Thurg's defeat at the hands of this smooth-skinned stranger.

'Let us not fight,' continued Thandar. 'We are alone upon the island. I have seen no other than you since the Great

Nagoola came forth and destroyed the people. Let us be friends, hunting together in peace. Otherwise one of us must kill the other and thereafter live always alone until death releases him from his terrible solitude.'

Roof peered over Thandar's shoulder toward the wood behind him.

'Are you alone?' he asked.

'Yes – have I not told you that all were killed but you and I?'

'All were not killed,' replied Roof. 'But I will be friends with Thandar. We will hunt together and cave together. Roof and Thandar are brothers.'

He stooped, and gathering a handful of grass advanced toward the American. Thandar did likewise, and when each had taken the peace offering of the other and rubbed it upon his forehead the ceremony of friendship was complete – simple but none the less effectual, for each knew that the other would rather die than disregard the primitive pact.

'You said that all were not killed, Roof,' said Thandar, the ceremony over. 'What do you mean?'

'All were not killed by the Great Nagoola,' replied the bad man. 'Thurg was not killed, nor was she who was Thandar's mate – she whom Thurg would have stolen.'

'What?' Thandar almost screamed the question. 'Nadara not dead?'

'Look,' said Roof, and he led the way to the foot of the cliff. 'See!'

'Yes,' replied Thandar, 'I had noticed that body, but what of it?'

'It was Thurg,' explained Roof. 'He sought to reach your mate, who had taken refuge in that cave far above us. Then came some strange men who made a great noise with sticks and Thurg fell dead – the loud noise had killed him from a great distance. Then came the strange men and she whom you call Nadara went away with them.'

'In which direction?' cried Thandar. 'Where did they take her?'

'They took her to the strange cliff in which they dwelt — the one in which they came. Never saw man such a thing as this cliff. It floated upon the face of the water. About its face were many tiny caves, but the people did not come out of these they came from the top of the cliff, and clambering down the sides floated ashore in hollow things of wood. On top of the cliff were two trees without leaves, and only very short, straight branches. When the cliff went away black smoke came out of it from a short black stump of a tree between the two trees. It was a very wonderful thing to see; but the most wonderful of all were the noise-sticks that killed Thurg and Nagoola a long way off.'

Not half of Roof's narrative did Thandar hear. Through his brain roared and thundered a single mighty thought: Nadara lives! Nadara lives! Life took on a new meaning to him now. He trembled at the thought of the chances he had been taking. Now, indeed, must he live. He leaped up and down, laughing and shouting. He threw his arms about the astonished Roof, whirling the troglodyte about in a mad waltz. Nadara lives! Nadara lives!

Once again the sun shone, the birds sang, nature was her old, happy, carefree self. Nadara was alive and among civilized men. But then came a doubt.

'Did Nadara go willingly with these strangers,' he asked Roof, 'or did they take her by force?'

They did not take her by force,' replied Roof. 'They talked with her for a time, and then she took the hand of one of the men in hers, stroking it, and he placed his arm about her. Afterward they walked slowly to the edge of the great water where they got into the strange things that had brought them to the land, and returned to their floating cliff. Presently the smoke came out, as I have told you, and the cliff went away toward the edge of the world. But they are all dead now.'

'What?' yelled Thandar.

'Yes, I saw the cliff sink, very slowly when it was a long way off, until only the smoke was coming out of the water.'

Thandar breathed a sigh of relief.

'Point,' he said, 'to the place where the cliff sank beneath the water.'

Roof pointed almost due north.

'There,' he said.

For days Thandar puzzled over the possible identity of the ship and the men with whom Nadara had gone so willingly. Doubtless some kindly mariner, hearing her story, had taken her home, away from the terrors and the loneliness of this unhappy island. And now the man chafed to be after her, that he might search the world for his lost love.

To wait for a ship appeared quite impossible to the impatient Thandar, for he knew that a ship might never come. There was but one alternative, and had Waldo Emerson been a less impractical man in the world to which he had been born he would have cast aside that single alternative as entirely beyond the pale of possibility. But Waldo was only practical and wise in the savage ways of the primitive life to which circumstance had forced him to revert. And so he decided upon as fool-hardy and hair-brained a venture as the mind of man might conceive. It was no less a thing than to build a boat and set out upon the broad Pacific in search of a civilized port or a vessel that might bear him to such.

To Waldo it seemed quite practical. He realized of course that the venture would be fraught with peril, but would it not be better to die in an attempt to find his Nadara than to live on forever in the hopelessness of this forgotten land?

And so he set to work to build a boat. He had no tools but his crude knife and the razor the sailor of the *Sally Corwith* had given him, so it was quite impossible for him to construct a dug-out. The possibilities that lie in fire did not occur to him. Finally he hit upon what seemed the only feasible form of construction.

With his knife he cut long, pliant saplings, and lesser branches. These he fashioned into the framework of a boat. Roof helped him, keenly interested in this new work. The ribs were fastened to the keel and gunwale by thongs of panther skin, and when the framework was completed panther skins were stretched over it. The edges of the skin were sewn together with threads of gut, as tightly as Thandar and Roof could pull them.

A mast was rigged well forward, and another panther skin from which the fur had been scraped was fitted as a sail, square rigged. For rudder Thandar fashioned a long, slender sapling, looped at one end, and the loop covered with skin laced tightly on. This, he figured, would serve both as rudder and paddle, as necessity demanded.

At last all was done. Together Thandar and Roof carried the light, crude skiff to the ocean. They waded out beyond the surf, and upon the crest of a receding swell they launched the thing, Thandar leaping in as it floated upon the water.

The sail was not taken along for this trial. Thandar merely wished to know that this craft would float, and right side up. For a moment it did so, until the sea rushing in at the loose seams filled it with water.

Thandar and Roof had great difficulty in dragging it out again upon the beach. Roof now would have given up, but not so Thandar. It is true that he was slightly disheartened, for he had set great store upon the success of his little vessel.

After they had carried the frail thing beyond high tide Thandar sat down upon the ground and for an hour he did naught but stare at the leaky craft. Then he arose and calling to Roof led him into the forest. For a mile they walked, and then Thandar halted before a tree from the side of which a thick and sticky stream was slowly oozing. Thandar had brought along a gourd, and now with a small branch he commenced transferring the mass from the side of the tree to the gourd. Roof helped him. In an hour the gourd was filled. Then they returned to the skiff.

Leaving the gourd there Thandar and Roof walked to a clump of heavy jungle grasses not far from the cliff where their cave lay. Here Thandar gathered a great armful of the yellow, ripened grass, telling Roof to do likewise. This they took back to the skiff, where, by rolling it assiduously between their hands and pounding it with stones they reduced it to a mass of soft, tough fiber.

Now Thandar showed Roof how to twist this fiber into a loose, fluffy rope, and when he had him well started he daubed the rope with the rubbery fluid he had filched from the tree, and with a sharp stick tucked it in every seam and crevice of the skiff.

It took the better part of two days to accomplish this, and when it was done and the gourd empty, the two men returned to the tree and refilled it. This time they built a fire upon their return to the skiff, Roof spinning a hard wood splinter rapidly between toes and fingers in a little mass of tinder that lay in a hollowed piece of wood. Presently a thin spiral of smoke arose from the tinder, growing denser for a moment until of a sudden it broke into flame.

The men piled twigs and branches upon the blaze until the fire was well started. Then Thandar taking a ball of the viscous matter from the gourd heated it in the flames, immediately daubing the melting mass upon the outside of the skiff. In this way, slowly and with infinite patience, the two at last succeeded in coating the entire outer surface of the canoe with a waterproof substance that might defy the action of water almost indefinitely.

For three days Thandar let the coating dry, and then the craft was given another trial. The man's heart was in his throat as the canoe floated upon the crest of a great wave and he leaped into it.

But a moment later he shouted in relief and delight – the thing floated like a cork, nor was there the slightest leak discernible. For half an hour Thandar paddled about the harbor, and then he returned for the sail. This too, though rather heavy and awkward, worked admirably, and the balance of the day he spent in sailing, even venturing out into the ocean.

Much of the time he paddled, for Waldo Emerson knew more of the galleys of ancient Greece than he did of sails or sailing, so that for the most part he sailed with the wind, paddling when he wished to travel in another direction. But, withal, his attempt filled him with delight, and he could scarce wait to be off toward civilization and Nadara.

The next two days were spent in collecting food and water, which Thandar packed in numerous gourds, sealing the mouths with the rubbery substance such as he had used to waterproof his craft. The flesh of wild hog, and deer, and bird he cut in narrow strips and dried over a slow fire. In this work Roof assisted him, and at last all was in readiness for the venture.

The day of his departure dawned bright and clear. A gentle south wind gave promise of great speed toward the north. Thandar was wild with hope and excitement. Roof was to accompany him, but at the last moment the nerve of the troglodyte failed him, and he ran away and hid in the forest.

It was just as well, thought Thandar, for now his provisions would last twice as long. And so he set out upon his perilous adventure, braving the mighty Pacific in a frail and unseaworthy cockleshell with all the assurance and confidence that is ever born of ignorance.

CHAPTER TEN

THE HEAD-HUNTERS

Nature so far, had been kind to Waldo Emerson Smith-Jones. No high winds or heavy seas had assailed him, and he had been upon the water for three days now. The wind had held steadily out of the south, varying but a few points during this time but even so Waldo Emerson was commencing to doubt and to worry. His supply of water was running dangerously low, his food supply would last but a few days longer; and as yet he had sighted no sail, nor seen any land. Furthermore, he had not the remotest conception of how he might retrace his way to the island he had just quitted. He could only sail before the wind. Should the wind veer around into the north he might, by chance, be blown back to the island. Otherwise he never could reach it. And he was beginning to wonder if he had not been a trifle too precipitate in his abandonment of land.

In common with most other landsmen, Waldo Emerson had little conception of the vastness of the broad reaches of unbroken water wildernesses that roll in desolate immensity over three quarters of the globe. His recollection of maps pictured the calm and level blue dotted, especially in the south seas, with many islands. Their names, often, were quite reassuring. He recollected, among others, such as the Society Islands, the Friendly Islands, Christmas Island. He hoped that he would land upon one of these. There were so many islands upon the maps, and they seemed so close together that he was not a little mystified that he had failed to sight several hundred long before this.

And ships! It appeared incredible that he should have seen not a single sail. He distinctly recalled the atlas he had examined prior to embarking upon his health cruise. The Pacific had been lined in all directions with the routes of long established steamer lanes, and in between, Waldo had felt, the ocean must be dotted with the innumerable tramps that come and go between the countless ports that fringe the major sea.

And yet for three days nothing had broken the dull monotony of the vast circle of which he was always the center and the sole occupant. In three days, thought Waldo, he must have covered an immense distance.

And three more days dragged their weary lengths. The wind had died to the faintest of breezes. The canoe was just making headway and that was all. The water was gone. The food nearly so. Waldo was suffering from lack of the former. The pitiless sun beating down upon him increased his agony. He stretched his panther skin across the stern and hid beneath it from the torrid rays. And there he lay until darkness brought relief.

During the night the wind sprang up again, but this time from the west. It rose and with it rose the sea. The man, clinging to his crude steering blade, struggled to keep the light craft straight before the wind which was now howling fearfully while great waves, hungry and wide jawed, raced after him like a pack of ravenous wolves.

Thandar knew that the unequal struggle against the mighty forces of the elements could not endure for long. It seemed that each fierce gust of brutal wind must tear his frail boat to shreds, and yet it was the very lightness of the thing that saved it, for it rode upon the crests of waves, blown forward at terrific velocity like a feather before the hurricane.

In Thandar's heart was no terror – only regret that he might never again see his mother, his father, or his Nadara. Yet the night wore on and still he fled before the storm. The sky was overcast – the darkness was impenetrable. He imagined all about him still the same wide, tenantless circle of water, only now storm torn and perpendicular and black, instead of peacefully horizontal, and soothingly blue-green. And then, even as he was thinking this there rose before him a thunderous booming loud above the frenzied bedlam of the storm, his boat was lifted high in air to dive headforemost into what might be a bottomless abyss for all Thandar knew. But it was not bottomless. The canoe struck something and stopped suddenly, pitching Thandar out into a boiling maelstrom. A great wave picked him up, carrying him with racehorse velocity within its crest. He felt himself hurled pitilessly upon smooth, hard sand. The water tried to drag him back, but he fought with toes and fingers, clutching at the surface of the stuff upon which he had been dropped. Then the wave abandoned him and raced swiftly back into the sea.

Thandar was exhausted, but he knew that he must crawl up out of the way of the surf, or be dragged back by the next roller. What he had searched for in vain through six long days he had run down in the midst of a Stygian night. He had found land! Or, to be more explicit, land had got in front of him and he had run into it. He had commenced to wonder if some terrible convulsion of nature had not swallowed up all the land in the world, leaving only a waste of desolate water. He forgot his hunger and his thirst in the happiness of the knowledge that once more he was upon land. He wondered a little what land it might be. He hoped that dawn would reveal the chimneys and steeples of a nearby city. And then, exhausted, he fell into a deep sleep.

It was the sun shining down into his upturned face that awoke him. He was lying upon his back beside a clump of bushes a little way above the beach. He was about to rise and survey the new world into which fate and a hurricane had hurled him when he heard a familiar sound upon the opposite side of his bush. It was the movement of an animal creeping through long grass.

Thandar, the cave man, came noiselessly to his hands and knees, peering cautiously through the intervening network of branches. What he saw sent his hand groping for his wooden sword with its fire-hardened point. There, not five paces from him, was a man going cautiously upon all fours. It was the most horrible appearing man that Thandar had ever seen – even Thurg appeared lovely by comparison. The creature's ears were split and heavy ornaments had dragged them down until the lobes rested upon its shoulders. The face was terribly marked with cicatrices and tattooing. The teeth were black and pointed. A head-dress of long feathers waved and nodded above the hideous face. There was much tattooing upon the arms and legs and abdomen; the breasts were circled with it. In a belt about the waist lay a sword in its scabbard. In the man's hand was a long spear.

The warrior was creeping stealthily upon something at Thandar's left. The latter looked in the direction the other's savage gaze was bent. Through the bushes he could barely discern a figure moving toward them along the edge of the beach. The warrior had passed him now and Thandar stood erect the better to obtain a view of the fellow's quarry.

Now he saw it plainly – a man strangely garbed in many colors. A yellow jacket, soiled and torn, covered the upper part of his body. Strange designs, very elaborate, were embroidered upon the garment which reached barely to the fellow's waist. Beneath was a red sash in which were stuck a long pistol and a wicked-looking knife. Baggy blue trousers reached to the bare ankles and feet. A strip of crimson cloth wound around the head completed the strange garmenture. The features of the man were Mongolian.

Thandar could see the warrior pause as it became evident that the other was approaching directly toward his place of concealment, but at the last moment the unconscious quarry turned sharply to his right down upon the beach. He had discovered the wreck of Thandar's canoe and was going to investigate it.

The move placed Thandar almost between the two. Suddenly the native rose to his feet – his victim's back was toward him. Grasping his spear in his left hand he drew his wicked-looking sword and emerged cautiously from the bushes. At the same moment the man upon the beach wheeled quickly as though suddenly warned of his danger. The native, discovered, leaped forward with raised sword. The man snatched his pistol from his belt, levelled it at the on-rushing warrior and pulled the trigger. There was a futile click – that was all. The weapon had missed fire.

Instantly a third element was projected into the fray. Thandar, seeing a more direct link with civilization in the strangely apparalled Mongol than in the naked savage, leaped to the assistance of the former. With drawn sword he rushed out upon the savage. The wild man turned at Thandar's cry, which he had given to divert the fellow's attention from his now almost helpless victim.

Thandar knew nothing of their finer points of sword play. He was ignorant of the wickedness of a Malay parang – the keen, curved sword of the head-hunter, so he rushed in upon the savage as he would have upon one of Thurg's near-men.

The very impetuosity of his attack awed the native. For a moment he stood his ground, and then, with a cry of terror turned to flee; but he had failed to turn soon enough. Thandar was upon him. The sharp point entered his back beneath the left shoulder blade, and behind it were the weight and sinews of the cave man. With a shriek the savage lunged forward, clutching at the cruel point that now protruded from his breast. When he touched the earth he was dead.

Thandar drew his sword from the body of the head-hunter, and turned toward the man he had rescued. The latter was approaching, talking excitedly. It was evident that he was thanking Thandar, but no word of his strange tongue could the American understand. Thandar shook his head to indicate that he was unfamiliar with the other's lanugage, and then the latter dropped into pidgin English, which, while almost as unintelligible to the cultured Bostonian, still contained the battered remnants of some few words with which he was familiar.

Thandar depreciated his act by means of gestures, immediately following these with signs to indicate that he was hungry and thirsty. The stranger evidently understood him, for he motioned him to follow, leading the way back along the beach in the direction from which he had come.

Before starting, however, he had pointed toward the wreck of Thandar's canoe and then toward Thandar, nodding his head questioningly as to ask if the boat belonged to the cave man.

Around the end of a promontory they came upon a little cove beside the beach of which Thandar saw a camp of nearly a score of men similar in appearance to his guide. These were preparing breakfast beside the partially completed hull of a rather large boat they seemed to have been building.

At sight of Thandar they looked their astonishment, but after hearing the story of their fellow they greeted the cave man warmly, furnishing him with food and water in abundance.

For three days Thandar worked with these men upon their craft, picking up their story slowly with a slow acquirement of a bowing acquaintance with the bastard tongue they used when speaking with him. He soon became aware of the fact that fate had thrown him among a band of pirates. There were Chinese, Japanese and Malays among them – the offscourings of the south seas; men who had become discredited even among the villainous pirates of their own lands, and had been forced to join their lots in this remoter and less lucrative field, under an unhung ruffian, Tsao Ming, the Chinaman whose life Thandar had saved.

He also learned that the storm that had cast them upon this shore nearly a month before had demolished their prahu, and what with the building of another and numberous skirmishes with the savages they had had a busy time of it.

Only yesterday while a party of them had been hunting a mile or two inland they had been attacked by savages who had killed two and captured one of their number.

They told Thandar that these savages were the most ferocious of head-hunters, but like the majority of their kind preferred ambushing an unwary victim to meeting him in fair fight in the open. Thandar did not doubt but that the latter mode of warfare would have been entirely to the liking of his piratical friends, for never in his life had he dreamed, even, of so ferocious and warlike a band as was comprised in this villainous and bloodthirsty aggregation. But the constant nervous tension under which they had worked, never knowing at what instant an arrow or a lance would leap from the shades of the jungle to pierce them in the back, had reduced them to a state of fear that only a speedy departure from the island could conquer.

Their boat was almost completed, two more days would see them safely launched upon the ocean, and Tsao Ming had promised Thandar that he would carry him to a civilized port from which he could take a steamer on his return to America.

Late in the afternoon of the third day since his arrival among the pirates the men were suddenly startled by the appearance of an exhausted and blood smeared apparition amongst them. From the nearby jungle the man had staggered to fall when halfway across the clearing, spent.

It was Boloon – he who had been captured by the head-hunters the day before Thandar had been cast upon the shore. Revived with food and water the fellow told a most extraordinary tale. From the meager scraps that were afterward translated into pidgin English for Thandar the Bostonian learned that Boloon had been dragged far inland to a village of considerable size.

Here he had been placed in a room of one of the long houses to await the pleasure of the chief. It was hinted that he was to be tortured before his head was removed to grace the rafters of the chief's palace.

The remarkable portion of his tale related to a strange temple to which he had been dragged and thrown at the feet of a white goddess. Tsao Ming and the other pirates were much mystified by this part of the story, for Boloon insisted that the goddess was white with a mass of black hair, and that her body was covered by the pelt of a magnificent black panther.

Though Tsao Ming pointed out that there were no panthers upon the island Boloon could not be shaken. He had seen with his own eyes, and he knew. Furthermore, he argued, there were no white goddesses upon the island, and yet the woman he had seen was white.

When this strange tale was retold to Thandar he could not but recall that Nadara had worn a black panther skin, but of course it could not be Nadara – that was impossible. But yet he asked for a further description of the goddess – the color of her eyes and hair – the proportions of her body – her height.

To all these questions Boloon gave replies that but caused Thandar's excitement to wax stronger. And then came the final statement that set him in a frenzy of hope and apprehension.

'Upon her left hand was a great diamond,' said Boloon.

Thandar turned toward Tsao Ming.

'I go inland to the temple,' he said, 'to see who this white goddess may be. If you wait two days for me and I return you shall have as much gold as you ask in payment. If you do not wait repair my canoe and hide it in the bushes where the man hid who would have killed you but for Thandar.'

'I shall wait three days,' replied Tsao Ming. 'Nor will I take a single *fun* in pay. You saved the life of Tsao Ming – that is not soon to be forgotten. I would send men with you, but they would not go. They are afraid of the head-hunters. Too, will I repair your canoe against your coming after the third day; but,' and he shrugged, 'you will not come upon the third day, nor upon the fourth, nor ever, Thandar. It is better that you forget the foolish story of the frightened Boloon and come away from this accursed land with Tsao Ming.'

But Thandar would not relinquish his intention, and so he parted with the pirates after receiving from Boloon explicit directions for his journey toward the mysterious temple and the white goddess who might be Nadara; and yet who could not be.

Straight into the tangled jungle he plunged, carrying the spear and the parang of the head-hunter he had killed, and in the string about his loins one of the long pistols of a dead pirate. This latter Tsao Ming had forced upon him with a supply of ammunition.

CHAPTER ELEVEN

THE RESCUE

It was dusk of the second day when Thandar, following the directions given him by Boloon, came to the edge of the little clearing within which rose the dingy outlines of many long houses raised upon piles. Before the village ran a river. Many times had Thandar crossed and recrossed this stream, for he had become lost twice upon the way and had to return part way each time to pick up his trail.

In the center of the village the man could see the outlines of a loftier structure rearing its head above those of the others. As darkness fell Thandar crept closer toward his goal – the large building which Boloon had described as the temple.

Beneath the high raised houses the cave man crept, disturbing pigs and chickens as he went, but their noise was no uncommon thing, and rather than being a menace to his safety it safeguarded him, for it hid the noise of his own advance.

At last he came beneath a house nearest the temple. The moon was full and high. Her brilliant light flooded the open spaces between the buildings, casting into black darkness the shadows beneath. In one of these Thandar lurked. He saw that the temple was guarded. Before its only entrance squatted two warriors. How was he to pass them?

He moved to the end of the shadow of the house beneath which he spied as far from the guards as possible; but still discovery seemed certain were he to attempt to rush across the intervening space. He was at a loss as to what next to do. It seemed foolish to risk all now upon a bold advance – the time for such a risk would be when he had found the goddess and learned if she were Nadara, or another; but how might he cross that strip of moonlight and enter the temple past the two guards, without risk?

He moved silently to the far end of the building, in the shadows of which he watched. For some time he stood looking across at his goal, so near, and yet seemingly infinitely farther from attainment than the day he had left the coast in search of it. He noted the long poles stuck into the ground at irregular intervals about the structure. He wondered at the significance of the rude carving upon them, of the barbaric capitals sometimes topped by the headdress of a savage warrior, again by a dried and grinning skull, or perhaps the rudely chiseled likeness of a hideous human face.

Upon many of the poles were hung shields, weapons, clothing and earthenware vessels. One especially was so weighted down by its heterogeneous burden that it leaned drunkenly against the eaves of the temple. Thandar's eye followed it upward to where it touched the crudely shingled roof. The suggestion was sufficient – where his eye had climbed he would climb. There was only the moonlight to make the attempt perilous. If the clouds would but come! But there was no indication of clouds in the star shot sky.

He looked toward the guards. They lolled at the opposite end of the temple, only one of them being visible. The other was hidden by the angle of the building. The back of the fellow whom Thandar could see was turned toward the cave man. If they remained thus for a moment he could reach the roof unnoticed. But then there was the danger of discovery from one of the other buildings. An occasional whiff of tobacco smoke told him that some of the men were still awake upon the verandahs where most of the youths and bachelors slept.

Thandar crawled to where he could see the only verandah which directly faced the portion of the temple he had chosen for his attempted entrance. For an hour he watched the rising and falling glow of the cigarettes of two of the native men, and listened to the low hum of their conversation. The hour seemed to drag into an eternity, but at last the glowing butt of first one cigarette and then another was flicked over into the grass and silence reigned upon the verandah.

For half an hour longer Thandar waited. The guards before the temple still squatted as before. The one Thandar could see seemed to have fallen asleep, for his head drooped forward upon his breast.

The time had come. There was no need of further delay or reconnaisance – if he was to be discovered that would be the end of it, and it would not profit him one iota to know a second or so in advance of the alarm that he had been detected. So he did not waste time in stealthy advance, or in much looking this way and that. Instead he moved swiftly, though silently, directly across the open, moonlit space to the foot of the leaning pole. He did not cast a glance behind nor to the right nor left. His whole attention was riveted upon the thing in hand.

Thandar had scaled the rickety, toppling saplings of the cliff dwellers for so long that this pole offered no greater difficulties to him than would an ordinary staircase to you or me. First he tested it with eyes and hands to know that it rested securely at the top and that beneath his weight it would not move noisily out of its present position.

Assured that it seemed secure, Thandar ran up it with the noiseless celerity of a cat. Gingerly he stepped upon the roof, not knowing the manner of its construction, which might be weak thatching that would give beneath him and precipitate him into the interior beneath.

To his surprise and consternation he found that the roof was of wood, and quite as solid as one could imagine. It had been his plan to enter the temple from above, but now it seemed that he was to be thwarted, for he could not hope to cut silently through a wooden roof with his parang in the few hours that intervened before dawn.

He stooped to examine the roof minutely with eyes and fingers. The moonlight was brilliant. In it he could see quite well. He pulled away the thin palm frond thatch. Beneath were shingles hand hewn from billian. In each was a small square hole through which was passed a strip of rattan that bound the shingle to the frame of the roof.

Thandar lifted away the thatching over a little space some two feet square. Then he inserted the point of his keen parang beneath a rattan tie string, and an instant later had lifted aside a shingle. Another and another followed the first until an opening in the roof had been made large enough to easily admit his body.

Thandar leaned over and peered into the darkness beneath. He could see nothing. His own body was between the moon and the hole in the roof, shutting out the rays of the satellite from the interior.

The man lowered his legs cautiously over the edge of the hole. Feeling about, his feet came in contact with a rafter. A moment later his whole body had disappeared within the temple. Clinging to the edge of the hole with one hand, Thandar squatted upon the rafter above the temple floor.

Now that his body no longer closed the aperture in the roof the moonlight poured through it throwing a brilliant flood upon a portion of the floor at the opposite side of the interior. The balance was feebly lighted by the diffused moonlight.

The temple seemed to consist of a single large room. In the center was a raised platform, and also about the walls. From the rafters hung baskets containing human skulls – one swung directly in the moonlight beneath Thandar. He could see its grisly contents plainly.

His eyes followed the moonlight toward the area which it touched upon the far side of the room. It reminded Waldo Emerson of a spot light thrown from the gallery of a theater upon the stage.

Directly in the center of the light a woman lay asleep upon the platform. Thandar's heart stood still. About her figure was wrapped the glossy hide of Nagoola. Over one bare, brown arm billowed a wealth of thick, black hair, fine as silk, upon the third finger of the left hand blazed a large solitaire. The woman's face was turned toward the wall – but Thandar knew that he could not be mistaken – it was Nadara.

From the rafter upon which he squatted to the floor below was not over twelve or fifteen feet. Thandar swung downward, clinging to the rafter with his hands, and dropped, catlike, upon his naked feet to the floor below.

The almost noiseless descent was sufficient, however, to awaken the sleeper. With the quickness of a panther she swung around and was upon her feet facing the man almost at the instant he alighted. The moonlight was now full upon her face. Thandar rushed forward to take her in his arms.

'Nadara!' he whispered. 'Thank God!'

The girl shrank back. She recognized the voice and the figure; but – her Thandar was dead! How could it be that he had returned from death? She was frightened.

The man saw the evident terror of her action, and paused.

'What is the matter, Nadara?' he asked. 'Don't you know me? Don't you know Thandar?'

'Thandar is dead,' she whispered.

The man laughed. In a few words he explained that he had been stunned, but not killed, by the earthquake. Then he came to her side and took her in his arms.

'Do I feel like a dead man?' he asked.

She put her arms about his neck and drew his face down to hers. She was sobbing. Thandar's back was toward the doorway of the temple. Nadara was facing it. As she raised her eyes to his again her face went deadly white, and she dragged and pushed him suddenly out of the brilliant patch of moonlight.

'The guard!' she whispered. 'I just saw something move beyond the door.'

Thandar stepped behind one of the tree trunks that supported the roof, looking toward the entrance. Yes, there was a man even now coming into the temple. His eyes were wide with surprise as he glanced upward toward the hole in the roof. Then he looked in the direction of the platform upon which Nadara had been sleeping. When he saw that it was empty he ran back to the doorway and called his companion.

As he did so Thandar grasped Nadara's hand and drew her around the opposite side of the temple where the shadows were blackest, toward the doorway. They had reached the end of the room when the two warriors came running in, jabbering excitedly. One of them had passed halfway across the temple, and Thandar and Nadara had almost reached the door when the second savage caught sight of them with drawn parang.

As the fellow rushed forward Thandar drew the pistol the pirates had given him and fired point blank at the fellow's breast. With a howl the man staggered back and collapsed upon the floor. Then his fellow rushed to the attack.

Thandar had no time to reload. He handed the weapon to Nadara.

'In the pouch at my right side are cartridges,' he said. 'Get out several of them, and when I can I will reload.'

As he spoke they had been edging toward the doorway. From the street beyond they could already hear excited voices raised in questioning. The shot had aroused the village.

Now the fellow with the parang was upon them. Thandar was clumsy with the unaccustomed weapon with which he tried to meet the attack of the skilled savage. There could have been but one outcome to the unequal struggle had not Nadara, always quick-witted and resourceful, snatched a long spear from the temple wall.

As she dragged it down there fell with it a clattering skull that broke upon the floor between the fighters. A howl of dismay and rage broke from the lips of the head-hunter. This was sacrilege. The holy of the holies had been profaned. With renewed ferocity he leaped to close quarters with Thandar, but at the same instant Nadara lunged the sharp pointed spear into his side, his guard dropped and Thandar's parang fell full upon his skull.

'Come!' cried Nadara. 'Make your escape the way you

came. There is no hope for you if you remain. I will tell them that the two guards fought between themselves for me – that one killed the other, and that I shot the victor to save myself. They will believe me – I will tell them that I have always had the pistol hidden beneath my robe. Good-bye, my Thandar. We cannot both escape. If you remain we may both die – you, certainly.'

Thandar shook his head vehemently.

'We shall both go – or both die,' he replied.

Nadara pressed his hand.

'I am glad,' was all that she said.

The savages were pouring from their long houses. The street before the temple was filling with them. To attempt to escape in that direction would have been but suicidal.

'Is there no other exit?' asked Thandar.

'There is a small window in the back of the temple,' replied Nadara, 'in a little room that is sometimes used as a prison for those who are to die, but it lets out into another street which by this time is probably filled with natives.'

'There is the floor,' cried Thandar. 'We will try the floor there.'

He ran to the main entrance to the temple, and closed the doors. Then he dragged the two corpses before them, and a long wooden bench. There was no other movable thing in the temple that had any considerable weight.

This done he took Nadara's hand and together the two ran for the little room. Here again they barricaded the door, and Thandar turned toward the floor. With his parang he pried up a board – it was laid but roughly upon the light logs that were the beams. Another was removed with equal ease, and then he lowered Nadara to the ground beneath the temple.

Clinging to the piling, Thandar replaced the boards above his head before he, too, dropped to the ground at Nadara's side. The streets upon either side of the temple were filled with savages. They could hear them congregating before the entrance to the temple where all was now quiet and still within. They were bolstering their courage by much shouting to the point that would permit them to enter and investigate. They called the names of the guards, but there was no response.

'Give me the pistol,' said Thandar.

He loaded it, keeping several cartridges ready in his hand. Then, with Nadara at his side, he crept to the back of the temple. Pigs, routed from their slumbers, grunted and complained. A dog growled at them. Thandar silenced it with a cut from his parang. When they reached the edge of the shadow beneath the temple they saw that there were only a few natives upon this side of the structure, and they were hurrying rapidly toward the front of the building. A hundred yards away was the jungle.

Now a sudden quiet fell upon the horde before the temple doors. There was the sound of hammering then a pushing, scraping noise, and presently shouts of savage rage – the dead bodies of the guardsmen had been discovered. Now, from above, came the padding of naked feet running through the temple. The street behind was momentarily deserted.

'Now!' whispered Thandar.

He seized Nadara's hand, and together the two raced from beneath the temple out into the moonlight and across the intervening space between the long houses toward the jungle. Halfway across, a belated native, emerging from the verandah of a nearby house, saw them. He set up a terrific yell and dashed toward them.

Thandar's pistol roared, and the savage dropped; but the signal had been given and before the two reached the jungle a screaming horde of warriors was upon their heels.

Thandar was confused. He had lost his bearings since entering the village and the temple. He turned toward Nadara.

'I do not know the way to the coast,' he cried.

The girl took his hand.

'Follow me,' she said, and to the memories of each leaped the recollection of the night she had led him through the forest from the cliffs of the bad men. Once again was Waldo Emerson Smith-Jones, the learned, indebted to the greater wisdom of the unlettered cave girl for his salvation.

Unerringly Nadara ran through the tangled jungle in the direction of the coast. Though she had been but once over the way she followed the direct line as unerringly as though each tree was blazed and sign posts marked each turn.

Behind them came the noise of the pursuit, but always Nadara and Thandar fled ahead of it, not once did it gain upon them during the long hours of flight.

It was noon before they reached the coast. They came out at the camp of the pirates, but to Thandar's dismay it was deserted. Tsao Ming had waited the allotted time and gone. If Thandar had but known it, the picturesque cut-throat had overstayed the promised period, and had but scarce left when the fugitives emerged from the jungle beside the beach. In fact his rude craft was but out of sight beyond the northern promontory. A pistol shot would have recalled him; but Thandar did not know it, and so he turned dejectedly to search for the hidden canoe.

It lay behind the little clump of bushes that had hidden Thandar the morning that he had saved Tsao Ming's life, several hundred yards to the south.

All signs of pursuit had now ceased, and so the two walked slowly in the direction of the craft. They found it just where Tsao Ming had promised that it would be. It was well and staunchly repaired, and in addition contained a goodly supply of food and water. Thandar blessed Tsao Ming, the unhung murderer.

Together they dragged the frail thing to the water's edge, and were about to shove it out when, with a chorus of savage yells, a score or more of the head-hunters leaped from the jungle and bore down upon them. Thandar turned to meet them with drawn pistol.

'Get the canoe into the water, Nadara,' he called to the girl. 'I will hold them off until it is launched, then we may be able to reach deep water before they can overtake us.'

Nadara struggled with the unwieldy boat which the rollers picked up and hurled back upon her each time she essayed to launch it. From the corner of his eye Thandar saw the difficulties that the girl was having. Already the horde was halfway across the beach, running rapidly toward them. The man feared to fire except at close range since his unfamiliarity with firearms rendered him an extremely poor shot. However, it was evident that Nadara could not launch the thing alone, and so Thandar turned his pistol upon the approaching savages, pulled the trigger, and wheeled to assist the girl.

More by chance than skill the bullet lodged in the body of the foremost head-hunter. The fellow rolled screaming to the sand, and as one his companions came to a sudden halt. But seeing that Thandar was busy with the boat and not appearing to intend to follow up his shot they presently resumed the charge.

Thandar and Nadara were having all that they could attend to with the canoe and so the savages came to the water's edge before they realized their proximity. When he saw them, Thandar wheeled and fired again, then picking the canoe up bodily above his head he struggled out through the surf, Nadara walking by his side, steadying him.

After them came the savages – perhaps half a dozen of the bolder, when suddenly a great roller caught them all, pursuers and pursued, sweeping them out into deep water. Thandar and Nadara clung to the canoe, but the head-hunters were dragged down by the undertow.

Upon the beach, yelling, threatening and gesticulating, danced thirty or forty baffled savages; but now Thandar and Nadara had crawled into the craft, which the outgoing tide was carrying rapidly from shore, and with the aid of the paddle were soon safely out upon the bosom of the Pacific.

Safely?

CHAPTER TWELVE

PIRATES

As the tide and wind carried the light craft out to sea, and the shore line sank beneath the horizon behind them, Waldo Emerson looked out upon the future as he did upon the tumbling waste of desolate water encircling them, with utter hopelessness.

Once before he had passed by a miracle through the many-sided menaces of the sea; but that he should be so fortunate again he could not hope. And now Nadara was with him. Before, only his own suffering and death had been possible; now he must face the greater agony of witnessing Nadara's.

The wind, blowing a steady gale, was raising a considerable sea. The vast billows rolled, one upon the heels of another, with the regularity of infantry units doubling at review. The wind and the sea seemed to have been made to order for the frail vessel that bore Thandar and Nadara. It rode the long, ponderous waves like a cork; its crude sail caught the wind and bellied bravely to it, driving the boat swiftly over the water.

And scarce had the shore behind them sunk forever from their sight than dead ahead another shore line showed. Thandar could scarce believe his eyes. He rubbed them and looked again. Then he asked Nadara to look.

'What is that ahead?' he asked.

The girl half rose with an exclamation of joy.

'Land!' she cried.

And land it was. The wind, driving them madly, carried them toward the north end of what appeared to be a large island. Angry breakers pounded a rocky coast line. To strike there would mean instant death to them both. But would they strike? As they neared the point of the island it became evident to Thandar that they would be borne past it. Could he hope to stem the speed of the little craft and turn it back into the sheltered water in the lee of the land? The chances were more than even that the canoe would capsize the instant he cut away the sail and attempted to paddle across the wind, as would be necessary to come about the end of the island.

But there seemed no other way. He handed his parang to Nadara, telling her to be ready to cut the rawhide strips that supported the sail the instant that he gave the word. With his paddle clutched tightly in his hands he knelt in the stern, watching the progress of the canoe past the rocky point.

At this extremity of the island a narrow tongue of land ran far out into the sea. It was past the outer point of this tongue that the canoe was racing. When they had passed Thandar realized the rashness of attempting to turn the canoe into the trough of the sea even for the little distance that would have been necessary to make the shelter of the point, where, almost within reach, he could see the peaceful bosom of unruffled water lying safely behind the island.

And yet as he looked ahead upon the limitless waste of ocean before them he knew that one risk was no greater than the other, and then an alternative plan occurred to him. He would run a short distance past the point and then turn almost directly back and attempt to paddle the canoe in the calm water, running nearly into the face of the wind, thus avoiding the dangers of the trough.

There was but a single drawback to this plan – the question of his ability to drive the canoe against the gale. At least it was worth trying. He gave Nadara the word to cut down the sail, and at the same instant, the canoe being upon the crest of a wave, he bent to the paddle. As the panther skin tumbled at the foot of the rough mast the nose of the craft swung around in reply to Thandar's vigorous strokes.

So intent were both upon the life and death struggle that

they were waging with the elements that neither saw the long, low-lying craft that shot from the mouth of a small harbor behind them as they came into view upon the lee side of the island.

For a moment the canoe hung broadside to the wind. Thandar struggled frantically to carry it about. Down they dropped into the trough of a great sea. Above them hung the overleaning tower of the wave's crest ready to topple upon them its tons of water. The canoe rose, still broadside, almost to the crest of the wave – then the thing broke upon them.

When Thandar came to the surface his first thought was for Nadara. He looked about as he shook the water from his eyes. Almost at his side Nadara's head rose from the sea. As her eyes met his a smile touched her lips.

'This is better,' she shouted. 'Now we can reach shore,' and turning she struck out for land.

Just behind her swam Thandar. He knew that Nadara was like a fish in water, but he doubted her ability as he doubted his own to reach the shore in the face of both wind and tide. A wave carried them high in air, and from its crest both saw simultaneously a long craft in the hollow beneath them, and noted the fierce aspect of her crew.

Nadara, fearing all men but Thandar, would have attempted to elude the craft, but the glimpse that the man had had of those aboard her had convinced him that he had fallen by good fortune into the company of Tsao Ming and his crew.

'They are friends,' he screamed to Nadara, and so they let the boat come alongside and pick them up; but no sooner had Thandar obtained a good look at the occupants than he discovered that never a face among them had he seen before.

They were of the same type as Tsao Ming's motley horde, nor did Waldo Emerson need inquire their vocation – thief and murderer were writ upon every countenance. They jabbered questions at Nadara and Thandar in an assortment of dialects which neither could understand, and it was only after the craft had been anchored in the little bay and the party had waded to shore that Thandar tried speaking with them in pidgin English. Several among them understood him, and he was not long in making it plain to them that they would be paid well if they carried him and Nadara to a civilized port.

The leader, who seemed to be a full blooded negro, laughed at him, ridiculing the idea that an almost naked man could pay for his liberty. At the same time the fellow cast such greedy glances at Nadara that Thandar became convinced that the fellow, for reasons of his own, preferred not to believe that they could pay in money for their liberty.

It seemed that the party had been about to embark for another portion of the western coast of the island where the main body of the horde lay. They had but been waiting for three of their crew who had gone inland hunting, when they had seen the canoe and put out to capture its occupants. Now they returned to the little harbor to pick up their fellows, and continue toward the main camp.

The black was for dispatching Thandar at once as their boat was already overcrowded, but there were others who counselled him against it, reminding him of the probable anger of their chief, who saw only in a dead prisoner the loss of a possible ransom.

At last the hunters returned and all embarked. Soon the boat had passed out of the bay and was making its way south along the west coast of the island. It was almost dark when her nose was turned toward shore and the long sweeps brought into play as the sail sagged to the foot of the mast.

Between two small, overlapping points that hid what lay behind, they passed into a landlocked harbor. As the boat breasted the end of the inner point, Thandar sprang to his feet with a cry of joy and amazement. Not a hundred yards away, riding quietly upon the mirror-like surface of the water, lay the *Priscilla*.

The pirates looked at their prisoner in astonishment. The black rose with clenched fists as though prepared to strike him.

'*Priscilla ahoy!*' shrieked Waldo Emerson. 'Help! Help!'

The negro grinned. There was no response from the white yacht. Then the men told Thandar that they had captured the vessel several weeks before, and were holding her crew prisoners upon land awaiting the return of the chief who had been unaccountably absent for a long time. When Waldo Emerson told them that the yacht belonged to his father the black was glad that he had not killed him, for he should bring a fat ransom.

It was dark when they landed, and Thandar and Nadara were forced into squalid huts that lay side by side with several others just above the beach. For a long time the man could not sleep. His mind was occupied with doubts as to the fate of his father and mother. Nadara had told him that both had been aboard the *Priscilla*. She had said nothing of the treatment accorded her by Mrs Smith-Jones, but Waldo had guessed near the truth, and he had seen that the sight of the *Priscilla* had awakened no enthusiasm or happiness in the girl.

After a while he dozed only to be awakened by the sound of movement outside his hut. There was something sinister in the stealthiness of the sound. Silently Thandar rose and crept to the door. The pirates had made no attempt to secure their prisoners – there was no possibility of their escaping from the island.

Thandar put his head out into the lesser darkness of the night. He muttered a little growl of rage and fear, for what he saw was the huge, dark bulk of a man crawling into Nadara's hut. Instantly the American followed. At the door of the girl's shelter he paused to listen. Within he heard a sudden exclamation of fright and the sound of a scuffle. Then he was within the darkness, and a moment later stumbled against a man. Thandar's fingers sought the throat. He made no sound. The other wheeled upon him with a knife. Thandar had expected it. His forearm warded the first blow, and running down the forearm of the other his hand found the knife wrist. Then commenced the struggle within the Stygian blackness of the interior of the hut. Back and forth across the mud floor the two staggered and reeled – the one attempting to wrench free the hand that held the knife – the other seeking a hold upon the throat of his antagonist while he strove to maintain his grip upon the other's wrist. The heavy breathing of the two rose and fell upon the silence of the night – that and the scuffling of their feet were the only sounds of combat. Nadara could not assist Thandar – she knew that it was he who had come to her rescue though she could not see him.

At last, with a superhuman effort, the night prowler broke away from Thandar. For a moment silence reigned in the hut. None of the three could see the other. From beneath his panther skin Thandar drew the long pistol that Tsao Ming had given him, but he dared not fire for fear of hitting Nadara, nor dared he ask her to speak that he might know her position, for then would he have divulged his own to his antagonist.

For minutes that seemed hours the three stood in utter silence, endeavoring to stifle their breathing. Then Thandar heard a cautious movement upon the opposite side of the room. Was it his foe, or Nadara. He raised his pistol level with a man's breast, and then very cautiously he too moved to one side. At the slight sound of his movement there came a sudden flash and deafening roar from across the hut – the enemy had fired, and in the flash of his gun all within the interior was lighted for an instant, and Thandar saw the giant black not two paces from him, and to the man's left stood Nadara, safe from a shot from Thandar's pistol.

The black, not knowing that Thandar was armed, had not guessed that his chance shot was to prove his own death messenger. The instant that the flash of the other's gun revealed his whereabouts Thandar's pistol gave an answering roar, and simultaneously Thandar leaped to one side, running swiftly to grapple with the black from the side; but when he came to him, instead of meeting with ferocious resistance as he had expected, he stumbled over his dead body.

But now the whole camp was awake. The pirates were running hither and thither shouting questions and orders in their many tongues. Confusion reigned supreme, and in the midst of it Thandar grasped Nadara's hand and ran from the hut. Back of the other huts he ran until he had passed the end of the camp. Then he turned down toward the water. It was his intention to reach a boat and make his way to the *Priscilla*.

Behind them the confusion of the camp grew as the pirates searched the huts for an explanation of the two shots – there could have been no better opportunity for escape. Drawn up on the beach was one of the *Priscilla*'s own boats. Together Thandar and Nadara pushed it off, and a moment later were rowing rapidly toward the yacht.

It was with a feeling of unbounded security and elation that Waldo Emerson clambered over the side and drew Nadara after him; but his elation was short lived for scarcely had he set foot upon the deck than he was seized from behind by half a dozen brawny villains who had been upon guard on board the *Priscilla* and had seen the two put off from shore, watched their flight toward the yacht and lain in wait for them as they clambered over the side.

The balance of the night they were kept prisoners upon the *Priscilla*; but early the next morning they were taken ashore. There they found all the pirates congregated outside one of the huts. Within were the passengers and crew of the *Priscilla*. As Thandar and Nadara approached they were seized and hustled toward the doorway – with an accompaniment of oriental oaths they were pushed into the interior.

Standing about in disconsolate and unhappy groups were the crew of the *Priscilla*, Captain Burlinghame and Mr and Mrs Smith-Jones. As his eyes fell upon the last, Waldo Emerson ran toward her with outstretched arms.

With a horrified shriek Mrs Smith-Jones dodged behind

her husband and the captain. Waldo came to a sudden halt. The two men eyed him threateningly. He looked straight into his father's face.

'Don't you know me, Father,' he asked.

John Alden Smith-Jones' jaw dropped.

'Waldo Emerson,' he cried. 'It cannot be possible!'

Mrs Smith-Jones emerged from retreat.

'Waldo Emerson!' she echoed. 'It cannot be!'

'But it is, Mother,' cried the young man.

'What awful apparel!' said Mrs Smith-Jones after she had embraced her son. Then her eyes wandered to Nadara, who had been standing in demure silence just within the doorway.

'You?' she gasped. 'You are not dead?'

Nadara shook her head, and Waldo Emerson hastened to recount her adventures since Stark's attack upon her on the deck of the *Priscilla*. Mrs Smith-Jones approached the girl. She placed a hand upon her shoulder.

'I have been doing a great deal of thinking since last I saw you,' she said, 'and the result of it is that I am going to do something that I have never before done in my life – I am going to ask your pardon; I treated you shamefully. I do not need to ask if my son loves you – you have already told me that you love him – and his eyes have told me where his heart lies.

'For long nights I lay awake thinking of the horror of it, and almost praying that he might be dead rather than come back to find you waiting for him in Boston – that was before you went overboard. You had no birth or family, and that to me meant everything; but since I thought that you were both dead I discovered that I recalled many things about you that were infinitely to be preferred over birth and breeding.

'I cannot tell you just what they are – only I cannot blame my son for loving you. Only you must discard that horrible garment for something presentable.'

'Mother!' shouted Waldo Emerson, as he threw his arms

about her. 'I knew that you would love her, too, if you ever knew her.'

Just then the door opened and one of the pirates entered.

'Come,' he said.

They filed out past him. From those outside they learned that it had been decided to kill them all and after looting the *Priscilla*, sink her, as a man-of-war had been sighted cruising off the coast early in the morning. In their terror they had decided to wait no longer for the absent chief, and all thoughts of ransom were forgotten in the mad desire to erase every vestige of their piracy.

The victims looked at one another in horror. They were entirely surrounded by the pirates, and one by one were securely bound that there might be no chance of any escaping. The plan was to lead them inland to the densest part of the jungle and there to cut their throats and leave their corpses to the vultures. The pirates appeared to derive much pleasure in recounting their plan to the prisoners.

At last all were bound and the death march commenced. The last of the long line of hope forsaken prisoners and brutal, gibing cut-throats had disappeared in the jungle when a rude craft made its way into the harbor. At sight of the *Priscilla* it hesitated and prepared to fly, but seeing no sign of life aboard it, approached, and finding the decks deserted, mounted. In the cabins the newcomers discovered two Malays asleep. These they awoke with much laughter and rude jests.

The two guards leaped to their feet, feeling for their pistols; but when they saw who had surprised them they grinned broadly and jabbered volubly. They addressed all their remarks to a huge and villainous fellow whom they called chief. He it was whom the pirates had awaited, and whose prolonged absence had resulted in the determination to execute the prisoners of the *Priscilla*.

When the chief learned of what was going on in the jungle he cursed and bellowed in rage. He saw many thousand liangs of sycee evaporating before his eyes. Shouting orders to his fellows to follow him he leaped into the craft that had brought them to the *Priscilla*, and a moment later was pushing rapidly toward the shore. Without waiting to draw the boat upon the beach the chief plunged into the jungle, his men at his heels.

Far ahead of him trudged the weary and fear-sickened prisoners, lashed onward with sticks and the flats of murderous parangs. At last the pirates halted in a tangled mass of vegetation.

'Here,' said one; but another thought they should proceed a little further. For a few minutes the two men argued, then the first drew his parang and advanced upon Thandar.

'Here!' he insisted and swung the blade about his head.

A sudden crashing of the underbrush and loud and angry shouts caused him to turn his eyes in the direction of the interruption. The prisoners, too, looked. What they saw was not particularly reassuring – only another very ferocious appearing and exceeding wrathful pirate followed by a half dozen other villains.

He rushed into the midst of the group, knocking men to right and left. The wicked looking fellows who had bullied and cowed the frightened prisoners but a few moments before now looked the picture of abject terror.

The chief came to a halt before the man with the bared parang. His face was livid, and working spasmodically with rage and excitement. He tried to speak, and then he turned his eyes upon Thandar, standing there bound ready for decapitation. As his gaze fell upon this prisoner his eyes went wide, and then he turned upon the would-be executioner, and with a mighty blow felled him.

That seemed to loose his tongue, and from his mouth flowed a torrent of the most awful abuse the prisoners had ever heard. It was directed toward the men who had dared contemplate this thing without his sanction, and principally against the cowering unfortunate who had not dared rise from where his chief's heavy fist had sprawled him.

'And you would have killed Thandar,' he shrieked. 'Thandar, who saved my life!'

And then he fell to kicking the prostrate man until Thandar himself was forced to intercede in the wretch's behalf.

With the coming of Tsao Ming the troubles of the prisoners evaporated in thin air, for when he found that the owner of the *Priscilla* was Thandar's father he restored the yacht and all the loot that his men had taken from it to their rightful owners. Nor would he have stopped there had they permitted him to have his way, which was no less than to behead half a dozen of his unfortunate lieutenants who had been over-zealous in the performance of their piratical duties.

Tsao Ming's picturesque villains replenished the water casks of the *Priscilla* and carried aboard her a sufficient stock of provisions to ensure her company a plentiful table to Honolulu, the port they had chosen as their first stop.

And when the preparations were completed a dozen piratical prahus escorted the white yacht a hundred miles upon her northward journey, firing a farewell salute with volley after volley from the little, brass six-pounders in their bows.

As the tiny fleet diminished to mere specks astern, disappearing beneath the southern horizon, a white flanneled man with close cropped blonde hair, and a slender, black haired girl in simple shirt waist and duck skirt watched them from the deck of the *Priscilla*.

An involuntary sigh escaped the lips of each, and they turned and looked into one another's eyes.

'We are leaving a cruel world that has been kind to us,' said the man, 'for with all its cruelties it gave us each other and reunited us when we were separated.'

'Will civilization be more kind?' asked the girl.

Thandar shook his head.

'I do not know,' he replied.

CHAPTER THIRTEEN

HOMEWARD BOUND

At Honolulu Waldo Emerson Smith-Jones and Nadara were married. Before the ceremony there had been some discussion as to what name should be used in describing Nadara in the formal contract.

'Nadara' alone seemed too brief and meaningless to the precise Mrs Smith-Jones; but Waldo Emerson and the girl insisted that it was her name and all-sufficient. So, in lieu of another name, it was finally decided by all that 'Nadara' could not be legally improved upon.

Prior to the ceremony, which took place on board the *Priscilla*, Mr and Mrs John Alden Smith-Jones, Captain Cecil Burlinghame, several invited guests from amongst officials and friends in Honolulu, and the crew of the *Priscilla* presented gifts to the bride.

Captain Burlinghame in presenting his proffered a few words in explanation of it.

'To you, Nadara,' he said, 'these trinkets will hold a deeper meaning and a greater value than to another, for they come from your own forgotten island, where they lay for twenty years until, by chance, I picked them up close by the sea. The poor lady to whom they once belonged you never knew – it is quite possible that she never was upon your savage coast – and how her jewels came there must always remain a mystery. But two things you hold in common with her, for she was a lady and she was very beautiful.'

He held toward Nadara in his open palm a little worn bag of skins of small rodents, sewn together with bits of gut. At sight of it both the girl and Waldo Emerson exclaimed in astonishment.

Nadara took the bag wonderingly in her hands and dumped the contents into her palm. Waldo pressed forward.

'Did you know to whom those belonged?' he asked Burlinghame.

'To Eugenie Marie Celeste de la Valois, Countess of Crecy,' replied the captain.

'They belonged to Nadara's mother,' returned Waldo. 'Her foster parents were present at her birth and took these jewels from the poor woman's body after she had passed away. She was washed ashore in a boat in which there was only a dead man beside herself – Nadara was born that night.'

And so, when the clergyman had performed the marriage ceremony he entered upon the certificate in the space provided there for the name of the woman: Nadara de la Valois.

And they are living in Boston now in a wonderful home that you have seen if you ever have been to Boston and been driven about in one of those great sight-seeing motor buses, for the place is pointed out to all visitors because of the beauty of its architecture and the fame that attaches to the historic and aristocratic name of its owner, which, as it happens, is not Smith-Jones at all.

SCIENCE FICTION

0352   Star

396644	Roger Elwood (Editor) **CONTINUUM 1**	60p*
396555	**CONTINUUM 2**	60p*
396563	**CONTINUUM 3**	70p*
397837	Sam J. Lundwall **2018 A.D. OR THE KING KONG BLUES**	50p*
397845	Michael Moorcock (Editor) **BEFORE ARMAGEDDON**	60p
398949	Michael Moorcock & Michael Butterworth **THE TIME OF THE HAWKLORDS**	70p
39501X	Edgar Pangborn **MIRROR FOR OBSERVERS**	75p*
398655	Joanna Russ **PICNIC ON PARADISE**	50p*
398469	Kilgore Trout **VENUS ON THE HALF SHELL**	50p*

SCIENCE FANTASY

0352   Star

397675	Edgar Pangborn **DAVY**	75p*
397683	**WEST OF THE SUN**	65p*
397691	**THE COMPANY OF GLORY**	60p*
398523	W.W. **QHE: PROPHETS OF EVIL**	50p

0426   Tandem

177347	Edgar Rice Burroughs **BEYOND THE FARTHEST STAR**	50p*
177266	**THE MONSTER MEN**	50p*
148401	**OUT OF TIME'S ABYSS**	35p*

The Fantastic Gor Series

144961	John Norman **ASSASSIN OF GOR**	45p*
167821	**CAPTIVE OF GOR**	60p*
147952	**HUNTERS OF GOR**	45p*
17531X	**MARAUDERS OF GOR**	60p*
144880	**NOMADS OF GOR**	45p*
167740	**PRIEST-KINGS OF GOR**	50p*
124235.	**RAIDERS OF GOR**	40p*
143736	**TARNSMAN OF GOR**	75p*
181476	**TRIBESMEN OF GOR**	95p*
130553	**OUTLAW OF GOR**	80p*

*Not for sale in Canada.

0352   Star

30006X	THE MAKING OF KING KONG B. Bahrenburg	60p*
398957	THE MARRIAGE RING ("COUPLES") Paddy Kitchen & Dulan Barber	60p*
397276	MURDER BY DEATH H. R. F. Keating	60p*
398825	McCOY: THE BIG RIP-OFF Sam Stewart	50p*
398035	PAUL NEWMAN Michael Kerbel	75p
397470	ODE TO BILLY JOE Herman Raucher	60p*
398191	THE ROCKFORD FILES Mike Jahn	50p*
397373	THE SCARLET BUCCANEER D. R. Benson	60p*
398442	THE SIX MILLION DOLLAR MAN 3: THE RESCUE OF ATHENA ONE Mike Jahn	45p*
398647	THE SIX MILLION DOLLAR MAN 4: PILOT ERROR Jay Barbree	50p*
396490	SIX MILLION DOLLAR MAN 5: THE SECRET OF BIGFOOT Mike Jahn	60p
396652	SPACE 1999: (No.2) MIND BREAKS OF SPACE Michael Butterworth	60p
396660	SPACE 1999 (No. 1) PLANETS OF PERIL Michael Butterworth	60p
398531	SPANISH FLY Madelaine Duke	50p
398817	SWITCH Mike Jahn	50p*
398051	THE ULTIMATE WARRIOR Bill S. Ballinger	50p*

0426   Tandem

180240	AT THE EARTH'S CORE Edgar Rice Burroughs	50p
180321	THE LAND THAT TIME FORGOT Edgar Rice Burroughs	50p
164164	LENNY Valerie Kohler Smith	50p*
16184X	ONEDIN LINE: THE HIGH SEAS Cyril Abraham	60p
132661	ONEDIN LINE: THE IRON SHIPS	60p
168542	SHAMPOO Robert Alley	50p

*Not for sale in Canada.

0352 Star

396881	**A STAR IS BORN** Alexander Edwards	60p
396792	**THE BIONIC WOMAN (No. 1)** **DOUBLE IDENTITY** Maud Willis	50p*
39689X	**BIONIC WOMAN (No. 2)** **A QUESTION OF LIFE**	50p*
398175	**THE BLACK BIRD** Alexander Edwards	45p*
398256	**CANNON: THE FALLING BLONDE** Paul Denver	50p*
398728	**CANNON: IT'S LONELY** **ON THE SIDEWALK**	50p*
396687	**CARQUAKE** Michael Avallone	60p
397349	**COLUMBO: ANY OLD PORT IN A STORM** Henry Clement	50p*
398183	**COLUMBO: A CHRISTMAS KILLING** Alfred Lawrence	45p*
300795	**COLUMBO: THE DEAN'S DEATH**	40p*
30099X	**DIRTY HARRY** Phillip Roch	60p
396903	**EMMERDALE FARM (No. 1)** **THE LEGACY** Lee Mackenzie	50p
396296	**EMMERDALE FARM: (No. 2)** **PRODIGAL'S PROGRESS** Lee Mackenzie	60p
397489	**ESCAPE FROM THE DARK** Rosemary Anne Sisson	50p
398744	**GABLE AND LOMBARD** Joe Morella & Edward Z. Epstein	60p*
397160	**HARRY & WALTER GO TO NEW YORK** Sam Stewart	50p*
398493	**HAWAII 5-0: THE ANGRY BATTALION** Herbert Harris	50p*
300876	**HAWAII 5-0: SERPENTS IN PARADISE**	45p*
396288	**HEAVEN HAS NO FAVOURITES** Erich Maria Remarque	75p
398477	**HUSTLE** Stephen Shagan	60p*
398574	**INNOCENTS WITH DIRTY HANDS** Richard Neely	60p*
397500	**INSERTS** Anton Rimart	60p
397438	**KOJAK: GIRL IN THE RIVER** Victor B. Miller	50p*
397357	**KOJAK: GUN BUSINESS**	50p*
397446	**KOJAK: MARKED FOR MURDER**	50p*
398671	**KOJAK: TAKE-OVER**	50p*

*Not for sale in Canada.

Wyndham Books are obtainable from many booksellers and newsagents. If you have any difficulty please send purchase price plus postage on the scale below to:

Wyndham Cash Sales,
44 Hill Street,
London W1X 8LB

While every effort is made to keep prices low, it is sometimes necessary to increase prices at short notice. Wyndham Books reserve the right to show new retail prices on covers which may differ from those advertised in the text or elsewhere.

Postage and Packing Rate
U.K. & Eire
One book 15p plus 7p per copy for each additional book ordered to a maximum charge of 57p.

These charges are subject to Post Office charge fluctuations.